She was cool and smooth.

Like marble. Like a statue he'd seen in Italy. That image pleased C.J.

As he crossed the room to meet her, he admired the unruffled sweep of her shoulder-length brandy colored hair. Her face was gently rounded. Not beautiful, maybe, by some standards. Her nose was a little too long, her mouth a little too wide. But she was elegant.

He watched her stiffen, sensed the reserve that settled over her. When he held his hand out to her, he thought he saw a moment of uncertainty.

Then she placed her hand in his, and her eyes—the same distinctive color as her hair—flared with temper.

He revised his image. Marble had no spark like that . . . and it certainly didn't stir him the way she just had.

Dear Reader,

Welcome to the Silhouette **Special Edition** experience! With your search for consistently satisfying reading in mind, every month the authors and editors of Silhouette **Special Edition** aim to offer you a stimulating blend of deep emotions and high romance.

The name Silhouette **Special Edition** and the distinctive arch on the cover represent a commitment—a commitment to bring you six sensitive, substantial novels each month. In the pages of a Silhouette **Special Edition**, compelling true-to-life characters face riveting emotional issues—and come out winners. Both celebrated authors and newcomers to the series strive for depth and dimension, vividness and warmth, in writing these stories of living and loving in today's world.

The result, we hope, is romance you can believe in. Deeply emotional, richly romantic, infinitely rewarding—that's the Silhouette **Special Edition** experience. Come share it with us—six times a month!

From all the authors and editors of Silhouette **Special Edition**,

Best wishes,

Leslie Kazanjian,
Senior Editor

PATRICIA McLINN
Hoops

Silhouette Special Edition

Published by Silhouette Books New York

America's Publisher of Contemporary Romance

To my family, for believing.
To my friends, for listening.
To my fellow writers, for helping.

SILHOUETTE BOOKS
300 East 42nd St., New York, N.Y. 10017

ISBN: 0-373-09587-2

First Silhouette Books printing March 1990

All the characters in this book are fictitious. Any
resemblance to actual persons, living or dead, is
purely coincidental.

®: Trademark used under license and
registered in the United States Patent and
Trademark Office and in other countries.

Printed in the U.S.A.

PATRICIA McLINN

says she has been spinning stories in her head at least since childhood, when her mother insisted she stop reading at the dinner table. As the time came for her to earn a living, Patricia shifted her stories from fiction to fact—she became a sports writer and editor for newspapers in Illinois, North Carolina and the District of Columbia. Now living outside Washington, D.C., she enjoys traveling, history and sports but is happiest indulging her passion for storytelling.

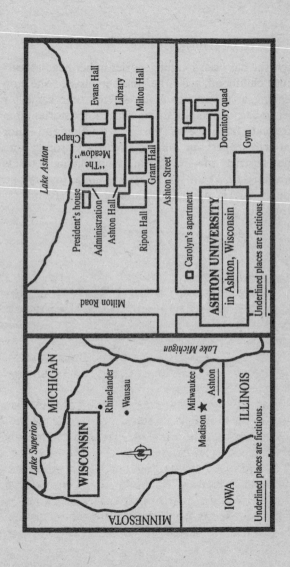

Lake Ashton

Chapel

Evans Hall

"The Meadow"

Library

Milton Hall

President's house

Administration

Ashton Hall

Grant Hall

Ripon Hall

Dormitory quad

Gym

Ashton Street

Milton Road

☐ Carolyn's apartment

ASHTON UNIVERSITY
in Ashton, Wisconsin

Underlined places are fictitious.

Lake Superior

MICHIGAN

Rhinelander

• Wausau

Lake Michigan

WISCONSIN

MINNESOTA

Milwaukee

Madison ★

Ashton

IOWA

ILLINOIS

Underlined places are fictitious.

Chapter One

He was hard to miss.

Carolyn pushed open the door, and there he sat, his jean-clad legs stretched out, practically filling the reception area.

During her past five months in Europe, she'd often thought about Ashton University—about paths bordered with daffodils in the spring and chrysanthemums in the fall, sailboats skimming the lake, stately stone buildings, her colleagues, her friends.

Never once did she think about finding someone like this sitting in the university president's outer office. The Ashton U. sweatshirt, the jeans, faded to a dusty blue, and the white athletic shoes befitted a student. But only the most casual student would wear that outfit to the president's office. And this, Carolyn Trent told herself, was no student.

Mid-thirties, she'd say from the sharp angles and planes of his face. Even in the shadows of the far corner where he sat, his features added up to self-assurance. Surprise mingled in his expression with something else she couldn't identify. But it most definitely wasn't self-consciousness. If he was at all aware of the incongruity of his attire against the backdrop of burgundy leather and walnut paneling, he gave no sign of it.

He didn't fit. And that jarred her. Here at Ashton everything was supposed to be the way it always had been—orderly and steady. Here, she'd told herself, she'd shake the discontent that kept scratching at her just when everything was going so well.

"She'll be back in a minute," said a distinctive voice, a mixture of gravel and drawl, like a slow rumble of rocks. "The secretary," the man added with a slow nod to the empty desk. "She said she'd be right back."

She felt an unaccustomed flush sweep her face. She'd been staring. And he knew it. "Thank you."

"Have an appointment?"

She shook her head. If the room had been empty, or if Marsha had been alone out here, Carolyn would have gone straight in to surprise Stewart. But not with an audience. Not that the informality would have bothered this man.

"Shouldn't be long. He's not too tied up this afternoon," he offered optimistically, nodding toward the double doors to the inner office. "That's what the secretary said."

Carolyn sank straight-backed into a wing chair. What would it be like to be as unconcerned about the proprieties as he seemed to be? She gave another small shake of her head, this time at herself. Whatever it was like, it wouldn't be appropriate for an Ashton University professor of English literature.

"Carolyn! Welcome back," an older female voice exclaimed. Stewart Barron's secretary was in the doorway with a folder in one hand, mail in the other, and a wide smile.

"Hello, Marsha. It's good to be home."

"How was the seminar? How was England? And Paris? Oh, how I envy you." She sighed, not waiting for answers. "You must have had a wonderful time. All the cafés, the shops..."

Just the word *Paris* and Carolyn saw Marsha conjuring up romantic fantasies. But it wasn't like that. She'd spent half her time at the Louvre and half at the Musée d'Orsay, soaking in line and color after months devoted to the written word.

"The seminar was excellent—very worthwhile. But now I'm eager to find out what I'll be doing and to get started."

She was more than a little curious. In retrospect, Stewart's dodging the topic during the two-and-a-half-hour drive back from the airport late last night struck her as odd.

"Of course you are. I'll go in and let him know you're here," said Marsha, hurriedly setting the mail on her desk.

Carolyn watched the older woman disappear into Stewart's office with growing uneasiness. She'd known Marsha Hortler for more than seventeen years, ever since Stewart and Elizabeth had assumed guardianship of Carolyn and brought her back to Ashton at the age of eleven. But Marsha almost seemed to be avoiding her.

Or maybe Marsha wanted to avoid the subject of her assignment this semester. She frowned. Missing six weeks meant she couldn't have her usual class load, but why this mystery?

Her gaze slid to the tall stranger, then immediately jerked away. He was studying her openly. Perhaps she deserved that after the way she'd stared. But that didn't mean she'd just sit there. She turned back to him and smiled, pleasant but distant, the small smile so effective at keeping her male students at arm's length.

He grinned, a genuinely amused, lopsided grin that showed a slash of white teeth. Shifting in her chair, she automatically pulled the hem of her cognac wool skirt over her knees. The grin deepened in apparent appreciation of the shape that showed between her just-lowered skirt and matching pumps.

What was the matter with her? What did a little staring from a stranger matter?

A stranger. Of course. Marsha would never discuss faculty matters in front of a stranger. That must be the explanation for her manner. But then why had Stewart acted so oddly last night?

"He'll see you now, Carolyn. Come in," Marsha said, emerging from the double doors to Stewart Barron's office.

"Carolyn! Come in. Come in, my dear!" With his pin-stripe suit fitted precisely to his tall, rangy form and distinguished by white wings at the temples of his dark hair, Stewart Barron presented the perfect picture of a university president.

"Hello, Stewart." She returned his hug with vigor, but watched him closely as he resumed his seat behind the mahogany desk. "How are you feeling today?"

"Me?" He waved aside the irrelevancy. "The question is, how are you? You're the one who's returned from adventuring, seeing the wide world. And—" his voice deepened to an ominous note "—the one who wasn't supposed to report to work for another five days. Haven't you heard of jet lag? You should be collapsed in bed somewhere."

"I'm not the type for the vapors," she answered with mock indignation. "There's no cause for me to take to my bed."

At least he didn't look as lost or alone as he had last spring. Carolyn sat back in her chair. He'd insisted she go to the seminar; still, she'd worried about leaving him alone less than a year after Elizabeth's death.

Well, not alone, precisely. Everyone at Ashton cared about him, of course. And Elizabeth's cousin Helene, who'd helped nurse her over the final months, stayed on to help with his social obligations. But Helene was so different from Stewart, and Carolyn worried he'd miss talking to someone who could share his concerns about Ashton.

"I wasn't referring to having the vapors, and you'll note I didn't say *whose* bed."

"Stewart." She clicked her tongue in feigned disapproval. "Someday you're going to say something like that in front of the wrong person, and they're going to think you're trying to encourage me into a hedonistic life."

"I am." He slid his dark-framed glasses back onto his nose. "Maybe that would balance the twenty-eight years of seriousness you've lived so far! Dedicated teachers don't always have to be serious, Carolyn. I wish I could convince you of that. Your parents knew it." He looked over the top of his glasses at her.

He always did that when he wanted to make a particular point, Carolyn thought—as if he believed he could see her reaction more clearly without the magnification of the lenses. Strangely enough, she believed he could.

She stood up and moved to the full-length window that looked out on the Meadow, an open grassy area framed by maples gathering color for a final, vibrant burst of Wisconsin autumn. Students strolled along paths that connected the Administration Building, the classroom buildings and the chapel. One young couple was stretched out on the grass, the girl's head resting on the boy's chest, and both stared up at the puffs of white drifting across the blue.

The scene had formed part of her life for so many years, but today she seemed out of sync. She felt like someone

trying to jump on a merry-go-round already in motion.
Maybe it came from missing the start of the school year.

No. She shouldn't try to excuse it that way. In England
she'd tried to put it down to longing for Ashton—plain old
homesickness. But the feeling had poked at her even before
the trip. Part of her grieving for Elizabeth, she'd thought at
first. Now she wasn't so sure.

Whatever the cause, working hard would leave less time
to fret about it. Barely conscious of her own sigh, Carolyn
turned back and put the question directly, "What do you
have planned for me, Stewart?"

"Since you're so eager, the first thing is Homecoming this
weekend."

He ignored her half groan as she sank back into the chair.
The informal tea Thursday afternoon, the parade and rally
Friday, the Saturday football game, the evening's dinner-
dance, and Sunday's farewell brunch made Homecoming a
command performance for faculty members.

"You enjoy it. Admit it—even the football game," he
said.

Sheepishly she acknowledged a fondness for the hoopla.
She was concerned that people would look askance at a
professor who liked fight songs, cheers, tackles and touch-
downs. "But I've already missed so much of this semester.
I want to get started."

Stewart Barron removed his glasses to rub the bridge of
his nose before replacing them. "You know it's difficult with
the semester already so advanced . . ."

She crossed her knees and waited for him to go on. He
didn't. "We discussed that before I went," she reminded
him. "We agreed the seminar would be worthwhile because
of the opportunity."

"Of course," he acknowledged. "And since you're one
of the few from this country ever invited, I know several

publications eager to have articles from you. That's good exposure."

"Yes, I'll need to write several. And the organizers asked me to contribute an essay for a collection they're publishing, but now—"

Now she wanted to teach. She missed it. The prestige of the seminar, the essay, the articles—all those were things any professor should value. They helped advance her standing in the academic world. How many people had told her how proud her parents would have been? Those words were always a reassurance: she was on the right track. These people, who'd been her parents' colleagues and now were hers, certainly valued her accomplishments. Lately, though, she'd found the accomplishments less satisfying than she'd expected.

"I'll write in my spare time. Until I get my own classes next semester, I thought I'd guest-lecture for the English literature courses." She leaned forward. "And if the graduate students—"

"That would be difficult, Carolyn. All the syllabuses are set, and you know how some of the professors get if anything interferes. Maybe next semester—"

"Next semester? I don't want to wait—" Catching herself, she sat back with a conscious effort to stifle her disappointment. She couldn't expect to be respected as a professional if she acted like a child. Knowing someone as long as she'd known Stewart, though, sometimes she expressed herself too emotionally. "What would I do the rest of this semester?"

As the words left her mouth, she wished she could snatch them back. She'd stepped into a trap. She wasn't sure what kind, but his bland expression didn't fool her. If he were a chess player, she'd say he'd just lined up the checkmate he'd been plotting.

"This is an unusual situation. Your department head wasn't sure how to handle it, so he's let me make arrangements. We can't let you sit around, can we? It might be bad for morale."

She sat up straighter. This was getting worse and worse. Now he was cajoling. "What do you have in mind, Stewart?"

"There's a group of students I want you to work with, Carolyn. A special group."

Oh, Lord, please, not house mother, she pleaded to herself.

"About ten or eleven. It won't be as impressive on your résumé as the seminar, but you don't need any help there. And it would be interdepartmental—not only English."

Carolyn relaxed. Ten or eleven. That might not be so bad. And working across departmental lines might be interesting. Perhaps he had a point. Perhaps a short break to try something a little different wouldn't hurt. It might provide an antidote for this restlessness.

Stewart Barron's glasses dropped down his nose just enough for him to peer at her. "I've assigned you as academic adviser to the men's basketball team."

Her first inclination to chuckle faded at the look on his face. He was serious. "The basketball team!"

"It's something Coach Draper and I have decided—"

"The basketball team!" Something a little different, yes. But this was outlandish. "I'm a professor. I teach. English. Literature. I don't want to assist some ridiculous game!"

"You like the *football* games."

"That's because the board isn't trying to 'upgrade' football. So far the Ashton *football* players are still students—"

"These *basketball* players are students—"

"Barely. They—"

"Carolyn."

The single word stopped her.

"They're students," he repeated, "at Ashton University. As such, they deserve the best education we can deliver. I know your opinion of the board's decision to return to top-division competition in basketball."

She winced inwardly. The two of them had started arguing the issue as soon as the board had proposed that Ashton move to Division I basketball, with its scholarships, bigger budget and top-level schedule. In Carolyn's memory they'd never disagreed before on what course Ashton should follow.

"But the administration and the *faculty* have an obligation to honor that decision and to nurture these students."

"They're here because they can bounce a round ball. Why should we pretend otherwise?"

"Whatever the reason, they *are* here. That's the point. You wouldn't deny these young men an education *because* they play basketball, would you?"

That wasn't fair. He knew she couldn't resist such an appeal to one of her most basic values.

"What do you expect me to do, Stewart?" She aimed for a dignified tone, but wasn't sure she'd achieved it.

"I want you to teach them the best way you know how."

She gave him a skeptical look, despite the flow of warmth at his confidence.

"You won't be in a classroom situation. You'll be overseeing the players' overall class load, helping them find specific help if they need it, guiding them on study habits, advising them on next semester's schedule. It will mean dealing with a very wide range of backgrounds, abilities and interests. Coach Draper recommends—"

"Wait a minute. Who's Draper? Didn't the board hire someone else last year? I met him. Didn't I?"

He sighed heavily. "Coach Roberts quit last April, just before you left for England. Don't you remember?"

"No."

She was no absentminded professor, but she did save her memory for things that counted. Basketball coaches didn't fall into that category.

"His alma mater hired him. I can't blame him. It's one of the top programs in the country, but it left us in rather a difficult position."

"Why? Anyone with sense should be honored to come to Ashton. This is an excellent university."

Admiration and exasperation mingled in his face. "Your loyalty is wonderful, Carolyn, but sometimes I fear we shut you in this ivory tower when you were much too young. Maybe we were wrong to bring you here—"

"Nonsense." He'd fretted about that more and more in the past few years—and so unnecessarily. She'd become what she was meant to be. If her parents had been alive, she wouldn't have spent six years on her grandparents' farm before Stewart and Elizabeth brought her back; she would have spent all her formative years at Ashton. It was what her parents would have wanted. Carolyn spread the fingers of her right hand on the leather arm of her chair and gripped it. "This is where I belong. You and Elizabeth saw that, and I will always be grateful to you."

Stewart gave another deep sigh, then returned to the subject. "However fine an academic institution this is, Ashton isn't an athletic powerhouse. I know you don't think that's important, but I, for one, enjoy sports."

He sounded so defiant that she had to smile.

"I liked playing them and I like watching them. Oh, I know some programs get out of hand—very much out of hand. But there are schools that maintain high academic standards *and* field competitive teams. I want Ashton to be one. I want our students to have opportunities for all the good things a university can offer, and sports is one of them."

She'd liked sports, too, especially her years in competitive swimming. But following her parents' footsteps had required eliminating distractions, and sports was one. "With so fervent a champion, I think any coach would jump at the opportunity to come here," Carolyn said dryly.

"I'm afraid I don't offset the drawbacks. In the basketball conference we've joined, we're the smallest school among state schools that have five times as many students. That makes recruiting difficult. Our academic standards make it even more difficult—"

"There! You just admitted it: high academic standards are a drawback when you field a Division I basketball team."

Stewart frowned at her, but doggedly continued, "We don't pay the salary a coach can command elsewhere. With the gym needing repairs, we don't even have enough in the budget for a real assistant coach until next season—only Dolph Reems when he's not running the athletic department and a couple of student team managers. We were extremely fortunate to get C.J. Draper."

"Why?" She laced the bald question with her doubt that getting any coach warranted the label *fortunate*.

"He was a standout in college and led his team to the national tournament Final Four two years in a row. Then he had four good years as a professional. Experts were touting him as the next big star—until he hurt his knee. He came back when nobody thought he could, but he never played quite as well. He hung on for a couple of years, going from team to team. Then he played a year in an Italian league. A couple of years ago he signed on as assistant coach with one of his old pro teams."

"So when he could no longer do, he decided to teach. Is that it?" She knew Stewart had recognized the bite in her words. She'd gone too far.

With his crossed forearms resting on the desk, Stewart leaned forward. "Professor Trent, C.J. Draper is Ashton University's basketball coach. As such, he's a member of this university and will be accorded the same respect every other member receives."

Carolyn said nothing.

"I believe C.J. Draper is a good coach, a good *teacher*," Stewart continued. "And the fact that he's requested an academic adviser for his players shows me that he has their educational good at heart. That should be encouraged. Don't you agree?"

"By all means, Stewart."

He nodded, apparently satisfied with her neutral tone. Carolyn knew that Stewart was too accomplished an administrator to expect more than acquiescence at this point.

He pushed the intercom button. "Marsha, please send Coach Draper in."

Carolyn couldn't sit still. She went to the window again. The sky-gazing couple was gone. The broken clouds seemed to have dropped closer to the chapel's bell tower. Walkers pulled sweaters and jackets more tightly around them and hurried their steps. A shiver ran up her spine as she heard the double doors from the outer office open and shut.

"Afternoon, Stewart. How are you?"

She grimaced out the window at the newcomer's casualness. She should have guessed his words would be delivered in that gravelly drawl.

Perhaps she *had* guessed. Somehow it fitted that the man who'd made her feel so uncomfortable outside was both the prominent figure in the new basketball program she'd fought and the instigator of this job she didn't want.

"Very well, thank you. How are you, C.J.?"

"Fine. Just fine."

She heard the words of greeting, but held her position. As long as she could, she'd delay facing this.

"C.J., I'd like you to meet Professor Carolyn Trent. Carolyn, this is Coach C.J. Draper."

She turned, prepared for a cool exchange across the expanse of the office. But she should have known Coach Draper wouldn't wait for such formalities. With hand extended, he stood in front of her, new Ashton sweatshirt, worn jeans, white athletic shoes, lopsided grin and all.

"Pleased to meet you, Professor Trent." His grin cut grooves in his cheek, deeper by his mouth, then shallowing as they rippled higher.

She had no choice; dignity demanded she meet his handshake firmly. A kind of disquiet pushed her heartbeat faster for an instant as her hand disappeared in his large grasp. His palm, slightly roughened with calluses, encompassed her cold fingers like a scratchy woolen blanket. He returned her grip solidly.

He was even taller than he'd appeared at first, at least a foot over her five foot six, and lean to the point of lankiness. But his shoulders were broad enough to block her view of the room, and his handshake promised strength. The sun through the window picked out streaks of gold and bronze and even a strand or two of gray in the straight sandy brown mop of hair that fell across his forehead, ending just above his eyes—the brightest, bluest eyes she'd ever seen.

Their corners crinkled. "And here I thought you might be a student out there in the waiting room," he said.

Almost gratefully she felt anger sweep away the disquiet. *He'd* thought *she* was a student? Him, with his sweatshirt

and sneakers? At least she wore a suit, an outfit appropriate to the office of the president of Ashton University.

"I don't know, Stewart." C.J. addressed the university
president, but his grinning gaze was focused on Carolyn.
"She looks awfully young. You think she'll be able to handle my guys?"

C.J. had known who she was right away. He'd had an
appointment with Stewart Barron to talk about an academic adviser, and she'd been called in to the president's
office before him. It didn't take much skill to come up with
the right solution to that equation.

Besides, he'd remembered her from his first visit to the
school. Dolph Reems, the athletic director, had been showing him around the compact campus, and C.J. had spotted
her.

He had stopped Dolph right in the middle of explaining
his dream plans for a new arena. He didn't seem to mind. In
fact, he'd been nearly as loquacious extolling the attributes
of Professor Carolyn Trent as he had of his mirage arena.

C.J. half suspected the older man knew he'd been talking a pipe dream—this school wasn't likely to ever reach the
big time. Settled into the fertile hills of southern Wisconsin, it was about a two-hour drive from Milwaukee and not
much more from Chicago—if you measured in miles per
hour. Otherwise, it was a world apart. Still, it just might
turn out to be his ticket to the big time.

Odd that he'd picked her out right away like that. Not
really his type at all. "Women gotta be feisty, flashy and
fiery. What's the fun if there isn't some sizzle?" That was
what Rake used to say when they roomed together. C.J.
hadn't followed the pattern as closely, or as often, as Rake,
but looking back he could see he'd tended toward women

who moved on a lot. Or was he the one always moving on? Well, one way or another, it didn't last.

But this Carolyn Trent was a different kind entirely. Cool and smooth, like marble. Standing at the window in Stewart Barron's office staring out like that, she looked like a statue he'd seen in Italy.

The image pleased him. As he crossed the room to meet her, he admired the unruffled sweep of her straight shoulder-length hair, as if newly sculpted from some warm golden-brown stone by a meticulous craftsman. Her face was gently rounded with a bone structure Michelangelo might have created. Not beautiful, maybe, by some standards. Her nose was a little too long, her mouth a little too wide. But she was elegant.

That realization made it easier to understand why his eye had been drawn to her all those months ago. Her kind of elegance wasn't a common commodity in his world. No wonder he'd noted it.

On the other hand, close up she seemed about as warm as one of those marble statues. He watched her stiffen when she turned to him, and sensed the reserve that settled over her. She had the kind of nose designed for looking down— long, straight and narrow. He was just glad nature fixed it so she'd have to look up before looking down on him.

He didn't usually let a haughty attitude get to him; why it did with her, he didn't know. Maybe he'd forgotten how it felt because he'd gotten past all that after five months at Ashton. Maybe he was just tired.

When he held his hand out to her, he wondered if he only imagined a moment of uncertainty beneath that surface, just as he thought he'd seen out in the waiting room. Both times it disappeared so quickly that he couldn't be sure. Just as before, a disapproving coolness dimmed the glimmer of light in her eyes.

Then she placed her hand in his, and her eyes—the same distinctive color as her hair—flared with temper for an instant at his comment. He revised his image.

Marble had no spark like that...and it certainly didn't stir him the way she had just done.

Chapter Two

How dare he think her too young? How dare he question her ability? she fumed as they left Stewart's office. As for "handling his guys," she could teach, and teach she would, even if she didn't have a classroom. C.J. Draper or no C.J. Draper.

"I suggest, since Stewart has left the details to us . . ." To her irritation she hesitated over the common pronoun, drawing a grin from her companion. That stiffened her back, and her voice. He found her amusing, did he? "I suggest we go to my office and discuss this program. It would be best if we both knew exactly where we stand."

"Sure," he agreed. He followed her out of the Administration Building's main door and down the shallow granite steps. But there he stopped. "If you want to know about the guys' courses and grades and all, we'll have to go to my office first."

Carolyn held in her impatience with determination. Why couldn't he have said that in the first place?

They fell into step along a path that led across campus, then up the slope to the ridge where the Physical Education Building sat. It irritated her to realize he was shortening his long, easy stride to accommodate her smaller step. It irritated her further that besides the disadvantage of a foot in height, she had to contend with a restrictive straight skirt and mid-heel pumps while he swung along completely comfortable in jeans and sneakers.

"It would be helpful, Mr. Draper, if you came to our next meeting prepared."

"Why, Professor Trent, I came prepared to this one—all prepared to meet you. And that's what I did," he said, his drawl seeming to slow along with his pace.

She looked up. "Meet me?"

"Of course. I wanted to meet the guys' academic adviser."

"You might have considered what would happen after you met me."

Carolyn lengthened her stride until it stretched taut the material of her skirt. His pace automatically and effortlessly adjusted.

"I guess I just didn't count on you being such a gym rat."

"I beg your pardon?" She heard the tone in her voice that said if C.J. Draper were smart, he'd start begging *her* pardon. She sounded like someone she hardly recognized—and didn't particularly like. That didn't matter, she decided grimly, if her attitude helped make it clear from the start that she'd brook no impairment of Ashton's academic reputation. Ashton was too much a part of her, her history, her heritage, to not defend what it had always stood for.

"Sorry, Professor. That's basketball talk for a workaholic. Some guy who spends all of his time in the gym shooting hoops—that's a gym rat."

"Hoops?" she inquired coolly.

"Baskets, basketball," he translated as he held a side door open for her at the Physical Education Center.

Carolyn noticed the return of the lopsided grin, and she regarded it with some suspicion.

But he gave her no time to investigate its meaning. He strode away down a dim, narrow hall that echoed faintly of voices, sneakers squeaking on hardwood and bouncing balls. She'd barely caught up when he turned into a doorway, then swung the door open for her to enter his tiny office.

The furniture was worn just short of disrepute. Patches rubbed nearly raw marred a leather couch pushed against one wall, but it stretched long enough for even C.J. Draper's comfort. Green metal filing cabinets, dented and scratched but neatly labeled, marched across the back of the room. On the walls hung blackboards covered with x's and o's drawn in miniature basketball courts and lists of numbers and abbreviations she couldn't decipher. A door to the left opened to Dolph Reems's office. Through it she saw another door labeled simply Gym.

"Have a seat." C.J. gestured toward the couch as he squatted down to search a bottom filing cabinet.

The room really wasn't that small, Carolyn realized. It only appeared that way because of C.J. Draper's long frame. Even crouched over the drawer he dominated the room. She caught herself staring at worn jeans stretched tightly over hard thighs and abruptly spun away, moving toward his desk.

She intently surveyed the stacks on top to block the memory of her previous view. The files, envelopes and VCR tapes were orderly; their owner would know where to find whatever he wanted.

Two photographs in frames stood apart from the clutter. One showed two women and a young boy with C.J.—a family group. The woman on his right must be his mother; they had a resemblance not so much of features but expression and posture. The boy, tall and gangly with adolescence, shared enough similarities to link him to both C.J. and the older woman.

The other woman was harder to classify. A wife? C.J. Draper wore no wedding ring. Was he the kind who would? Carolyn didn't pause to consider the uncharacteristic observation of ringless hands. Maybe a sister or sister-in-law.

Absently she picked up the other frame. She instantly recognized C.J. in the brief uniform of professional basketball. He was lean and polished, the muscles and sinews of his arms and legs standing out in the instant after he'd released the ball that hung two inches beyond his fingers. A black man in the same uniform was poised to receive the pass, his powerful body bunched to go soaring to the basket above, a cocky smile already evident. Between them, a player in a different uniform stood, the realization of how he'd been duped just making an imprint on his face.

"Hard not to smile back at ol' Rake, isn't it?"

The words from over her shoulder jolted her into an uncomfortable realization: she was actually smiling. She started to put down the photograph but he intercepted her, taking it from her hand, their fingers not quite touching. She let out a breath.

He was so big. That was why she'd reacted that way, she decided. When someone a foot taller stood near your shoulder, close enough to stir your hair with his words, close enough to breathe in the clean scent of his soap, you had to be aware of him.

"That was my last game with the Tornadoes. Last game with anybody for more than a year."

He moved to stand next to her. What had Stewart said about his pro career? A serious injury? So it must have been in that game. Yet he smiled warmly at the photograph and its memories. She had to admire his ability to remember the good things.

"Rake and I worked that play to perfection. Rake's one of the greats. You must've heard of him—Rake Johnson. Just retired after last season... Well, maybe *you* wouldn't have heard of him. Rake'd be devastated."

He put down the picture and picked up the other. Casually he answered the questions she wouldn't have asked. "This is my family. My mom, my sister Jan and my nephew Jason. They're in Florida now."

As he reached across her to replace the picture, his arm brushed hers and feathered the side of her breast. Resolutely she ignored the clamoring of her nerve endings. It was ridiculous to react to incidental contact, something that could just as easily happen in a crowded elevator.

She had to think of something else, so she focused on the picture C.J. had put down and wondered briefly about the missing father. Briefly was all the time she had to wonder because C.J. suddenly seemed in a hurry.

"You ready? I figure you'll want to keep these in your office, so we might as well head over there." He slid a stack of file folders under his arm and headed out the door.

Annoyance swamped her other feelings as she struggled to keep pace with his long strides, which turned their cross-campus route to her office into an endurance test. He was doing it on purpose, damn him. He was trying to unsettle her. Well, she wouldn't give him the satisfaction. In her office, she would control the discussion of her role as academic adviser.

"Won't you sit down, Mr. Draper?" Carolyn asked as they entered her office. In her own territory she held an advantage. Right now she appreciated even the subtle edge gained by sitting in her big wooden desk chair, and leaving C.J. Draper in the chair a colleague said reminded him of applying for a bank loan. That was exactly how she wanted this man to feel.

But C.J. Draper didn't sit down. He wandered the room with long strides, examining titles in the orderly bookshelves, twiddling the cord to the blinds, running a hand along her uncluttered desk. And bothering her.

No sense lying to herself. He'd shown a knack for disconcerting her from the moment he'd caught her staring at him in Stewart's office. She suspected he'd been cultivating the knack ever since.

Steeling herself, she began to speak. She made her points, and he agreed. After the introductory meeting tomorrow, she'd begin scheduled meetings with the ten members of the Ashton basketball team, as a group and individually. She'd be given access to all material on their academic backgrounds and progress. She would serve as liaison with individual professors if that need arose. She would have the right to declare a player academically ineligible, with the time period subject to Stewart's final approval.

C.J.'s only contribution was the stipulation that any questions from the media be directed to him. She had no trouble agreeing to that.

She raised one eyebrow when she counted out only nine folders. After checking them, he said he must have missed Frank Gordon's, and he'd send it to her. There was one final area to clarify. Now she'd find out what he really had in mind. "Mr. Draper, why did you request an academic adviser?"

Deliberately she let her challenge speak louder than the question, and it stilled him. He turned from looking out the window and flipped the blinds closed. "I don't have anything against academics." She accepted that with a slight nod; that was what Stewart said of him. "Not like you have against basketball," he added. Then his usual drawl became less pronounced. "I've been meaning to ask, Professor Trent, just what *do* you have against basketball? Or is it me?"

At the last words, she looked up and saw anger in his eyes . . . and some other element behind it. "I have nothing against basketball, Mr. Draper. When the team played under Dolph Reems at the lower level of competition, I had no objection at all—"

"Gracious of you," he murmured.

She ignored him. "What I do object to is Ashton becoming one of those schools where academic standards are subordinated to the athletic program."

"And that's where I come in?"

She let her silence answer.

"What makes you think I'd do that?"

"Are you an ambitious man, Mr. Draper?"

"Yes." The flat neutrality of the word carried more weight than passion would have.

"Your ambition, I'm certain, extends beyond Ashton. So this is only a stepping-stone to you. Somewhere to win at all costs, make a name for yourself and move on. How many schools has that happened to? How many schools are better known for athletic scandals than academic achievement? I won't have that happen to Ashton, Mr. Draper."

"So you want to get rid of this program—and me—at any cost? Without giving it a chance, without giving me—" He broke off abruptly. He seemed to sweep all emotion away except an amusement that gently mocked them both. "Maybe that's why I asked for an academic adviser."

The drawl had returned. She could almost imagine it had never lapsed.

"Maybe I figure the best way to keep the academic community happy is to let one of their own right inside where she could keep us in line. Like one of those treaty inspectors who get in there to make sure the Russians really are destroying their missiles." He moved slowly to the door. "Maybe that's the way I figured it. Maybe..." He touched the doorknob, but made no move to turn it as his gaze took in her office once more.

"Mr. Draper. Mr. Draper," she repeated with emphasis to reclaim his wandering attention. "Is there something wrong with my office? I have the impression you don't approve."

She meant him to be nonplussed. This time she wouldn't be the one off balance.

"Oh, it's not that I don't approve, exactly." He seemed willing to clarify his thoughts, if only he were sure of them himself. "It's just, it's so..." He shrugged. Whatever anger he'd felt before seemed gone.

He swung the door open and crossed the threshold into the hall before producing a resounding snap of his fingers. It took only one long stride to bring him back into the office and half a second to close the door behind him.

"Monochromatic. That's the word I wanted. Your office is monochromatic. I bet you thought I wouldn't know a word like that, didn't you, Professor? Nothing more complicated in this head than pick-and-roll, right?"

She couldn't have said, since she had no idea what pick-and-roll meant, but he seemed to have followed the drift of her thoughts.

"Monochromatic. That's just what your office is." He looked around with seeming satisfaction, then down at her again. "Just like you."

"Like me?" The words were out before she could stop them.

"Uh-huh." He leaned over her desk and gently lifted a lock of her hair across two fingers. "Your hair's the exact same color as your eyes. And that outfit's nearly the same color again. Monochromatic."

She twisted away from his hand, and he let the hair slip across his fingertips.

"It's a nice enough color," he continued, his eyes on the lock of hair, swinging softly along the side of her neck. "But you know what they say about too much of a good thing. You ought to wear colors. Red. Green. Blue. Let 'em see you, instead of blending in."

"Mr. Draper—" His gaze lifted from her throat to her lips, then to her eyes, and Carolyn suddenly couldn't remember the stinging rebuke she intended to deliver.

"I know. I shouldn't say things like that, Professor. I just got so caught up with everything about you being the same color—what do you call that color, anyway?"

"Mr. Draper—" she tried again, but this time his words instead of his eyes stopped her.

"Now don't tell me it's brown, because dead leaves are brown, and that's not it. No, I'll bet all those European men have been telling you all sorts of things. You know, I lived in Italy a couple of years, and I know some of the things they're likely to say." The sparkle in his blue eyes contradicted the earnestness of his tone. "I'll bet they've been calling it polished oak, or old brandy, or fine leather. And they'd all come close, but none of 'em is quite right." He studied her closely, his head slightly tilted.

She pulled in a breath to stop this silliness, but he was off again, opening the door wide before turning. "Nope, I just don't have it. But I'll come up with it, Professor. And when I do, I'll be sure to let you know."

Carolyn stopped outside her front door and turned to look back. Her apartment occupied the second floor of a forty-year-old house that sat on a rise above the campus. The small covered porch at the top of the exterior stairway provided a wonderful view of the university, a view shared by the living room and bedroom. That was why she had chosen the apartment.

She could clearly see the rectangular-shaped Meadow. Three sides of it were enclosed by the Administration Building, the original classroom building and the chapel. The fourth side sloped away to Lake Ashton, which glinted in late-afternoon sun. Beyond this core, the campus expanded in concentric rings of buildings, each ring older than the larger one beyond it.

Despite the university's growth, huge trees and large, open areas remained. The grass had faded, but the trees displayed their prewinter bravura of color. Yellows skittered away down pathways and roads, while the oranges and reds would time their flaming peak perfectly for Homecoming.

She needed no such dramatics to make her own homecoming pleasant, Carolyn thought as she stepped inside. No signs of disorder betrayed her return from a five-month trip. She'd unpacked immediately. Clothes had gone back to their accustomed spots. Presents waited on the dining table to be distributed to friends. Only books presented a problem.

She eyed the shelves that covered one wall of the living room and dining area, interrupted by the generously cushioned couch and the door to her bedroom. More shelves lined a tiny bedroom office she'd created from a walk-in closet. All the shelves were full. She'd have to rejuggle her collection to accommodate her European purchases, with the spillover going to her campus office.

Carolyn arranged her suit jacket on a padded hanger in the closet across from the front door. With a steadying hand on the small table next to the door, she slipped her shoes off, then padded across the soft nap of the buff carpeting.

The beige cotton-covered couch, matched by two over-stuffed chairs facing it across a bleached pine coffee table, tempted her. What luxury to curl up and enjoy the panorama of Ashton through the picture window. But she should change first.

To the left of a pine table and chairs that made a dining area of one end of the living room was a compact kitchen with white cabinets and butcher-block countertops. She switched on a burner under the teapot and took a spoon from the drawer.

Just one, she told herself, scooping a heaping spoonful of Heavenly Hash ice cream directly from the carton in the freezer to her waiting mouth. She murmured with pleasure. If there was one thing she'd missed most in Europe, this was it.... Five months was a long time without true Wisconsin ice cream, she justified as she took a second spoonful. And a third.

Resolutely she rinsed the spoon and started toward the bedroom. The ringing phone hurried her back to the kitchen. She caught it on the second ring, barely beating her answering machine. Her breathless hello drew a laughing response.

"If I didn't know better, I'd say you'd just run all the way from Europe. But I hear you've already punched in for work—before you've even taken the time to tell me about all the fashions from Paris. How are you, Carolyn? Tell me all about the trip. Have you decided what you're going to wear to the dance Saturday? Did you like that hotel I recommended in Paris? I hope it hasn't changed too much over the years. One time I went back to a hotel after ten years and discovered it had converted to the hourly trade, if you know what I mean—no luggage necessary. So, how are you? Tell me everything. Oh, how silly, I didn't tell you who this is. It's Helene.''

Who else could it be? Carolyn smiled, switching off the burner. "How are you, Helene?"

Five months or five years away, no one could mistake Helene Ainsley's scattergun conversational style. It was as different from Elizabeth Barron's as the two cousins' lives had been. A former model and fashion consultant, Helene's bone structure still gave her a claim to beauty at age fifty.

When Elizabeth had become ill three years ago, Helene had left New York without a question to nurse her. She'd stayed at Ashton after Elizabeth's death fourteen months ago, saying that she might as well retire there as New York, especially since the air was a whole lot better in Wisconsin.

"I'm fine. I always am. I wish I could get Stewart to take it easier, though. That man works too hard, just like you. What you both need is a good course in having fun."

"Taught by Helene Ainsley, I presume."

"Could be, could be. Who better?"

"No one, I'm sure." The laugh faded from Carolyn's voice. "How has Stewart been, Helene? Before I left, he seemed so—"

"I know. When Liz died, I wondered... But these past few months I think he's better. Do you know he even took a vacation up to the lake house? A whole week of just sitting around and fishing. Best thing for him. Now, when are you going to do what's good for you?"

"Helene—" Carolyn tried to ward off the imminent lecture with little hope of success.

"What you need is someone to show you a good time, someone to light you up, make you glow. You're too... I don't know, steady, I guess. You think too much. Everything neatly ordered, including your love life. I don't suppose you did any high living over in England, did you?" Helene sighed deeply into the brief silence—silences were always brief with Helene. "No, I knew you wouldn't. Probably not even in Paris, heaven help you. What am I going to do with you?"

"Well, you could start by going shopping with me," Carolyn offered as a diversion from the you-need-a-man-in-your-life theme she knew would follow. "I need something for the dinner-dance Saturday."

Perhaps a new belt or scarf to complement her black sheath. But she'd wait to tell Helene that. It would only start a lecture about her boring clothes.

C.J. Draper's drawl floated into her head. *You ought to wear colors. Red. Green. Blue. Let 'em see you, instead of blending in.*

She shook her head, and the voice was once more Helene's.

"Done. Though why you didn't buy some marvelous dresses while you were in Paris, I can't understand. But I did see a few things at that new boutique at the mall that just might do. Pick you up in half an hour."

From the foot of her bed Carolyn contemplated the shopping bags cluttering its surface. What had possessed her?

Helene, of course. She'd been caught up in a shopping tornado that had accumulated the most unlikely objects in its funnel cloud of fashion and deposited them here on her bed. And if she wanted to go to sleep, she'd have to clear away the debris.

The first bag held a silky undergarment unlike any Carolyn had ever owned. She needed it because of the nearly backless teal dress Helene had convinced her to buy.

Carolyn gave a little sigh of pleasure at the crackle of the taffeta skirt as she pulled the dress out of its wrapping and carefully placed it on a padded hanger. The maneuver required care, because with no back, the tight-fitting bodice tended to fall off the hanger. At least she'd had the sense to withstand Helene's first choice: a red silk dress cut so low that it was nearly front-less.

Perhaps she shouldn't have given in to the teal dress, either. She could always return it. She'd think about it tomorrow, decide rationally and reasonably whether the dress was too, well, too something, for a professor at Ashton. And then she could always wear her black sheath.

She frowned as she folded a soft new royal blue sweater into the drawer. But perhaps some changes in style were in order, she thought as she hung up a red blazer. She didn't want to become stagnant.

Maybe that explained her twinge of dissatisfaction when she'd surveyed her living room while waiting for Helene. The beige of her upholstery, drapes and carpet usually soothed her, but today it seemed bland.

She pulled three vibrantly colored pillows—red, yellow and blue—out of their bags and headed for the living room. These ought to fix that.

She tried multiple combinations before settling on the red pillow on one armchair and the yellow and blue pillows layered in the far corner of the couch. She ran her hand over the texture of the blue pillow.

Monet blue. The blue of the sky sharing the canvas with a sun-bright field of Monet tulips. The blue of a lake caressing serene water lilies...like C.J. Draper's eyes.

Carolyn snatched her hand away and stood up. Where had that come from? She hadn't thought about him since he'd walked out of her office that afternoon.

At least she'd tried not to. But Helene extolling his virtues practically the whole evening had made it rather difficult. She'd heard how C.J. Draper had charmed the alumni; how he'd formed a team under difficult circumstances; how he'd won allies on the faculty; how he'd convinced Stewart to spend a week fishing.

Carolyn knew very well the purpose of that exercise. Helene meant to remind her, none too subtly, that C.J. Draper possessed charms her usual escorts lacked.

Helene had unstintingly described the visiting sociology lecturer Carolyn had dated, before leaving for Europe, as boring with a capital *B*. "And that anthropology professor before him wouldn't cause a tremor on any Richter scale of excitement, either," she'd told Carolyn after an unsuccessful dinner. "Come to think of it, the last one worth mentioning was the redhead who hung around Liz and Stewart's house that summer I spent here. Whatever happened to him?"

"Tony Reilly?" Laughter and exasperation had warred in Carolyn. "I was fourteen that summer and Tony Reilly was fifteen."

"So? Now you're twenty-eight and he's twenty-nine."

"Yes, he's also married with a child or two and selling insurance, I believe."

"He could be selling cemetery plots and he'd be more exciting than these poker faces you've been seeing," Helene had insisted.

To herself, Carolyn had admitted Helene might have had a point. Especially when it came to lovemaking. Either she couldn't figure out what all the fuss was about, or her few ventures were far below standard.

But the men she dated were long on academic credentials. She had concluded that if their company left her rather dissatisfied, then she must have failed, not them. Being reminded of that failing counted as one more item to chalk up against Ashton's new basketball coach.

What he represented was bad enough. But to call her too young! He'd tried to rile her on purpose, too. And worse, he'd succeeded. But then there had been that easy friendliness when he'd told her about the photographs and, nearly as surprising, the moment she'd sensed another person half revealed in that flash of anger in her office.

She snapped the light off in the living room with unnecessary force. It was probably all an effort to keep her at a disadvantage. Sure, that was it. He knew she disapproved of the basketball program, and he wanted to keep her from watching him too closely.

Well, she wouldn't fall for it.

And the reason she was haunted by vibrant blue eyes, a set of broad shoulders and that crazy, lopsided grin? Jet lag. That was all. Simple jet lag.

Carolyn looked across the Meadow toward Lake Ashton from the window of the small classroom in Ripon Hall. Waiting to meet the basketball team elicited an odd mixture of assurance and uncertainty that she always felt before the first session of a class. But she was ready.

She'd gone over their files and noted points to cover. She'd carefully chosen her suit of russet brown gabardine and effectively disposed of the box of toffee that she'd found on her desk this morning, along with a note from C.J. Draper saying he hoped he'd found the right color.

She'd thrown the note out and contributed the toffee to the English department secretary's sweet tooth. She would just as efficiently ignore any lingering thoughts about the donor.

The pen she held between her index and middle fingers tapped rapidly against the window ledge. She knew her ability; she knew she was a good teacher. That represented the known in this equation. The unknown consisted of ten young men who would walk through that door in the next few minutes. She'd already done her homework, she thought with an inner smile. Now it was their turn.

Their files had been a pleasant surprise. Six of the players were upperclassmen, juniors or seniors who had chosen Ashton well before the return of big-time basketball there. They had solid academic credentials. That left the four players recruited by C.J. Draper.

One had a strong academic background. A smile tugged at her lips. Thomas Abbott III might play basketball, but his admission essay made it quite clear he'd set his sights on law school and politics. He wouldn't jeopardize that with poor grades.

Ellis Manfred was another situation. He'd graduated from a strict parochial school in a poor section of St. Louis. Though unspectacular, his grades and test scores showed steady ability. Steadiness from a student in that kind of neighborhood said a lot.

She wished Ellis Manfred could share some of that stability with Brad Spencer. Roller-coaster grades linked with test scores that widened her eyes meant getting Brad Spencer to produce could rank as a full-time project by itself.

That left Frank Gordon. She knew only two things about him: he was a junior transfer from a two-year school in

Pennsylvania, and it was his file that C.J. Draper had somehow overlooked. That in itself roused suspicion. She could just imagine Frank Gordon—he'd probably be closer to twenty-five than eighteen, he'd be overgrown—body and ego—and his knowledge would be limited to street smarts and basketball courts. Probably a troublemaker. Just the sort of player she'd expect C.J. Draper to bring in. Setting Frank Gordon straight would be her first priority.

The door swung open and two players came in. With a surge of adrenaline and nerves, she moved to her customary position in front of the teacher's desk to start matching faces with names and backgrounds.

She also made a mental note to find somewhere else to meet. From the players' expressions, classroom desks took the leap from discomfort to torture when you were over six feet.

C.J. Draper's four recruits were last. Ellis Manfred was the composed, polite black with intelligent eyes that didn't miss a thing. Thomas Abbott III wore faded designer jeans, a faded blue work shirt and a white cashmere sweater, which Carolyn guessed cost as much as her suit. Brad Spencer, his blond hair casually styled, walked with a hint of a bounce on the toes of bright red high-tops that jammed up the bottoms of his black jeans. He needed the bounce to keep an arm hooked around the white-shirted shoulders of the player he came in with.

This last one must be Frank Gordon; no one else was left. He was certainly tall enough to play major college basketball; he had to be nearly seven feet. Other than that, he wasn't at all what she'd anticipated. This was no rough troublemaker. With close-cropped brown hair and wide brown eyes, he seemed a sweet-faced boy. And he obviously felt ill at ease at being caught even at the periphery of the attention that Brad Spencer was now basking in like a cat in sunshine. While Brad exchanged good-natured gibes with the others, Frank slipped into a desk at the back of the group as unobtrusively as someone his size could.

She'd expected Bill Sikes and in walked an overgrown Oliver Twist. Chalk up another surprise from C.J. Draper.

Carolyn leaned back against the desk with a hand at either side of her and drew in a breath. "Good morning. I'm Carolyn Trent. I'm a professor of English literature...." Her introduction trailed off as ten faces shifted from her to the doorway.

"Morning, Professor," C.J. greeted her. He sauntered in with his hands tucked into the front pockets of his jeans, pulling them even tighter around his lean hips. "Thought I'd sit in on this first session."

Think again, Mr. C.J. Draper, she silently advised him with one raised eyebrow. She had no intention of sharing this forum with him. From the start she wanted it clear that to her these ten young men were students. His presence could only remind them of basketball.

The grooves in his cheek deepened as he met her look, but his lips didn't betray the smile she was certain he'd suppressed. He started past the front desk, then stopped to look at her more closely.

She didn't flinch. Not even when he shook his head and said that now that he'd seen her again, he had to admit toffee wasn't quite right. Not even when the players chuckled a little, amused without knowing what he meant.

She wouldn't let C.J. Draper get to her. She watched him fold into a desk chair with difficulty but without awkwardness. If he succeeded in getting a rise out of her in front of the players, she would lose a lot of ground she might never make up. He would get no rise out of her.

"Before you leave, Mr. Draper," she said with emphasis, "would you like to say something to your—" she wouldn't call them his team; she wouldn't fall into that mentality "—to the students?"

He met her steady gaze with a faintly quizzical air, then he seemed to bow to her determination. He nodded in apparent acquiescence. "Well, if you don't want me around . . ." His slightly plaintive murmur drew chuckles. She caught several quick glances from the students, and the chuckles abruptly died.

Slowly he unwound his legs. Slower still he levered his long body out of the chair. Apparently in no hurry to get there, he walked to the front of the room to stand right in front of Carolyn.

She looked him squarely in the eyes and waited. If he thought he'd intimidate her with some body language, he was wrong. She'd taken her stance carefully to show her authority; she wouldn't relegate herself to the side of the room to leave him in charge.

The corner of his mouth twitched as he looked down at her, but other than that he remained solemn. He turned around and lowered himself onto the edge of the desk, his hip missing Carolyn's hand by no more than an inch. It took all her self-control not to snatch her hand away. She would hold that position if he talked until doomsday.

"You guys know why you're here. You know you gotta have the grades to play ball. *I* want you to be able to play. *You* want to be able to play. So you gotta have the grades. Professor Trent here is going to keep an eye on you to see that you have them." He paused and looked from face to face.

With a teacher's experienced eye, Carolyn classified them as not quite bored but prepared to lapse into that state the moment the situation warranted it.

C.J.'s conversational manner never varied. "The way I figure it, it's pretty simple. You can be here at Ashton and have a whale of a time—party every night, play a little ball, spend time with the guys, maybe go after the women. And you can stay here one semester." He paused again. "Or you can have a little less fun, work hard and stay eight semesters. It's up to you."

He pushed off from his perch slowly until he towered above Carolyn, then stretched out a hand. "Thank you, Professor," he said, shaking her uncooperative hand. Then he added, as if it had been his intention all along, "Guess I better be getting along now." He headed out the door. "See you, guys."

The air came out of her lungs in a slow exhalation. He'd left without a fight. More than that. She'd prepared to battle him for the players' attention. But the faces that turned toward her told her there would be no battle, not even a skirmish. At least not here, not yet.

Most of these players had chosen Ashton because of its academics in the first place. But the others—the ones recruited by C.J.—had heard his message loud and clear. As if they'd spoken aloud, their expressions said that his words had struck a chord.

She would have appealed to their thirst for knowledge; he went straight to common sense. His way worked. She gave him credit for that.

She smiled. "The first thing is the schedule that Mr. Draper and I have agreed on. I don't imagine it will surprise any of you much to know you have no say in the matter."

They smiled back at her.

Chapter Three

The irregular rhythm of ten sets of lungs trying to replenish depleted oxygen stores grated into C.J.'s consciousness. The players lagged, made mistakes because their bodies didn't obey the right commands. He knew the law of diminishing returns as well as any economist. There was just so damn much left to accomplish. If only the human body didn't cause so much trouble.

"Okay. Listen up." The gymnasium instantly stilled. "Gordon, Manfred, Spencer stay. The rest of you take off." The emancipated shuffled toward the locker room without a backward glance. "Same time tomorrow. Be ready to work."

The admonition drew groans. After working Frank, Ellis and Brad another hour, C.J. acknowledged they had cause to groan.

He knew he pushed them hard. He had to. Especially these three. They formed the core of his team this season and next, the core of his program at Ashton.

At his gesture they flopped down at midcourt. He sat facing them, elbows hooked around bent knees. "We've got to be a team that outsmarts opponents. There aren't a lot of teams we can beat on pure physical ability."

They nodded, acknowledging the kind of soaring, sprinting and leaping that set the stars apart from the likes of them.

"We've got to always use our heads. Mental and physical. Together. The two of them together, times the ten of you on the team, can stand up to almost anybody."

He looked directly into Ellis Manfred's serious dark eyes. "You're my brain out there, Manfred. You've got to know what I want in a situation as well as I do because the situation changes on a basketball court in a split second. You've got to adjust and make the right decision."

Ellis nodded.

"If you don't shoot, you can't win. But only about five minutes each game is shooting. Most often it's the other thirty-five minutes that determine whether you win or not. Okay. Back to work."

C.J. stifled a grimace of pain as he stood up, but he refused to favor his aching left knee. What was the good of the damn brace if it didn't let him practice for a couple of hours?

"I have to go, Coach," objected Ellis. "I have a hundred-page reading assignment due tomorrow."

His expression didn't change under C.J.'s glare. "Okay." What else could a coach say? Especially with an academic watchdog on the case. An image of Carolyn Trent's face appeared before his eyes. Oddly his scowl lightened. "How about you, Brad?"

"Sure, I'll stay."

A gym rat, C.J. thought. The cheerfulness gave him away. "Frank?"

Frank looked after Ellis's retreating back as if for support, then back. "I'll stay."

When C.J. dismissed them forty minutes later, Frank left practically before he'd said the words. Brad lingered, trailing him to the office and talking. C.J. recognized the heavily casual questions as an effort to pump him about his playing days. There had been a time he'd encountered it often. These days it was a rarity.

"I saw you in Chicago the next year," Brad said after one anecdote of the Tornadoes' championship season. "I'll never forget the way you drove the lane like nothing in the world could keep you from that basket. You dished off to Rake Johnson, and he got the slam. It was so smooth. I've never seen anything so smooth. I went home and practiced that move for months. I never did get it." He paused, a wave of embarrassment at his own enthusiasm abruptly stopping his flow. "I mean, I was just a kid then."

"Hey," C.J. objected. "I'm not that old. My last season with the Tornadoes didn't happen during the Dark Ages."

He glanced at the photo on his desk. *My last season.*

He was still looking at it when he added, "My old high school coach used to say, 'Drive the lane like the Indy 500. Go all out, but put on the brakes before you crash into a wall.' The one time I didn't put on the brakes, I crashed in flames. Remember that when you practice that move." He gestured with his clipboard. "Now get outta here. Hit the showers. I've got work. And you've got books to crack."

Half an hour later, when Brad came past and said goodnight, C.J. looked up from his notes for the first time. The interruption reminded him he was hungry. Packing up six game tapes to review that night, he headed to the apartment he called home.

When he got there, he swallowed the last of a half gallon of milk while he flipped through his mail. Then he crunched through an apple while he read the only thing that interested him: a letter from his mother full of the small news of a peaceful life. He heated leftover pizza as he set up the VCR.

Videotapes, clipboards and notebooks were the only accessories in the minimalist decorating scheme of his furnished apartment. As long as the functioning parts met his needs, he was happy. The couch stretched long and firm, so he ignored the raucous paisley cover that even clashed with white. The end table showed a dent and two burn marks, but it had a drawer for pens and clipboards and a shelf underneath for videotapes.

He knew it was ugly, and when he really looked at it, he winced. But he wasn't here much, and even when he was, he seldom really looked.

There had been a woman when he played for the Tornadoes who had wanted to decorate his place in Chicago. Kim had said he should think of his image. The way things had been going, he probably would have let her redecorate eventually. Then the injury.

He gave her credit, though. She didn't disappear when his knee—and his career—shattered. But seven months into the rehabilitation she'd told him she couldn't compete any longer with machines, exercises and strength tests. It was just as well it had ended there; it never would have survived his swing through the league, to Italy, then back. And if by some miracle she'd still been around, the relationship surely would have withered at Ashton.

The thing was, he knew himself well enough to recognize that the challenge here affected him much the way the challenge of rehabilitation had. He hadn't really minded when Kim had left. To be honest, he'd barely noticed. He'd had a mission.

Now the mission was to give Ashton a decent basketball program and give himself a shot at the big time. For five months he'd been going practically nonstop. He'd looked at every player, every highlight tape that had come his way, hoping to find the remaining recruiting nuggets the swarms of prospecting coaches had somehow missed. He'd studied tapes until he'd known each twist and turn.

Sometimes, like tonight, he felt permanently attached to a VCR. He rubbed his eyes as he pulled a tape out. He wouldn't have minded it so much if his eyes would just stop superimposing an image over the screen—a smooth sweep of amber-brown hair surrounding a serious face. Carolyn Trent could develop into a real thorn in his side if he let her.

This morning he'd thought his presence might show the guys how seriously he took the adviser program. But she'd made it damn obvious she didn't want him around.

The toffee? Just a little friendly joke. A little teasing to see if she'd come out from behind that marble facade.

And that moment in his office yesterday when he'd stood close enough to smell the hint of spice and flower in her hair? Or when his arm had absorbed the slight contact with the swell of her breast like a branding iron?

The memory tightened his body.

C.J. cursed emphatically and shoved the next tape into the machine. Definitely a thorn.

Doing her Homecoming duty wasn't so bad. Being outdoors in the brisk sparkle of an autumn afternoon was nice, and the colors and noise swirling around the football field and stands were wonderful. Oh, the level of play fell below what television audiences would expect, but that suited her fine. This was the way college sports were supposed to be.

Carolyn just wished that doing her duty didn't include sitting on these bleachers in front of C.J. Draper. Not when his long legs—the only ones clad in jeans in the entire presidential party—put his shins within tempting reach of providing the backrest her body craved. She shifted for the third time in two minutes.

"See, that's the problem with football games," C.J. said, leaning over from the row behind her to speak directly into her ear. "No backs on the seats."

"There are no backs on the seats at basketball games, either, Mr. Draper."

Turning to confront him was a mistake. His eyes were so close that she felt wrapped in blue. Against the brisk air the touch of his breath was warm on her cheek. His lips slanted into a grin inches from hers, showing strong white teeth. She turned back to the field, fighting the disturbing sensation that a feather had lodged in her throat.

"I guess not, but I've never sat through a basketball game. I've always played." She couldn't detect even a note of bragging. "You think maybe that's why people are jumping up all the time at these games? It's not so much that they get excited, as they just can't stand to sit still?"

Before she could answer, Stewart, seated to her left, spoke up. "Don't forget about the dinner-dance tonight at the Ashton Club, C.J. It's one of the best parties at Ashton. Isn't it, Helene?"

Helene, sitting on the other side of Stewart, agreed with a laugh. "I guess I think all parties are good, but the dinner-dance and the cocktail party at Mrs. Dawton's beforehand are something special. She has the most wonderful house up on the Heights with a marvelous view. And she always has such elegant hors d'oeuvres."

"Do you have the directions, C.J.?" Stewart asked.

"I've got the address. I'll find my way."

Stewart looked concerned. More concerned than the situation called for, Carolyn thought. He's up to something. She shifted for a better view of his face.

"It can be very difficult to find. It's very confusing up there on the Heights. What might work best—" Carolyn became fully alert when she heard the calculated blandness in Stewart's voice "—is if you and Carolyn drove up together."

"That's an excellent idea, Stewart," Helene seconded quickly, confirming Carolyn's suspicion. This was a setup.

"I'm sure Mr. Draper will have no difficulty finding it, Stewart. He has, after all, traveled extensively."

"Carolyn," objected Helene, "you know how confusing it is up there with all those streets twisting and turning on themselves. Why, I've been there hundreds of times, and I still get lost, so imagine how hard it would be for someone new."

"I do have a tendency to get lost," murmured C.J.

Carolyn shot him a dark look under frowning brows. He returned one of utter innocence.

Stewart took the cue. "Then, of course, it certainly would be better—"

"But I'm sure Mr. Draper has a guest he's bringing tonight. I don't want to intrude—"

"Nope. No guest," he contradicted cheerfully.

"There. It's all settled." Satisfaction suffused Helene's face.

"No, it's not settled," Carolyn said. "I think I should go with you and Stewart as planned."

"If you're concerned about driving with C.J. up those roads, Carolyn, I can assure you, I've ridden with him, and he's an excellent driver," Stewart said.

Carolyn opened her mouth for another attempt at escape, but C.J.'s drawl intruded. "I don't think it's the driving that's worrying the professor. I think it's the arriving. You see," he explained, "if we *arrive* together, people might think we're *together* and that could be awkward for the professor."

Stewart and Helene turned questioning eyes to her, and Carolyn felt her shoulders sink under the hopelessness of extricating herself.

It wasn't that she didn't want people to think they were together; she was just uncomfortable with him. She hadn't worked out yet in her own mind why—an oddity in itself. But she knew she definitely didn't want it brought up now. How he'd stumbled so close to the truth, she didn't know. But since he had, she could only deny it.

"Not at all, Mr. Draper," she said, looking away quickly from the laughter in his blue eyes before she lost her temper. "Of course I'll drive with you. Heaven knows we wouldn't want to risk our new basketball coach driving off a cliff, would we?"

Graciousness and stoicism are the keys to getting through this with dignity, Carolyn told herself as she smoothed the taffeta skirt of her new dress. She'd put the black sheath on first. But she'd seen herself looking staid and boring in too many mirrors. In the end she'd flung the sheath on the bed and pulled on the teal dress with a tingling—and unaccustomed—sense of daring.

The color added glow to her hair and heightened the natural pink blush of her fair skin. The tight bodice molded to the curves of her breasts and the narrowness of her waist. The skirt crackled around her with whispering touches against her silk-hosed legs. She felt the headiness of a woman who knew she looked good. But it didn't prevent a surge of nerves at the sound of her doorbell.

The porch light glinted on the fair strands of C.J.'s hair, and a smile barely pulled up the corners of his mouth. His double-breasted navy blue topcoat kept the perfect line of his squared shoulders and dropped without a wrinkle or fold. Beneath it the sharp crease of charcoal-gray slacks showed. The coat's V opening displayed a crisp white shirt and rich burgundy silk tie.

Wordlessly she stepped back as he entered.

"This is for you." He handed her a brown paper bag as he closed the door behind them. He shrugged out of his coat and laid it over the back of a chair. His suit jacket was as trim as the topcoat. The precise fit across the shoulders and down his long arms and torso proclaimed it tailored for him by a master.

"I can understand your surprise, Professor," he said with only the brightness of his eyes betraying his sympathetic expression. "But you really ought to do something about that—" he nodded toward the bag she still held "—before it drips on your dress."

Abruptly the cold penetrating her hands registered in Carolyn's mind. "What is it?"

"Ice cream. And I think it's melting."

"Ice cream! What on earth possessed you to bring ice cream?" For a moment she had an eerie feeling this man could see inside her. How had he divined her vice?

"The color. You better put it in the freezer first and ask questions later, Professor."

The bag was suspiciously limp. Carefully holding it away from her, she carried it to the kitchen, fully aware that C.J. was following her. Blocking his view of the Heavenly Hash carton already there and giving silent thanks that at least he wasn't a mind reader, she closed the freezer door on the ice cream, bag and all, then moved to the sink to wash her hands.

"That's quite a dress, Professor." His low voice came from right behind her.

She twisted around to hide her bare back and found herself no more than four inches away from him, and her eyes roughly on a level with his collar despite the three-inch heels she wore. His nearness startled her into a backward step, which was abruptly halted by the counter's edge.

His light grasp helped restore her balance, and her hands rested on his forearms for a moment as she steadied herself. Under her fingertips she felt the smooth warmth of his fine wool sleeve. Beneath it, the solid bulk of a muscular arm.

Carolyn resolutely ignored a thrumming in her veins to concentrate on the knot in his silk tie. He was so big. Standing like this, his body seemed a wall against the outside world. Cutting her off or protecting her?

She pushed the question aside and concentrated on her heartfelt gratitude that she hadn't let Helene talk her into the red dress. With that plunge front and from his vantage point . . . She glanced up quickly at his blue eyes sparkling with something she couldn't quite describe as mischief, and just as quickly looked down again. She didn't want to think of what he would have seen.

"Thank you," she said stiffly as she stepped around him. "Now, would you like to explain the ice cream?"

"It's mocha chip."

She waited, but that, apparently, was the extent of his explanation. "Is that supposed to have some significance?"

He nodded. "I saw the mocha chip in the ice cream store after the game, and I thought for sure I'd got something the

exact color of your hair and eyes." He shook his head for-
lornly. "But now I see that's not it, either."

Impatiently Carolyn headed toward the front hall.
"Really, Mr. Draper, don't you think this is rather silly?"

Scooping up his coat as he passed the chair where he'd
laid it, he started to follow. "Yeah, I should have known it
was too light. Guess I'll have to try something else."

In the mirror over the small hall table she watched his reflection as he smoothly pulled on his coat. Something on the
bookshelf next to the bedroom door caught his interest, and
he changed direction with an easy economy of motion.

He held it in one large hand before she realized what he'd
seen: the photograph of her as a little girl with her parents,
the last one taken of them. Their eyes met in the mirror, and
she saw his question. "My parents," she jerked out. She
remembered how easily he'd told her of his family.

"I've heard about them. Both professors here, weren't
they?"

She nodded.

"What happened?"

There was something in his voice. It couldn't be pity. Pity
never would have made her answer.

"They were killed in a car accident. Up north. Trying to
avoid a deer in the road. I was five." She turned away from
the mirror. "I lived with my grandparents until Stewart and
Elizabeth Barron brought me back to Ashton."

None of it was a secret. He probably knew it already;
anybody at Ashton could tell him the story. But *she* didn't
tell people. Why was she telling him?

And why was she feeling the urge now to tell him it had
been the end of being sure? The end of the security known
by that happy little girl holding hands with the two laughing adults.

"Everybody says how proud they'd be of you."

There it was in his voice again. Perhaps an echo of understanding? But why should his understanding mean anything to her? It didn't.

She turned to watch his gaze roam the living room, taking in the details the way he had in her office. "Monochromatic," she said with a snap. "Like me."

Confused by her own sharpness, she turned away to open the closet door, reaching for her coat to give herself time. She wished, for an irrational moment, that she could close the closet door behind her and hide in the dark awhile.

One large hand pushed her fingers aside as she fumbled with the hanger, deftly removing the coat. His other hand ran down the smooth slipperiness of the dress's tight-fitting sleeve to her wrist, then turned her so that she faced the mirror with her back to him.

She couldn't move; her muscles refused to heed her orders. She could only watch him survey the smooth, bare flesh of her back and feel herself become unaccountably heated by the look.

His eyes rose to meet hers in the mirror as he held her coat for her. "No room's monochromatic as long as you're there in this dress."

Stoicism and graciousness, Carolyn reminded herself as they headed down the stairs toward his car. Ignore him.

What about your reactions to him? asked a sneaky little voice from the back of her mind. *How are you going to ignore yourself?*

They reached the drive to Mrs. Dawton's estate and drew into the slowly advancing line of cars headed into the long, curving drive.

"Still worried about people thinking we're together?" C.J.'s voice was soft and sympathetic.

Carolyn looked over at him quickly; just as she thought, the grin lurked just beneath the surface. "I beg your pardon, Mr. Draper." Detached and calm, her own tone pleased her. Surely her coolness would penetrate eventually—if not to him, at least to herself.

"I guess I can see your point. You being a professor of literature and all." He eased the car forward, moving around a curve to the front of the sprawling stone mansion. At the door each car in turn discharged its passengers and a young man in an Ashton jacket took it away to leave room for the next. "And I hear this meeting thing you attended in England is pretty exclusive. Only for the best. Sort of an all-star game for literature professors."

She didn't bother to reply to that, but he didn't seem to notice.

"I'll tell you what. I'll make you a deal, Professor. We'll call it a bet, as long as you don't tell the guys—it wouldn't set a good example for them."

They were next in line. Once inside, she decided she'd convince Stewart and Helene to drive her to the dinner-dance.

"Now what should the bet be, Professor? How about if you can say something nice about basketball?"

"No." No need to answer more. Carolyn's door opened as C.J. stopped the car, and a gentlemanly hand extended to help her out.

"Professor Trent!" Frank Gordon's eyes widened.

She smiled at him and headed up the stairs. Knowing C.J. was close behind still didn't prepare her for the warmth of his big hand slipping under her elbow.

She turned to frost him with a look, but he seemed immune. She could have pulled away from the light grasp; it wasn't until much later that she came up with the explanation that it would have appeared blatantly rude.

"Okay, you pick the bet," he said. "And to make it interesting, we'll have a little something riding on it. How's that?"

For a moment Carolyn considered the satisfying temptation of telling him exactly what she thought of his idea. But parting to hand their coats to attendants gave her time to reconsider. C.J. immediately returned to her side. His palm cupped her elbow once more, guiding her to the end of the reception line.

He bent his head so that his low voice reached only her. "If you win, you'll be spared my company the rest of the evening. That's what you want, isn't it?"

His words surprised Carolyn even more than the rasp of his drawl and the tightening of his fingers. She looked up quickly to find his blue eyes disconcertingly close, and even more disconcerting in their directness. Once more he'd come closer to reading her feelings than she liked. She *did* want to be spared his company. She only hoped he didn't realize that the reason was the peculiarly unsettling effect he seemed to have on her.

His customary lightness replaced the slight harshness of his previous question, but his grip remained firm. "And if I win the bet, I continue to be your escort for the evening. And you dance with me—at least twice. Agreed?"

She opened her mouth to deny it, to end this immediately. But the pressure of his hand on her elbow turned her face-to-face with Mrs. Dawton. C.J. Draper had timed it perfectly.

Mrs. Dawton said a polite welcome to Carolyn, then gushed over C.J. There was no other word to describe it, Carolyn decided. And Mrs. Dawton wasn't the only one. In fact, the press of people trying to meet him ultimately succeeded in loosening his hold on her arm.

Just before she moved away, though, some impulse that took her by surprise pushed her up on her toes to bring her mouth closer to his ear, so only he could hear.

"You have to make a literary allusion before we leave for the club. An allusion that impresses a professor of literature. How's that, Mr. Draper?"

She caught a flicker of his surprise before she slipped past the encircling people eager to talk to the new basketball coach, and gave a short sigh of accomplishment. Maybe it indicated a weakness in her character, but turning his "bet" on him brought a certain satisfaction.

Glancing back through the thicket of shoulders to the shining head that topped all the others, her eyes caught C.J.'s. For an instant she thought a forlorn shadow crossed his face, and she felt an odd echo in her own heart.

"Carolyn, how nice to see you. And you look lovely. That's a wonderful color for you."

Shaking off the strange sensation, she turned to Mary Rollins, a longtime friend from the registrar's office.

There were so many people she hadn't seen since the spring, so many eager to hear about her travels and studies that she found herself postponing the moment when she would seek out Stewart and ask to join his party.

C.J. spent an hour talking basketball and wondering what had gotten into him. He listened to a board member's analysis of a top national team with flattering interest while watching Carolyn's progress through the room. Just remembering the urge he'd wrestled with earlier to stroke her ivory back made his fingertips tingle.

Why did he try to goad her that way? Sure, she hid behind a mask of chilly dignity. So what? People wore masks all the time.

Take this alum. He downplayed his position as a chief executive officer with carefully cultivated modesty. Behind that an ego drove him to succeed—and to retell glories of his athletic days.

Why did Carolyn's retreat behind her marble facade make him want to shake her? Smiling, he answered a professor of mathematics's question about a famous former teammate.

Was it because he wasn't really sure what was behind her pose as the distant academic? Or because he hoped the warmth and vulnerability he thought he'd seen were real? If he didn't know himself better, he'd say this thorn in his side might well become a full-blown infection.

With a mental sigh, C.J. wondered how much longer he needed to charm the influential guests. Better get used to it, Draper, he told himself. Coaching doesn't start on the court, and it doesn't end in the locker room.

He'd do his Homecoming duty, then he'd finish up a certain bet with Professor Carolyn Trent. And he'd beat her. Masks, thorns and all.

C.J. smiled broadly at the bragging alum.

"The seminar sounds like quite an outing, Carolyn," commented Edgar Humbert, a colleague from the English Department, as he lit a cigarette from the butt of the one he'd just finished. "And I hear they were quite impressed by you. You're going to make department head before you're thirty."

"Edgar, I'm honored," she teased. "That my name should be included on your academic grapevine—surely the most extensive one in the free world—is an honor indeed."

His slight bow acknowledged the compliment, and the truth of it. A wink, though, pricked any pomposity in his self-congratulations. "I'd like to have you in to lecture to my grads. Let's talk about a date." His eyes darted over her shoulder, and a smile flicked on his thin lips. "That is if you can spare time from your basketball players."

So the faculty grapevine already hummed with word of her new assignment.

"Hi, Ed," came C.J.'s near-drawl from behind her. He moved around to join them. It was the first time she'd seen him free of a crowd since their arrival. "'Fraid Caro's going to be busy with my guys. They'll take a lot of time. Isn't that right, Caro?"

"Caro?" Carolyn and Edgar chorused the name, Carolyn indignantly and Edgar questioningly.

"I don't believe I've ever heard Carolyn called that before," said Professor Humbert with avid curiosity and a distinct expression of puzzlement as he looked at C.J.

"Oh?" C.J.'s blue eyes looked with innocence from Carolyn to Edgar Humbert. "It just seemed to suit her. You know, sort of poetic?"

"Poetic?"

Edgar kept supplying C.J. with exactly the leads he wanted, and Carolyn wished she could have warned him—better yet, ordered him—to be quiet.

"Wasn't there a poem written to a Caro once? 'Remember thee! Remember thee! Till Lethe quench life's burning stream...'"

Edgar Humbert spluttered over his cigarette. "Byron, of course! But, C.J., do you know the rest?" Humbert didn't wait for an answer, but continued the quote:

"Remember thee! Aye, doubt it not.
And haunt thee like a feverish dream!
Remember thee! Aye, doubt it not.
Thy husband too shall think of thee:
By neither shalt thou be forgot,
Thou *false* to him, thou *fiend* to me!

"Byron wrote it about Lady Caroline Lamb when he'd ended the affair and she kept after him," Humbert offered, darting a look from Carolyn's stony stillness to C.J.'s dancing eyes. "Not very flattering to our Carolyn."

"No, indeed," said C.J. with exaggerated repentance. "I beg your pardon, Professor Trent. Now I know why no one calls you Caro!"

"See you at the club, Edgar." Carolyn spun on her heel and headed out, too angry to trust herself to say more.

A setup. She'd been set up. One way or another she'd been set up. She'd picked the test, but he'd been lying. All that drawling unsophisticated talk, all that nonsense of trying to find the right "color" for her, all that supposed friendly openness. All the while he was playing her for a fool by pretending to be an ill-educated jock.

She took four strides before she felt C.J.'s strong fingers grip her elbow.

"You're right. It's time we left for the club." His voice dropped to a laughing growl in her ear. "How'd you like that, Professor? Impressed two literature professors for the price of one." Then he said louder, "I was just coming to get you when we got into that very interesting literary discussion with Professor Humbert."

She ignored him, carefully avoiding his eyes as he escorted her to his car.

Why she even allowed that tacit acknowledgment that he'd won his silly bet, she couldn't imagine. The only possible reason was to use the trip to the Ashton Club to find out how much of a fool she'd made of herself.

"How much do you know about Byron?" She put the question to him when she could speak with the calm she expected of herself.

"Not much. You know, the affair with Caroline Lamb, rumors about him and his half sister, sleeping with pistols under his pillow during his honeymoon. When Professor Eggers got to the dissolute life-style, that's when I listened up.''

"George Eggers?'' His "Uh-huh'' confirmed he meant the man who'd been a fixture at the state university for decades. "George Eggers doesn't teach large lecture classes. Only seminars.''

C.J.'s murmur was noncommittal.

"You took a Byron seminar from George Eggers?''

He shrugged almost apologetically. "I needed one more English class to graduate. The one on Byron was the only one that fitted into my schedule. Coach finagled me in.''

"George Eggers wouldn't—'' She bit off the words.

"Wouldn't what?'' He was deceptively cordial. "Wouldn't take a jock in his class? Or wouldn't doctor a grade to pass me?''

"I didn't mean...'' She couldn't finish. She wasn't sure she hadn't meant just that.

"Rest easy, Professor.'' She thought she heard an edge to his voice, one so thin that it barely existed. "George Eggers's integrity is intact. I was no scholar, but I passed that course. Legitimately.''

Twisting in her seat, she looked at the large hands curled competently around the steering wheel and the profile resolutely faced forward, and came to a conclusion—she wasn't truly surprised he'd taken the course. Or that he'd passed. "Mr. Draper, you're a fraud.''

He turned to her, and she saw a trace of uncertainty in his eyes. Then the grin slid into place. "I guess I am a bit of a fraud. Aren't we all?''

She ignored that. "Why don't you tell people?''

"Tell them what? That I'm not stupid? The ones that want to see that, see it. Stewart saw it. He asked about my academic background, and I told him. Most of the people

here at Ashton, like Edgar Humbert, got to know me before forming any conclusions. The rest of them? Well, you
notice I'm not always asked for my opinions on art or literature or politics. It can make people real uncomfortable
if you don't meet their expectations."

She'd deserved that. She'd jumped to her conclusions and
she was wrong. No wonder Edgar had looked so puzzled by
C.J.'s behavior. Still . . . "But to let people think you only
know basketball—"

"Look, Professor—" his mouth held a grim line, his eyes
narrowed and the title never sounded so like an insult
"—basketball is what I do. And do damn well. There's
nothing 'only' about it. It gave me the chance for that education you value so highly. It gave me enough money to buy
my family a decent life. And now it's given me a job—a
challenging job."

Carolyn turned away. He'd misled her, apparently on
purpose. But she'd fully cooperated. He'd only made sure
to meet her expectations.

"I beg your pardon, Mr. Draper."

C.J. stretched his fingers until he steered only with his
palms. "I liked it better when you said it the other way."

"Said what what other way?"

"When you'd say, 'I beg your pardon,' as if you were
Queen Victoria and I were a chimney sweep."

Queen Victoria? He saw her as the strait-laced, sad-faced
monarch? Carolyn bristled at the notion. Then she contemplated his half of the image. Vividly and ludicrously she
envisioned C.J. Draper trying to get his long limbs and wide
shoulders up a chimney. She tried to stifle the laugh, but the
effort only added a gurgle to it.

She saw the undiluted blue of his eyes open wide on her
for a second, then narrow with the now-familiar grin.

"Anyone less like a chimney sweep I find it hard to imagine," she said, laughter still filtering through her voice.

Anyone less like a marble statue, he silently replied some time later, *I find it hard to imagine.*

Holding her in his arms on the dance floor at the Ashton Club, he could feel her body move to the slow rhythm of the music. No marble there.

For the first two dances he'd carefully kept his hand at her waist. But this was the third dance, one past the terms of their agreement.

He slid his hand along the smooth material of her dress to where nothing covered the bare flesh at the small of her back. Cool and soft, the contact of her skin with his warm palm lit a fuse of dynamite that ran up his arm, tightening every muscle along the way.

She felt it, too. He knew she did, because for an instant she arched toward him, as if her body craved more of the contact, as if she would meet his body all along their lengths. He imagined her thighs moving against his, her hips touching his, her breasts pressing against his chest. With more self-control than he knew he possessed, C.J. resisted the urge to accomplish that union.

What had possessed him to spout off like that to her in the car? When had he ever expected people to treat him like a rocket scientist? For that matter, what had possessed him to play the dumb jock as much as he had from their first meeting?

Why hadn't he just told her he'd worked like a dog in George Eggers's class, spurred by his own pride and the old man's rigid standards. And, amazingly, he'd found he'd liked it. Found he remembered it. Even found himself, every now and again over the years, picking up that tattered paperback volume of poetry for the pleasure of it.

So what if two days ago this woman had smiled at him the way someone dressed in white smiles at a muddy dog? So what if she wore masks piled one on top of the other a foot thick? So what if her marble-smooth skin pulsed with a life no statue knew? So what if her eyes glowed with an ember he longed to bring to a blaze? He thought he'd outgrown this sort of thing a long time ago.

And look where it had gotten him now. What was he supposed to do with a contrite Carolyn Trent? But his body knew just what it wanted to do.

If he said something to her, anything, she'd raise her face to look up at him and, as close as they were now, her mouth would be right there, just below his. That wide mouth with the full lower lip.

The song ended and they stepped apart as the final chord swallowed his sigh. C.J. wasn't sure if he was sighing from frustration or relief at a temptation withstood. Maybe both.

Chapter Four

Ten minutes. Then fifteen. At twenty minutes past the time Brad, Frank, Ellis and the other players should have checked in, Carolyn pulled on coat and gloves and marched up the cinder-strewn path through melting evidence of the season's first snow to the Physical Education Center.

Just because C.J. Draper wasn't the buffoon he'd chosen to pretend to be didn't mean she could be charmed out of doing her job.

She'd been friendly—maybe too friendly—at the Homecoming dinner-dance. Lulled by his easygoing manner and perhaps a little embarrassed by her unfair assumptions about him, she'd remained in his company most of the evening.

They'd danced five times. He'd held her closer after the first few dances, but not so close that she'd felt obligated to protest. She'd wondered if he might try to tighten his hold, or perhaps even kiss her, say, at the door when they returned to the apartment. Not that she would have permitted it. Still, she'd felt a trace of surprise when he had simply pressed her hand and said good-night, not even asking to come in. She was *not* disappointed. She'd simply felt a moment of surprise that he'd seemed so willing to cut short what had turned out to be, after all, quite an enjoyable evening.

Then some slyly teasing comments at the alumni brunch the next morning had brought her up short. She'd never been teased about her other escorts. She'd liked dancing with him, and he did make her laugh. But it had all been misunderstood.

On Sunday night she had eaten the entire quart of mocha chip ice cream and come to a few conclusions. She'd determined a long time ago to live by her mind, and the decision had worked well for her. She thought things out, assessed them rationally. Then, and only then, did she act.

Rational assessment had told her that her colleagues had seen her being cordial to C.J. and interpreted it as much more than it was. Which, of course, was ridiculous. Even if he did make her laugh, even if he wasn't the dumb jock she'd presumed, even if she was aware how his crooked grin and blue eyes could charm some women, he was still the leading proponent of top-level basketball at Ashton. As long as she dealt with him on that basis, there would be no misunderstanding, she'd decided then.

Nearly three weeks of peace had passed under that regimen. Three weeks when her only communication with him dealt with the ten players and their academic progress. Three weeks when her only contacts with him were brief, businesslike phone calls and even more businesslike memos.

But no phone call or memo would serve this time. Those players were twenty minutes late for the mandatory study period.

In the otherwise quiet PE Center she heard the muffled squeak of sneakers and the sharp tones of one voice coming from the gym. Her fast-clicking heels snapped across the foyer with echoing emphasis, but didn't drown out the noises from inside. She swung the door open wide, and the momentum of her anger carried her a third of the way down the length of the gym.

The players were all gathered in a tableau under the basket at the other end of the court, moving to C.J.'s directions, or trying to. He had his back to her, but she could see—all too clearly—the taut cords running down his neck to the broad, squared shoulders and disappearing into the ragged opening of an armless sweatshirt cropped just above his waist. His practice shorts revealed every inch of his long, muscular thighs. Sweat darkened the hair at the nape of his neck and glinted on his arms and legs. The moisture helped mold the thin material to his narrow hips when no help was needed at all.

She felt heat sweep over her, tingling her nerves and turning her own muscles to marshmallow. A strange sensation coiled in her abdomen, pulling tighter and tighter.... All the result of going from the cold outside to the steamy warmth of the gym, she told herself. It must be.

C.J. stood, hands on hips, his muscles tensed. No one could mistake his frustration, even without the voice. "Do it again, Gordo. On three. One. Two. Three."

Ellis Manfred stood beyond the end line, holding the ball. On the count of three the other players simultaneously moved, each spinning in a different direction, taking three quick steps one way before reversing just as rapidly. Twice Ellis started to throw the ball, and twice pulled back. It appeared as random, unmotivated movement to Carolyn.

"No. No! *No!* You're supposed to fake the defender, not invite him to the prom, Gordo. Watch." C.J., moving easily despite the brace on his left knee that she noticed for the first time, took Frank Gordon's spot and, with a wave of his hand, ordered the tableau to reform around him as she'd first seen it.

Again the count of three produced a flurry of movement, but this time, C.J. emerged alone, unshadowed, for just the moment it took for Ellis to send him the ball. He jumped to meet it and continued his leap, carrying the ball with him and gently dropping it into the basket.

The movement channeled power and grace to achieve a single objective. It was beautiful, Carolyn thought with bemusement.

"All right!"

"Way to go, Coach."

"Yeah!"

C.J. ignored the accolades. He focused on Frank Gordon. "Do you see, Gordo? You've got to give him the fake. Even when his mind knows it's coming, there aren't many guys who can stop from reacting for that split second. And that's all you need. You create your own opportunity, and then, by God, you'd better take it or it'll be gone. Now try again. On three."

Ellis Manfred spotted Carolyn moving toward the bench along the side of the court and nodded in her direction. She knew he'd pointed her out to his teammates when several heads turned. She stopped.

"One. Two. Three." Frank Gordon and two or three others started their moves, but the rest held stock-still. "What the—" C.J. broke off the oath and spun around to find the source of the interruption.

Carolyn saw the intense concentration on his face, and felt a pang of regret for disrupting them.

"Oh. It's you." Ichabod Crane showed more enthusiasm at seeing the Headless Horseman. "What do you want?"

Carolyn lifted her chin. "I want those students. You're in my time, Mr. Draper. We had an agreement."

She saw his irritation. She could practically hear him telling her what she could do with that agreement when it impinged on a practice where he was finally—finally—starting to get his point across.

He turned away. Over his shoulder she could see the players watching him. They were waiting for him to tell her to get lost. She could see it in their faces—some looking forward to it, some dreading it, some just curious. But all of them waiting for it. Knowing it was coming. They'd seen it before.

She straightened her shoulders, ready to do battle, her momentary regret at interrupting forgotten. Slowly he turned back to face her. He drew in air and held it, apparently unaware that the movement drew up the cropped sweatshirt to expose a strip of hard-muscled waist above the low-slung waistband of his shorts.

But she was aware of it. Vitally and basically aware. She tried to keep her eyes on his face, but they wouldn't cooperate. her breathing had somehow gotten out of kilter, and her pulse sprinted toward something she couldn't identify. She fervently wished he would hurry up and expel that breath.

When he did, the sound got lost in the intake of air behind him. "You're right, Professor Trent. I apologize. We all apologize. They'll be right there."

Silence.

He twisted to look over his shoulder at the statuelike players. "You heard me. Showers. Hustle it up. You've got books to crack."

That broke the spell. In two minutes the team manager wheeled a rack filled with basketballs out of the gym and the only two people left on the court were C.J. and Carolyn.

"So, was that satisfactory, Professor?" Neither had moved, ten feet of polished wooden floor separated them, but she could clearly see his crooked grin.

"Will you please stop calling me Professor when it's not appropriate?"

"Will you please start calling me C.J. when it *is* appropriate?"

Showcased by the sleeveless sweatshirt, muscles cupped his shoulders, indenting before the swell of his biceps. She swallowed the mental and conversational digressions. "It would have been more satisfactory if you'd ended practice on time, Mr. Draper." She spun on her heel and walked away.

Almost to the door, his voice reached her, and she could hear the grin in its mock servility. "Yes, Professor."

The conference room's large tables and chairs suited long bodies and legs, and the couches and armchairs around the room provided a spot for the sprawlers. After that first meeting she'd brought the players here for three-hour study sessions six days a week for the five weeks since she'd become academic adviser.

She decided that after the first of the year she'd make the daily sessions optional for the established students. Perhaps she'd make some changes in the schedule, too. But the structured schedule helped the freshmen and Frank Gordon.

Carolyn frowned as she looked at Frank hunched over a copy of the *Canterbury Tales*. He was in a lower level English class than she'd have expected for a junior, although that happened sometimes when a student lagged behind in one area. But this was mid-November. Shouldn't he be farther than that by now? And the boy looked miserable.

In fact, she thought as she looked around, they all looked miserable.

One of the upperclassmen kept flipping back through the pages he'd just read as if trying to reassure himself he'd actually seen the words. Ellis Manfred doodled over sheets meant for a midterm paper's outline. Thomas Abbott made no pretense of studying as he moodily stared out the window. Even Brad Spencer's usual cocky good humor seemed to have vanished as he started an algebra problem time after time, wadding each failed effort into a ball and lofting it toward the wastepaper basket. His latest effort spun on the edge with a thin, metallic sound, then dropped to the outside, landing on top of three others.

"Will you stop that? It's bad enough to have your misses all over the basketball court. Can't you spare us in here?" inquired a usually even-tempered upperclassman named Jerry.

"Yeah? How about your less than brilliant performance last night, huh?"

"Stop it. Both of you," Carolyn ordered, cutting across the rising tension. "Will someone please tell me what's the matter with all of you today?"

Ellis, she'd learned from Edgar Humbert, played a position called point guard. That was a position of leadership, he said. She could believe it. Every one of the other players looked at Ellis now, waiting for him to explain.

"We got beat last night, Professor Trent. In our first game of the season. By a team we should've beat."

"They were dog meat," muttered Brad.

"What does that make us?" asked Jerry with heavy sarcasm. "They beat us by twenty-two points."

"It's a good thing you didn't go last night, Professor Trent," said Frank.

Carolyn knew he meant that, but she felt a sudden shaft of guilt for not going. She'd considered it, but she hadn't wanted her position on the new basketball program misunderstood.

"We stunk." Thomas Abbott's forcefully delivered opinion drew some nods, but also a few smiles. The mood eased.

"Coach chewed our—" Brad swallowed the accustomed word and found a substitute "—fannies after the game."

"And this morning," added Jerry. "We had 6:00 a.m. practice," he explained to Carolyn. "He started off by holding up the ball and saying, 'This is a basketball, gentlemen. Just so everyone knows what we're talking about.'"

Together they winced at the memory.

She looked around at the faces, still glum, but not quite as miserable as before. "I can see you're not thinking about anything but basketball, so you might as well get out of here." They noisily welcomed the thirty-five-minute break.

Except Frank, she noted. He was in earnest conversation with Ellis and Brad when she left for her own office. She wasn't too surprised when the three of them arrived there a few minutes later.

"Professor Trent," began Ellis, not quite meeting her eyes. "We were wondering if you might have ideas to help us. See, we—" he waved to take in the three of them "—are having some difficulty adjusting to college classes and . . ."

Brad picked up his flagging teammate. "But it's different for all three of us. I've got this math cr—" again Carolyn saw him push back one word and select another "—crud that just doesn't connect in my head. Ellis here is being driven to distraction by some history wacko." She hid her smile at the description of Professor Wemler. "The guy's demanding he know all the ins and outs of the Battle of Waterloo. And Frank's got this old English book to read, only it turns out it's not English at all."

She studied the three faces in front of her. The players had accepted her to varying degrees and according to their individual personalities. They groaned over her supervision of their work, but mostly they complied. Only Brad caused real concern with missed assignments or meetings.

But Frank still seemed shy of her for some reason. On a shrewd guess she'd say that Frank really wanted the help now. But he didn't want to approach her or Edgar Humbert directly, so his teammates agreed, or volunteered, to serve as camouflage. If that was the way they wanted it, okay. But how could she best help Frank without exposing their ploy?

She waved them to chairs and came around the desk to perch on the corner. "Maybe we can address all three of your problems through something you already know very well—basketball."

"Basketball?" repeated Brad with more skepticism than hope.

"Yes," she said, putting more confidence behind the word than she felt. She wasn't at all sure this would work. "Take your math, for instance. Statistics are math. And I often hear you reciting statistics. Those numbers need more than simple arithmetic, don't they? You need formulas to figure out things such as averages and...and..."

She fervently wished for more knowledge of basketball at that moment.

"Percentages," supplied Ellis. "The way you figure that out is a sort of algebraic formula."

Brad looked at him with wide eyes. "Yeah," he said at last, "I guess it is."

Emboldened by that success, she picked up steam. "And your Battle of Waterloo, Ellis? That's just remembering strategy. That's your responsibility on the basketball court, isn't it? And you never forget that. So just try to think of history the same way."

She turned to Frank, feeling a little like the Wizard in *The Wizard of Oz*, handing out diploma, heart and courage to the Scarecrow, the Tin Man and the Cowardly Lion.

"Now, with the *Canterbury Tales*, what you've got is a language problem. You think it doesn't seem like English. But sometimes you players speak a language I'm *sure* isn't English, but it is. Only it's basketball English. Think about all the terms you use that have to do with basketball."

She racked her memory for phrases that C.J. had used. "Like pick-and-roll, or hoops, or point guard, or gym rat. All English, but each with a special meaning within the context of basketball. That's what's happening in the *Canterbury Tales*. So what you have to do is try to pick up the meanings from the sound because their spelling was very different then, so sometimes you won't recognize the word until you hear it. And the context should help."

A glimmer of hope showed in Frank's eyes.

"Then, whatever words you can't decipher, I'll try to help you with. Why don't you do that for two or three chapters tonight and bring a list, and we'll go over them in the morning between your classes." She held out her hand. "But only if you promise to do the same for me with basketball words. Is that a deal, Frank?"

He smiled as he shook her hand to seal the bargain. Then the ringing of the telephone cut their thanks short. Marsha Hortler said Stewart wanted to see her in his office.

When she got there, Marsha ushered Carolyn right in. But instead of Stewart, only C.J. Draper stood looking out the window at the Meadow.

With his hands dug into the front pockets of his jeans and his broad shoulders hunched slightly, he reminded her of the players. She wondered if, as he stared out at the almost-bare trees, his face held the same miserable expression theirs had.

An overwhelming urge to comfort him swept her into speech. "I hear last night's game was difficult. I'm sorry—"

"How the hell would you know? You didn't bother to come. Guess that's to be expected—it wouldn't add a line to your résumé."

He crossed from the window and dropped into one of the chairs in front of Stewart's desk. Dark smudges from lack of sleep dulled his eyes.

She stood stock-still. His words slapped at her, creating a stinging hurt that jolted her. Even more shocking was her impulse to reach out and smooth away his frown.

The desire to console and soothe him had no rational basis, but that wasn't what stopped her. His words stopped her, along with the certainty that he'd spurn any such gesture.

"I just bet you're sorry," he added harshly. "It would speed up your little program of getting rid of me and basketball if we can't win a game."

The door swung open and Stewart strode in, preventing any response, even if she'd been able to make one. He gave her limp shoulders a quick hug, then moved to his desk chair.

She felt groggy, as if she'd suffered a blow to the head. Slowly she sank into a chair.

"Tough loss last night, C.J.," Stewart said.

Carolyn waited for the explosion to rattle Stewart as it had her, but none came.

"I wouldn't mind losing if they'd just played some kind of game. They played like they didn't hear a word I'd said in a month of practice, Stewart."

She blinked, trying to get his reaction into focus. With her, he was bitter and angry. With Stewart, he sounded weary and disappointed. Why did that bother her?

Stewart nodded. "Sometimes it's that way in teaching, too. But if you persist, they'll get it." He turned to her. "That's why I asked you to come over, Carolyn. C.J. would like longer practices—"

Relief seeped into her. Dealing with the realities of her job as academic adviser returned her to solid ground. This she understood. "No."

C.J. gave a snort of disgust and raised his eyebrows to Stewart in a distinct "I told you so."

She ignored him and addressed herself to Stewart. "I just had three of the players in my office, asking for more help with classes at the very moment Marsha called. They came to me, Stewart. I'm not going to back off because he's lost a basketball game."

C.J. stood up. Under the lithe ease and laid-back drawl, she heard a band of anger. "This isn't going to work, Stewart. Professor Trent is more interested in putting up roadblocks for me than she is in helping the guys."

"That's not true. If you would look beyond your gymnasium—"

"No more, Carolyn." Stewart looked at her, then turned to C.J. "Sit down, C.J."

C.J. sat. She kept her eyes on Stewart as he removed his glasses and rubbed the bridge of his nose thoroughly before returning them to a spot where he could look over the top.

"I'm disappointed in you both. If either one of you would open your eyes, you'd see you both have the good of those players at heart. I think it's time you stopped bickering with each other and started putting those young men first. I expect the two of you to cooperate from now on. Is that understood?''

He got nods from both; reluctant nods, but definite acknowledgments.

"On this specific matter I hope you can start toward a workable solution right now."

Silence encompassed them.

Carolyn looked out the window, her peripheral vision absorbing the tired, discouraged lines of C.J.'s face. She cleared her throat. "What, specifically, does he . . . do you want in the way of changes?" She didn't quite look at C.J., but at least she'd saved herself from the absurdity of addressing her question through Stewart.

"I'd like more time—"

"More practice time is out—"

"Wait a minute, will you? Just for once, listen."

She met his glare with one of her own. "I'm listening," she snapped off after half a minute.

"What I was going to say is that I'd like more time, but if that won't work, at least having the practice time in one block instead of broken in two like it is now would help, for conditioning and continuity."

She did some quick figuring. "There wouldn't be time for the practice hours in one block and the study hall unless their dinner was pushed back."

"Pushing dinner back might cause a rebellion." The harsh lines in C.J.'s face eased a little as his grin flickered. "How about dividing up the study time. If you give me another hour and a half in the afternoon, I'll give you the time I've been using in the morning."

She couldn't argue with that. Two shorter periods a day could help keep them fresher for studying. And the morning meetings she'd been juggling between their classes would be easier to schedule.

"That's agreeable," she said with dignity. "As long as they come with their minds prepared to deal with something other than basketball. And with their anatomies intact."

She stood up, speaking to Stewart. "I believe the quote today was 'Coach chewed out our fannies.' Little studying was accomplished this afternoon."

"You must've made quite an impression on them, Professor Trent," C.J. drawled out, "that they gave you such a cleaned-up version."

She didn't look directly at him. But as she moved around the chair toward the door, she saw how C.J.'s cheek twitched with the effort to suppress a grin. "One more thing," she said. "I want Frank Gordon's file on my desk in the morning." She shut the door on that parting shot, so she missed the look C.J. exchanged with Stewart.

Into the silence C.J.'s sigh came heavy and tired. "I'm not sure this is going to work, Stewart."

"Give it time. I know you don't take losing well, but it's only their first game."

C.J. stifled a grimace. There was an axiom in basketball: players win games, coaches lose them. He'd lost.

Last night in bed he'd replayed every moment of that game, reviewing each maneuver in his mind to find where he'd failed. But what had gnawed at him as he'd stared at the ceiling until the dawn had turned it imperceptibly lighter was remembering how he'd scanned the crowd looking for Carolyn's face, and the disappointment he'd felt that she hadn't come.

"It's not the team. It's Professor Trent. I know she's got a great reputation, but how much good can she really do the guys when she hates basketball? And that's without even knowing everything."

"I don't know that she does hate basketball."

"All right, me, then," he retorted with the sharpness of sleeplessness. His mind replayed her expression after he'd blasted her when all she'd said was she was sorry they'd lost. He saw again the marble mask slip over the momentary softness. If she didn't hate him before, she surely did now.

"I don't know that she hates you, either," Stewart objected mildly.

He met Stewart's eyes across the desk and wondered what he was being told without words, if anything. But all Stewart put into words was his determination to continue with Carolyn as academic adviser.

When the file didn't arrive the next day or the day after, Carolyn sent another hot memo to C.J., this time with a copy to Stewart requesting approval to examine Frank Gordon's personal file in the registrar's office.

After a memo like that, no one could misconstrue her going to that night's home game. She wanted to make a gesture of support for the players. Only the players.

C.J.'s odd behavior in Stewart's office didn't really mean that her absence from the first game had hurt him. And she certainly felt no need to disprove his statement about her trying to get rid of his program by pulling for losses.

Still, her hands felt clammy even in the body-warmed heat of the gym. A natural reaction in unaccustomed surroundings, she told herself.

Students, faculty, townspeople and alumni packed the side of the gym reserved for Ashton's backers. She saw Stewart and Helene waving happily to her from a patch of faculty amid the students, but decided against trying to get to them. No seat merited fighting through all those bodies.

She went around and came in on the other side of the gym. She'd picked a spot on the edge of the bleachers near the door when she heard her name called. Edgar Humbert stood, waving to her, from the center of the bleachers, about halfway up.

"Good thing I saw you," he said when she'd made her way to him. He spoke around a wad of gum. "That's a terrible seat. You would have missed half the action. This is the best spot. I sit here every game. You can really see the game develop from here."

She watched in fascination as he folded another stick of gum into his mouth.

"No smoking in the gym," he said by way of explanation. Carolyn had never seen him without a cigarette before. "It's okay once the game starts. I forget about it, but until then this is the only thing that helps."

A roar nearly swallowed the last of his words. Ashton University's players sprinted out, shooting basketballs practically before they hit the edge of the court. She saw C.J.'s shining sandy mop above all the others as he and Dolph Reems, clad in red blazers in honor of Ashton, followed more sedately.

This basketball thing was more invigorating than she'd thought. The game hadn't even started and already her heart beat more heavily than usual.

Edgar mumbled away around the wad of gum about field goal percentages and zone defenses and shooting from the point.

She watched C.J.'s easy motions as he shook hands with the opposing coach and the officials in their black-and-white-striped shirts. He returned to the bench across the court from where she and Edgar sat. With his back to them, he removed the red jacket and carefully folded it over the end of the bench. Carolyn thought she saw his shoulders tense.

Then he turned and looked directly at her.

There was no vague, wandering gaze that happened to notice her. His eyes found her immediately and unerringly. The crooked grin would appear now, mocking her for coming at all. She waited, with her heart thudding fast and hard, and her chin raised. But he just looked at her.

At last he gave her a slow nod. She felt a wash of approval and appreciation and tried to tell herself she'd imagined it. She smiled a little, and an answering smile flickered onto his face.

Everyone stood for the "Star-Spangled Banner," snapped out by an Ashton band obviously eager to get the game started. Then a tidal wave of noise and confusion buffeted Carolyn as five players from each team took the court.

She wasn't a total novice to basketball. After all, she'd played from the time she'd started grade school. Baseball might be the American pastime, but basketball came as a godsend of all physical education teachers contending with energetic youngsters and inclement Midwestern weather.

But as she watched the speed and strategy unfold, she decided that the only thing this game had in common with the one she'd grown up with was that the score went up when the ball went into the basket.

At first that happened more frequently for the opposing team than Ashton. But late in the first half Brad hit three shots from so far away that the crowd oohed even before the ball swished through the net.

"That should loosen things up in the second half," Edgar said with satisfaction as the teams trooped off the court, with Ashton trailing by eight points.

"Why?"

"They've been packing in around Frank Gordon, but with Brad hitting from outside, they won't be able to do that. And Ellis is doing a good job breaking the press. See?"

Edgar Humbert tried. He even passed up his halftime cigarettes to try to explain the half-court press to her. Each time she started to get a grasp on it, however, his excitement would bubble up into another convoluted anecdote and set her adrift once more.

She did see what he meant about Brad's outside shooting opening up the game in the second half, though. For the first time Frank seemed to have some room to move under the basket, and soon he'd added enough points for Ashton to inch closer. Then ahead.

At game's end, with the scoreboard showing a five-point Ashton victory, Edgar turned to her with a big smile, made even bigger by the mass of gum in his cheek. "So, have any questions?"

She laughed as they climbed down the bleachers. "Edgar, I have *every* question."

And that included the one about why C.J. hadn't looked in her direction again. During the game she understood his total concentration on the play in front of him. But afterward she thought he might look up and share a smile.

How ridiculous, she chided herself. Why would she want him to look at her and smile? She pushed the question aside before some troublemaking part of her offered an answer.

"The only thing I know is the final score. But I made a deal with Frank Gordon, and I intend to make him keep his end of it tomorrow morning. He's going to explain this game to me if it kills both of us."

"Your end of the deal didn't happen to have anything to do with the *Canterbury Tales*, by any chance?"

"Yes. He asked for some help. I hope you don't mind."

He waved it aside. "That's the academic adviser's job. Actually, I'm pleased he's volunteering in class. The kid's bright. He's got some original ideas. You can tell he's really thought about what he's read. But sometimes a sort of unexpected gap in his basic knowledge seems to crop up.''

Carolyn considered Edgar's words as she walked across campus toward her apartment. She had the same impression of Frank. File or no file, she would ask him some questions the next day—right after she had him explain a half-court press.

She didn't have a chance to do either. She had just finished answering Frank's list of questions—shorter each day, Carolyn noted with pleasure—when a knock sounded at her office door.

In reply to her ''Come in,'' C.J. pushed open the door and said, ''Good morning.''

''Morning, Coach. I'm just leaving.''

''That's all right, Frank. Take your time.'' C.J.'s hand rested on Frank's shoulder briefly. ''I'll talk to the professor later.''

She saw the genuine affection between them, and a strong urge to please on Frank's part. ''No, honest, Coach, I'm leaving. We're all done, aren't we, Professor?''

He looked to her for confirmation. What could she say? *No, we're not done. I want to ask you what a half-court press is and, oh, by the way, I have a few questions about your academic background.*

She smiled at him. ''Yes, we're done for now. I'll see you with the rest at 2:30.''

C.J. watched the door swing closed behind Frank and turned to face Carolyn. Damn, she's lovely, he thought. He looked at the sleek golden brown hair and longed to let his hand smooth it. Then he would trace the bones of cheek, jaw, forehead and nose that created that elegant profile.

He met her eyes and knew by the startled look that came into hers that his face showed too much. From behind his back he produced the objects he'd brought and laid them on her desk: a small light brown teddy bear with soulful brown eyes, a brown button nose set slightly askew and a teal-green ribbon around his neck; and a manila folder labeled Frank Gordon.

She looked at the articles on her desk for a moment, then put the teddy bear aside to reach for the file. He'd known she would. It was enough that her fingers lingered for a furtive stroke of the soft brown fuzz.

"Darn, that's not quite right, either," he said with a sigh.

She schooled her expression to bland inquiry, but he saw that she knew exactly what he meant. "This little fella's not quite the right color, either. He doesn't have enough of the golden to his brown. Although," he added with a critical look at the wistful-looking bear, "I think that ribbon's a perfect match for your dress. What do you think?"

"I think it's about time you brought me this file."

"You should have it memorized by six tonight."

"Six? What's six?"

"That's what time I'll pick you up to go to the game I'm scouting. Edgar Humbert said he's turning your basketball education over to me. We start tonight."

He saw the tenuous truce they'd struck over the last twenty-four hours waver as she fought the temptation to tell him he was crazy. At least that was what he figured she wanted to do. Maybe not, because her refusal came out muddled and hesitant.

He'd never felt so good about a refusal.

He shrugged. "Okay. I just thought you'd decided that knowing more about your students, maybe learning a little about what's important in their lives, would help you as a teacher. Maybe not."

She drummed her fingers once across the manila folder. "I'll be ready at six."

"I'll pick you up at your place."

"I'll meet you at the gym."

He grinned at the teddy bear, then at her. "Yes, Professor."

They came to practice early that day. C.J. saw from their faces that they wanted his praise for the win the night before.

"Okay, guys. You've got a choice. You can hear how well you did last night." He bounced the basketball once, then held it still between his big hands. "Or you can hear how you can do better in the next game."

He watched disappointment sift through them and tried to stifle a twinge of guilt for withholding the praise they wanted. But dammit, they still had so far to go.

"Couldn't we have both?" Ellis asked softly. "Couldn't you tell us what we did right last night, then tell us how we can do better? We want to get better."

C.J. stared back at the composed, serious face in front of him. "Yes, we can do that." A grin crept in. "You could make a hell of a coach someday, Manfred."

"Yeah, he's already bossy enough," volunteered Brad.

"The best thing you did last night, Spencer, was keep your mouth shut," C.J. said.

The laughter quickly gave way to a technical discussion. Rather to his surprise, C.J. found no difficulty in remembering something good about each player's performance.

Then he put them to work on the box-and-one defense. They worked better together, and harder, than ever before. By the end, every shirt was soaked through and there were many weary legs, but they all knew they'd perform better the next time they used the box-and-one.

C.J. had already showered and changed in the tiny cubicle he and Dolph shared when Brad passed by the open door of his office to say good-night. C.J. responded and went back to his notes.

Soon it became apparent he wouldn't get much done. Mostly one by one, a couple of times in pairs, the players passed by the door and called good-night. Ellis came last. He paused before he said the words, then he smiled. It was, C.J. realized, the first time he'd seen Ellis smile.

Well, that was something. And seeing the improvement in the box-and-one was something. Even a single step brought satisfaction. Even when he knew how far they still had to travel.

Yes, there was satisfaction. But he'd dreamed such dreams of grander satisfaction. Sometimes, still, the past whispered the old dreams. He'd be a star. He'd be one of the best who'd ever played. He'd really be somebody and not just caught like a fly in a web.

He stood up so abruptly that his left knee buckled. He caught himself, awkwardly grabbing the edge of the desk with enough pressure to whiten his knuckles. He swore pungently.

I'm going to really be somebody, not just a fly caught in a web. Struggling all day long, being some kind of do-gooder just to get eaten in the end. Those weren't his words. They were the echo from a voice he wanted to forget. At one time he'd thought it would be better, far better, if he'd never heard his father's voice at all. He was stronger than that now. He'd been stronger than that even when his dream had come crashing down in the instant when his left knee had exploded into shards of agony.

He'd been strong enough to make his own opportunities from what had remained, strong enough to rebuild his left knee. One aching, straining movement at a time he'd rebuilt it from a piece of pudding to a joint that had carried him through two more years around the league and over to

Italy. It had carried him to enough respectable paychecks to set his family up in comfort and give him a cushion.

And he wasn't done yet. He was going to do more than dream and talk about getting somewhere.

He could have stayed in the pros as an assistant, worked his way up gradually. He'd gambled coming to Ashton. He could sink away from the attention of the basketball hierarchy as quickly as he had when his knee had gone. But a splash here, and he could have it made. He could be back headed for the top.

That would be satisfaction.

Chapter Five

Their truce seemed destined to end immediately when Carolyn discovered he'd said six o'clock so they'd have time to stop for dinner before the game. Even when he explained most reasonably that the restaurant was on the way, so it only made sense, she seemed inclined to object.

She said she'd eaten. It didn't take him long to discover her "dinner" consisted of ice cream and an apple snatched in the half hour between leaving her office and meeting him at the gym.

"How are you going to learn anything about basketball if you faint from malnutrition in the second quarter?" he asked, as he pulled into the restaurant parking lot. He recognized the warning signs when she straightened her shoulders and raised her chin. Hurriedly he added his clincher, "Besides, *I'm* hungry."

After he persuaded her to sample some of the restaurant's specialty prime rib, however, she agreed that the

dinner made the stop worthwhile. And she paid close attention when he spent time at dinner straightening out some of
her confusion about basketball. Once they got to the court,
he stayed too busy tracking the game on his scouting sheet
to answer many questions. In fact, she ended up providing
answers.

"Did you see who passed to the shooter?"

"Number twenty-four."

He grinned, even as his eyes followed the action on the
court. "You're handy to have around."

From then on she helped spot the numbers. A little ten-
tatively at first and then with growing confidence. He sensed
that she was pretty proud of herself, too. What a strange
woman, he thought, as he watched her intent profile from
the corner of his eye. A fast-track professor preening herself on spotting who'd taken a jump shot.

He could hear his mother saying that sometimes the
smallest things give you the most pleasure. He'd never have
thought he'd associate anything about Carolyn Trent with
his down-to-earth mother.

He explained more about basketball as they drove back
through a night howling with the promise of winter storms
to come. As her head started to nod, his voice lowered and
slowed. Just before she fell asleep he tugged her gently so
that her head rested on his shoulder. Even in the bulk of her
winter coat, she felt fine-boned, almost fragile.

He looked down at the lashes dark against her cheek. The
uneasiness between them had lessened. Gradually they were
learning to get along in some neutralized common ground
between academics and basketball—if they were careful.

They had to remain friendly, but not too friendly. Keep a
careful distance, he warned himself.

Careful. Distance. The words brought a twisted smile to
his mouth. Careful, as in the way he wanted to touch her all

the time. Distance, as in the way she slept against his shoulder as he drove through the night. Careful. Distance.

Carolyn saw C.J. and Dolph Reems coming toward her through the snow-covered campus before they saw her. She could still duck off to one side. But striking off from the shoveled path would look rather obvious. He'd know she was running away from him.

It was more than a week since she'd awakened with her head on his shoulder. She'd quickly wished him good-night and transferred to her own car. There had been no more invitations to scouting trips. Not that she'd expected—or wanted—any.

She'd seen him at the two games she'd attended. They'd said hello a few times, as now, when they'd passed on campus.

"Hello, Carolyn." Dolph Reems said, catching her in a bear hug. "How are you, my dear?"

His figure appeared even shorter and squatter than usual with the extra padding of his winter coat. C.J., long and lean with his bombardier jacket unfastened over jeans and sweater, emphasized the effect.

"It's great to see you at these last few games. We love to see supporters, don't we, C.J. Especially lovely ones."

She allowed one quick look at C.J., then she focused on Dolph.

"Her parents used to come to all the games," he told C.J. "They were great fans. And after they had her they'd bring her along, too. Just a baby, but she'd never cry during the games. Of course you were too young to remember that." Dolph gave Carolyn's shoulders another squeeze, then released her. "I used to think it was a sign you'd become a great athlete. And I still think I could've been right." He gestured toward her as he turned to C.J. "This one could've been a star swimmer. Olympics, I tell you. She was that good."

"I was never that good, Dolph," she said with a nervous laugh. Why did C.J. keep looking at her so solemnly? "And nowhere near that dedicated."

"Not to swimming, maybe, but to studying." He turned again to C.J. "Gave up swimming for studying. Can you believe it? Well, I guess that's how you get to be a professor at such a young age. Your parents sure would be proud of you, my dear."

No matter how often she heard the words, they always brought a kind of satisfaction, almost a validation of her accomplishments.

He gave a gusty sigh, then headed off with a quickness surprising in someone of his bulk. "Got to get to the Administration Building with these papers before Marsha Hortler has my hide. See you two later."

His departure left a wake of awkwardness.

"The...uh...the team looked good the other night," she offered after a desperate search for a topic. Ashton's win had given the Aces a 2-2 record.

"They're doing a little better." He cleared his throat. She glanced up and saw a faint echo of his grin. "They might improve even more if you didn't impinge on my time."

"What do you mean?"

He cleared his throat again. "You've got Gordo talking about 'basketball language' and Spencer doing formulas for statistics and Manfred—" His voice gathered confidence, the grin seemed surer. "I keep catching Ellis trying to turn my plays into the Battle of Waterloo." Her laugh slipped across the silent snow, and C.J.'s voice held an added huskiness as he said, "So you owe me. I want equal time."

"I guess that's only fair," she said without pause.

"Good. Dinner tonight. Angelo's. Seven-thirty. I'll pick you up." He started to back away down the path. She opened her mouth, but he forestalled her. "I know—you'll meet me there. Okay. Seven-thirty." He swung around and strode down the path.

She stared after him, feeling a little disconcerted by the abruptness of both his invitation and departure. Why did he leave so suddenly? Did he regret his impulsive invitation?

And why had she given him carte blanche? She didn't think. That was why. C.J. Draper didn't give her a chance to think things through. That had to change.

They ordered, and the waiter gathered the menus and departed. The bustle of arriving, the standard comments about the checked-tablecloth decor with candles dripping wax down wine bottles, the consultations over their selections—all that was used up.

This was the moment Carolyn always dreaded. This was the moment her escort's very impressive academic credentials became most obvious. This was the moment she told herself firmly that she admired that sort of conversation. But tonight, in the flickering candlelight of Angelo's, with the nubby texture of a checked napkin being pleated between her restless fingers, all that changed.

This was the moment she had no idea what to expect from C.J. Draper.

His eyes looked directly into hers. *Monet blue,* her thoughts whispered. She said the first thing that came into her mind, anything to break that look.

"I've gone through Frank Gordon's file. There are a few things missing." The information had largely confirmed her impression of Frank's strength in math and science, but told little about his background in several other areas, particularly English. "I thought you might have gotten them mixed up with some other papers."

He looked at her for a moment longer as if trying to read something in her face, then turned to flag the waiter as he said over his shoulder to her, "Sorry. I'll check. Practices have occupied me. I lose track of things sometimes."

While he spoke Italian with the waiter, she wondered if he was apologizing obliquely for keeping the players late that day two weeks ago.

"I'd forgotten to order the wine," he said after the waiter left. She started to protest automatically, but he stilled it. "You can't have Italian food without wine. It's like leaving out the pasta."

"Is that why you chose Angelo's? It reminds you of the restaurants when you lived in Italy?"

As he handed her the bread basket, he smiled, and grooves cut into his cheeks. "The restaurants they always took me to in Italy were American. They're nuts for Southern fried chicken and french fries over there."

She smiled back. "Isn't that absurd? You go to Paris and eat Chinese, but the Chinese want to eat French."

"When I played for the Tornadoes, we came up with a whole international route around the league: German in Milwaukee, French in Washington, Italian in Boston, Chinese in New York. But the best Chinese restaurant I ever went to was in Dublin."

"Ireland?"

He nodded. "It was terrific. At the end of the meal they served Irish coffee and fortune cookies." She started to laugh as he continued straight-faced, "Every Chinese restaurant should serve Irish coffee—but the fortune cookies were in Gaelic." His laugh joined hers, then lingered in his voice when he continued, "When I was growing up in East

St. Louis, I never would have expected to see the world the way I have.''

"St. Louis?"

He nodded. "East St. Louis, Illinois, actually. Just over the river. A tough neighborhood, especially for somebody with a name like mine."

"C.J.," she pronounced thoughtfully. She hadn't considered before that the letters meant anything more than *him*. "What does it stand for?"

He shook his head. "Sorry. I don't know you well enough to tell you that. I trust my name only to people I'd trust my life to—which came down to about the same thing where I grew up."

Despite his light tone, she wondered at the sort of childhood he'd had. "Do you go back?"

"Not a lot, but I've kept some ties. In fact, that's how I heard about Ellis Manfred. My old high school coach still goes to games all over the area. When I got this job, he called me up and said he knew this good kid and I'd better give him a scholarship."

"So you went to see Ellis play."

He shook his head solemnly as he took a breadstick from the napkin-lined basket. "I said, yes, sir, Coach. And that was that. Coach Gates is a tough old bird, and you don't question him. I got passed from him to another tough old bird at State U. Between Coach Gates and Coach Kenner, I was either going to grow up straight or die with the effort."

"What about your—"

She broke off as her mind caught up with her mouth. It was none of her business why these coaches seemed to stand in for the father he never mentioned. She had no right to ask questions about the things he didn't volunteer.

Carolyn watched the breadstick in his hands crumble to fragments. When she looked up, he met her eyes steadily. "Did you always play basketball?" she asked.

"You mean was I born with a ball under my arm? No. But there were always games going on in the neighborhood and I was always tall for my age, so I'd play with the older guys. Pretty soon I was as good as they were. Then I was better."

He started in on his salad, and Carolyn toyed with a forkful of greens and creamy dressing. "It kept you out of trouble?" She'd heard that about sports.

"Not entirely. More like a couple of basketball coaches got me out of trouble. Coach Gates and Coach Kenner dragged me up when I got too big for Mom to handle. I was a hellion, always in trouble. Mom tried her damnedest, but with working full-time to keep us alive, and with me bigger than her by the time I was twelve, it was tough. If it hadn't been for basketball, I'd probably be dead or in prison by now."

No fanfare. To him, just a simple statement of fact. And somehow Carolyn found herself believing him.

"So you decided basketball came before other things, before..." She took a bite of lettuce to cover the unfinished question. What? What did she know about the sort of things that had faced him or someone like Ellis Manfred?

She wondered again about the father so notably absent from his family pictures—the one on his desk and the one he drew now.

"Nope. Not on my own. Coach Gates found me in junior high. Told me basketball could be my ticket out, but every ticket's got to be paid for. I was going to pay for mine by hard work, keeping my grades respectable and clean living. It took a while, but he finally got through." He looked at her with a grin crinkling the corners of his eyes. "And, you know, eventually I found I kind of liked some of that classroom stuff. Not in big doses, of course.''

"Of course," she agreed dryly. "But please don't give that very moving testimonial on academics to your players, C.J."

Their eyes met in a shared smile, and he promised with a laugh.

As the waiter placed heaping dishes of rigatoni in front of them, she asked about his basketball career. He talked about the championships, the records, the achievements. But the warmth when he talked about his teammates and his game impressed her more.

She looked at the light in his eyes and his mobile mouth cutting grooves in his cheek with a smile. He loved basketball the way she loved teaching.

"Did you mean what you told Frank the other day about making your own opportunities—and if you don't take them, they're gone?"

The abrupt question brought a puzzled frown to his eyes. He didn't seem to remember saying that, but he obviously believed it. "Yes." He looked at her steadily. "Opportunity didn't come knocking where I grew up."

"So you went to look for it?"

"That's right." The light tone didn't eclipse his seriousness. "And when I found it, I followed it right out of that old neighborhood."

"And took your family along?"

"Yeah, but that took some doing, let me tell you," he said with an exaggerated sigh. "Mom's a nurse and she'd worked at a pediatric clinic in the area for years. I thought it would take a crowbar to get her away. She kept talking about how much they needed the help there, how much good she could do."

He leaned forward and lowered his voice to a conspiratorial undertone. "That's when I got sneaky. See, Jan and her son, Jason, lived with her by then, and I started pointing out how Jason was getting to be just like me at that age, just old enough to start being a problem."

Sitting back, satisfaction lit his face. "Poof! Like magic. Two weeks later she and Jan decided to let me help them get settled in Florida."

She laughed. "You are devious, aren't you?"

"You bet. And it worked out great. That was about four years ago. Now they've got a nice place near St. Pete. Mom's working with geriatrics, Jan's got a job nursing and Jason's playing junior varsity basketball. His grades aren't bad, either."

"Following his uncle's example, no doubt." Carolyn couldn't resist teasing him a little.

He was unperturbed. "His uncle's very *good* example," he expanded.

"What happened to..." The question about his father waited at the back of her tongue, but she wouldn't let it out. "Jason's dad?" she finished lamely.

He must have heard her stumble over the words. What would he make of it? And of her nosiness. She'd stopped the question about his father, only to blurt out something nearly as bad. She didn't have any right to ask. What if he didn't want to tell her? What if he told her it was none of her business? What if...

"Jack died eight years ago. He was in the army. Made it through Vietnam, then got shot when he walked into a convenience store that somebody was trying to rob late one night. Jack tried to stop him."

He shook his head, but Carolyn saw pain glinting in his eyes. "That was Jack. He and Jan were two of a kind. Took in every kind of stray—dogs, cats, runaway kids, homesick recruits—they sheltered them all. Jan stayed out in California for a while, but it was tough trying to work and raise Jason by herself. Jack didn't leave much besides the army benefits. So she moved back home with Mom to share expenses. That way Mom could help out with Jason, too.''

"You did, too, didn't you?'' Carolyn didn't know where the certainty had come from, but she spoke with utter conviction. C.J. Draper wasn't the kind of man to relegate his sister's fatherless son to Christmas gifts and birthday checks.

He met her eyes, and the look was charged. She could see his pleasure at her words. But also a challenge, as if he were telling her they'd crossed some frontier. That by recognizing that aspect of him, and expressing it, she'd pushed the conversation beyond the surface.

Perhaps she had, because she found herself beginning to open up about her own life. She told him about going to live with her grandparents at the age of five after her parents' death. She even laughed a little over her first encounter with a cow. She'd started swimming there on the farm in a pond, then had taken lessons and competed in her first meet through the county recreation association.

Her grandparents had her everlasting gratitude. They had opened their home to her and made many sacrifices of time and money for her. But, she said, it had worked out for the best when Stewart and Elizabeth, recognizing her ability, had brought her to Ashton to raise her in a more challenging environment. By her junior year in high school, she'd known what she wanted to do. Swimming and everything else had become secondary.

He listened so well.

He listened to the tale told with so little emotion in the words and so much in her eyes. He wanted more, but for now he'd take what she offered.

Wondering about all the things she didn't say, he knew exactly how she'd felt when she'd broken off those questions about his family that she'd started to ask. What would he have said if she'd asked?

He could give her the official line from his bio—his mother was a widow. He'd felt mostly relief when that had become the truth. Strangely, he didn't want to leave Carolyn with that partial reality. He knew he couldn't lie to her. But to tell the whole truth? No. A voice at the back of his mind added, *Not yet*.

He watched the flickering light change her face with the pattern of shadows. On the spur of the moment he'd chosen Angelo's because it was the first place he'd thought of with candles on the tables, and he'd wanted to see her by candlelight. He'd made the right choice. Candlelight gave her fair skin an ivory glow.

The sight acted on him in strange ways. Almost like hearing her laugh this afternoon. Standing there in the wind, surrounded by snow, then a simple sound had penetrated right through the Wisconsin cold and warmed him to his bones.

"And so you came to Ashton and became a professor and everybody says how proud your parents would have been," he finished for her gently.

She smiled, then let out a long breath. He saw that she didn't even recognize it as a sigh. But he did. And, to himself, he mourned a little for the girl who'd been working so hard to make her parents proud that she'd stopped playing games when she was sixteen years old.

"Well, if they do, it's all thanks to Stewart and Elizabeth. They were wonderful to me."

Worry put a single crease in the middle of her forehead, and he longed to smooth it with his fingertips. Or his lips. But he pulled himself away from the thought.

"But . . ." he prompted with a question in his voice.

"But," she picked up with a smile that quickly faded, "I wish I could do more now for Stewart. Since Elizabeth died, he's so lonely, so alone. I wish I knew better how to comfort him."

"That takes time. I think he's coming around. He's happier than when I first met him back in the spring."

She looked up hopefully. "You really think so? Helene said you went fishing with him right before the semester started. That was nice of you."

"I really think so. And it wasn't particularly nice of me. I was dying to get away to a quiet cabin for a while myself. I had as much fun as Stewart and Helene." He looked down into the liquid red velvet in his glass, then glanced up and let himself sink into the softer depths of Carolyn's eyes for an indulgent moment. "I think when he's ready there'll be somebody there to love him. He's damn lucky."

His drawl had become gravelly with a private implication he refused to examine. Then he saw the puzzlement on her face, the dawning recognition of his meaning.

"Helene?" As she struggled with the idea, he gestured for the check.

It couldn't be—not Helene and Stewart. Elizabeth was Stewart's perfect match, sharing his interests, his thinking. Helene was nothing like Elizabeth.

"Oh, I know they spend a lot of time together," she said. "And Helene has a wonderful heart. But Stewart . . . ?" Stewart was books, philosophy and education. "And Helene . . . ?" Helene was clothes, fun and fashion. "They're so totally different."

Was that really true? asked a voice inside her. Didn't they both like games and people and parties? Things that Stewart hadn't had much time for in recent years because of the demands of his job. But she remembered earlier years . . .

She moved to safer ground. "They come from such different backgrounds. They've led such different lives." Belatedly she saw he'd already paid the check—and she had been determined to pay her own way.

"Maybe so," he said, "but it seems to me they're good for each other. I know Helene's good for Stewart. Makes him forget the pressures a bit so he can go back and pick them up more easily the next time." He firmly waved away the money she tried to give him. "Besides, when you love you don't love the credentials. You love the person."

"Perhaps, but you can't fall in love without some things in common. Without sharing interests, priorities."

He came around to help her into her coat, his hands just brushing her neck as he freed her hair from the collar. "Can't you?"

Warmth from where his fingers touched her skin shot to her core. As they left the restaurant, she concentrated on directing her oddly spongy muscles into a dignified walk to the door and a smile at the proprietor.

In her mind C.J.'s words reverberated and echoed into another question: could you?

He insisted on walking her to her car, although she'd parked around back. He held open the car door. Just as she started to slide into the seat, she remembered her manners and turned to thank him for the meal.

She didn't expect him to be so close. She didn't expect to come up against his chest with such impact that she needed to hold on to him to steady herself. She didn't expect her fingers to instinctively cling to the wool sweater beneath his open jacket. She didn't expect the warmth of his body to push its heat through her veins.

C.J.'s large, roughened hands softly cradled each side of her head and tilted it back until she looked into his face above her. She saw his eyes on her mouth, then his face came closer. His mouth dropped swiftly to hers. He brushed gently across her lips once, then met her mouth completely.

That mobile mouth she'd watched these past weeks with suspicion or pleasure pressed against hers. Teasing, tantalizing, turning her bones to hot, languid liquid.

Her fingers opened, then curled tighter into the wool over his hard chest. She accepted the tribute of his lips, the caress of his hands sliding through her hair, cushioning her head. She felt the question in his touch and in his tongue's soft path along her bottom lip.

She couldn't answer. How could she? He'd erased all thoughts. And with no answer she could neither pull away nor pull closer. Then his lips left hers, and over the sound of her own heart she heard him breathing fast and shallow.

"Good night, Carolyn." His whisper came from just a breath away. He kissed her hard and quick, then spun away and strode off.

She sank to the car seat and sat staring at nothing. She felt so odd. Her head floated, but languor weighted her body. One finger traced the line of her lips where his had been just a moment before. Then she curved them upward in a smile.

"That was a foul, you jerk! You're blind! He fouled Ellis!"

Appalled, Carolyn snapped her mouth shut. Good Lord, what had gotten into her? Going to games to support the players and school was one thing. Yelling at officials was something else entirely. She looked around, prepared to meet expressions of condemnation for her outburst.

But no one paid her the least attention. Some yelled. Some shook their heads in disgust. Some described the referee's failure in heated terms to their equally irate neighbors. Some, like Edgar sitting next to her, booed. No one had noticed her lapse.

Outrage over that play still provided the main topic as
alumni, faculty and special guests mixed at a postgame
gathering hosted by Stewart Barron. An alumnus, Class of
'56, now senior partner of a top law firm in Chicago, alter-
nated comments to Carolyn about his business with la-
ments on how tonight's tough loss hung on one bad call.

Nodding and murmuring at the appropriate moments was
a well-honed skill. Carolyn let her attention freely wander
over the familiar setting of the university president's house.

The mahogany Chippendale pieces had furnished the
large room as long as she could remember. The style suited
the high ceiling, crown molding and formal carving that
framed the fireplace, doorways and windows. But the
arrangement was less regimented now, and the curtains and
carpeting bought a year ago were softer than their prede-
cessors, helping the room blend with the less formal area
that opened off the opposite end. She liked that. From
where she stood she could see the graduate student, happy
to earn extra cash by bartending, ensconced in a corner of
what had served as a family room when she was growing up
in the house. In those days the pocket doors between the two
areas were rarely open.

Helene moved to the doorway and stood, surveying the
scene for a moment before moving decisively toward the
group surrounding Stewart. For the first time Carolyn
wondered if Helene was responsible for the changes in the
president's house.

She admired the way Helene deftly eased an alumnus,
who'd had more than his share of consolation bourbon,
away from the group and toward the front door where his
wife waited, car keys in hand.

In a moment Helene returned to mix the guests into a new
configuration with the delicacy of a pastry cook folding in
a new ingredient. Everyone would go home feeling he or she

had had individual attention from the two most important people at the gathering—Stewart Barron and C.J. Draper. And they'd have Helene Ainsley to thank, Carolyn thought.

Perhaps she hadn't given Helene enough credit. The older woman possessed skills, valuable skills, she'd taken for granted. Perhaps Stewart recognized and appreciated those skills....

She watched Helene say a quick word to Stewart, and searched their faces carefully, but she saw nothing there to confirm what C.J. had said at Angelo's. He must have read more into the comfortable friendship than really existed.

Her reaction couldn't be described as relief, precisely— although she acknowledged to herself she had felt an instant of discomfort at the possibility. That was natural. A romance between Stewart and Helene would change things; would change her view of them, certainly, because in her mind the two kinds of people she'd always thought they were would never have a romance. Everything would be more complicated, and the lack of complications was what she'd hoped to rediscover at Ashton. She knew who she was, and who everyone else was.

Her gaze slid to where C.J., as always, topped the heads of those around him. He'd come in late. His duties to the team came first, but this appearance, too, was a duty. She noticed the slight slump of his shoulders and the way his grin never really hit its stride.

Annoyance at the people demanding his attention tugged at her. Couldn't they see he was tired?

"Bill Barrington, I was looking for you. What are you doing here off in the corner, chatting away with Professor Trent? Stewart said you'd be the very person to ask to help in setting up that trust for poor Armand Trettler's widow." Helene gripped the alumnus with one hand and Carolyn with the other and steered them smoothly across the room before either could draw a breath. She never stopped talking.

"You remember him, don't you, Bill? He ran Milton Hall for almost fifty years. Of course you know him. He used to tell such tales about your undergraduate days. I think you must have been one of his favorites. Well, when he died this summer we discovered he didn't leave any provision for his poor wife. We just didn't know what to do until we came up with your name. I'm sure you can help Stewart."

Helene slipped Bill Barrington in next to Stewart and headed toward the other group with Carolyn still in tow. "Excuse me, C.J., I hate to take you away, but you did say you'd give Carolyn a ride home." In response to the disappointed murmuring from the others, Helene lied sweetly. "Poor Carolyn has an eight o'clock lecture in the morning." In response to the stiffening of Carolyn's arm, Helene simply tightened her grip warningly.

The women's eyes met for a moment, and Carolyn saw Helene's well-meant intent. Someone else had seen the signs of weariness.

Carolyn watched C.J. look from Helene's innocent smile to her own disappearing frown. "Of course," he said.

They drove the miles in easy silence. Pulling into the driveway at Carolyn's place, he switched off the engine, pocketed the keys and let out a long, deep breath. His head dropped back to the headrest, and he hooked his elbows on either side of the top of the seat back.

"That was nice of Helene to give me an out back there." With his eyes closed he spoke to the roof of the car. "Thanks for going along."

"You're welcome." Somehow it didn't surprise her that he'd seen through the maneuver. "You must be tired." But she made no move to get out of the car.

He drew in another long breath and let it out with a soft curse. "I lost that game tonight, you know." He opened his eyes and turned his head to look at her.

"What do you mean?"

Lifting his head, he looked straight ahead. "I keep telling Manfred that he's the one who has to make the split-second decisions on the floor. That he has to know the team as well as I do so he can be my brain out there, so he's using *his* brain and not just following orders by rote. But when it came right down to it, I took the decision away from him."

An image of the players huddled around C.J. during a time-out with twelve seconds left in the game and the other team up by two points came to Carolyn's mind. She'd seen C.J. emphatically drawing on his clipboard. Ellis had looked at him for just an instant in surprise, then had nodded.

"I gave him a play and told him to run it." Frustration added gravel to his drawl. "The guys ran it just the way I told them, and it was the wrong damn play. If I'd just let 'em go, they might've had a chance."

He swore more vehemently. "When I played I could accept a loss, as long as I'd done my damnedest out there. But that's not enough in coaching. I'm not just responsible to myself. I'm responsible to those players. When I make a mistake I cheat them. All of them."

"Aren't you being hard on yourself? What would you have said to them if they'd run a play that didn't work? What would you have said to Ellis?"

"Thanks, Carolyn." He faced her, and for a moment, she wondered if he would kiss her again. She didn't have time to decide if she wanted him to before he turned away again. "But that's not really the point. What kind of coach tells his players one thing, then does something else."

It wasn't a question, but she murmured an answer. "Human."

"I tell them to use their minds so they'll know how to make their own decisions. So they'll know how to evaluate a situation in a split second and come up with the best way to handle it. That's what coaching's about."

Carolyn understood. That was how she viewed teaching. It wasn't teaching specific facts that gave her pleasure, but helping develop someone's skills so he could learn on his own.

"That's something Coach Gates and Coach Kenner sure as hell taught me. But first chance I get, I grab that decision right away from them. And Ellis just looks at me and says, 'Okay, Coach.'" He looked away from her. "Some coach I am."

A need to console him moved her hand to rest lightly just above his knee. "Why don't you ask your players what kind of coach they think you are before you go condemning yourself?"

His eyes came back to her. Their warmth began to kindle to heat. His hand covered hers, moving it a little higher on his thigh and holding it here. The lean strength she'd seen that day in the gym stretched taut and hard under her fingers now.

She'd intended the gesture to comfort; it had turned into something different. For both of them.

Memories resurfaced—muscular abdomen under the cropped sweatshirt that day in the gym, the feel of his hard chest under her hands as his lips tempted hers in Angelo's parking lot. Not looking at him, she slid her hand slowly out from under his and inadvertently caressed his thigh. She looked anywhere but at him, searching for a distraction from thoughts she was trying not to have.

"You know, you were right," he said.

She welcomed the change of subject, but his low words confused her. "Right about what?"

"That play. It was foul. That guy hacked Ellis."

Nonplussed, she stared at him. "You heard me? How could you hear me? Everybody was screaming at the same time."

"What was it you called the ref? Jerk, wasn't it?"

"How could you possibly hear me out of all those people?" she demanded.

"I seem to be tuned in to you."

He'd been teasing at first. But he'd meant those last words. She knew it from the tone. And the intensity of his blue eyes. And the way his breathing changed.

Her own breathing skittered, sending a tingling through oxygen-starved veins. "I...I..." She couldn't say anything as long as he looked at her that way. Turning away, she reached for the car door handle. "Thanks for the ride, C.J. Good night." She escaped the car and him.

From her living room window she watched him drive away and wondered if the distinction between cautiousness and cowardice might really be a blurred line.

Chapter Six

The second-floor corridor in Ripon Hall was cool and quiet after the student newspaper office, where voices shouted, phones rang and computers whirred—all at top speed. The next issue wouldn't be published for eight days, but with Thanksgiving three days away, not even the executive editor wanted to spend the weekend in the office.

Carolyn paused just outside the sturdy wooden door and enjoyed the peaceful contrast to the journalistic frenzy she'd left behind. A few steps down the dimly lit hall brought her almost to the stairwell.

Into the quiet came quick, sure footsteps on the stairs leading from the third floor. She glanced up and recognized C.J. smiling down at her. Her answering smile was spontaneous.

"See what I mean about being tuned in, Professor? I even find you in dark, deserted places like this." He hesitated, but so briefly she might have missed it. Then his smile frosted into one of determination as he joined her on the landing. "No, I forgot. You don't hold with that 'tuned in' idea, do you?"

Hold with it? How could she know when the idea of his being tuned in to her was scrambling her thoughts?

"What are you doing here, Professor?" he asked before she had any chance to consider either her own pleasure at seeing him or his abruptly changed mood.

"I dropped off an article on the seminar in England that the *Gazette* wanted to publish."

Belatedly, his question pierced her confusion. Behind his neutrality she heard what amounted to a demand for an answer—to a question he had no right to ask.

Lingering amity toward him disappeared in a rush of indignation. She didn't care one bit about talking to the media about the basketball team, but she wouldn't be dictated to by anyone. If he wanted to pick a quarrel—and she could almost believe he intended just that—she wouldn't deny him. "Why? What business is it of yours?"

"Since that's what you were doing, it's none of my business." He slipped a hand under her elbow, apparently to indicate a return to friendliness. But the gesture didn't mask his cool attitude.

She pulled away. "And if that wasn't what I was doing here?" she asked with deceptive calm.

"If it wasn't what you were doing here, I'd have to make sure you weren't here to talk to the press—even the Ashton University *Gazette*—about my team without my permission. And direction."

"Your team? Your direction? Your *permission*?" Icy indignation solidified around each word. Who did he think he was?

The man she'd eaten with at Angelo's and glimpsed the other night in his car vanished; in his stead stood an arrogant, tight-jawed jock.

He descended two steps before he seemed to realize she'd stopped for good. He turned and faced her, ascending one step to bring them nearly eye to eye, although he remained an inch or two above her. "Yes."

"What right do you think you have—"

"I have the right of knowing what I'm talking about." He overrode her without raising his voice. "Listen, Professor Trent, you're into a world here that you know absolutely nothing about. You're not going to run into your scholarly magazine types on the basketball beat."

A short sound of impatience escaped him while she maintained a rigid silence. "Not all the reporters are bad guys, but even the ones who aren't are looking for one thing—a story. If the media wants to talk to you about the guys, it's to get a story about the *team*. Not because they're students. Not because they're good kids or not good kids. But because they're basketball players. And that's *my* world. That's where I make the decisions. Not you. Understand?"

They glared at each other.

She knew whatever she tried to say at this moment would bear no resemblance to the well-reasoned, measured statements she expected of herself. So she held her tongue.

"Understand?" he repeated.

Not contradicting him this time stretched her self-control to the limit.

"Good." He nodded as if she'd satisfied him, breaking the stare. When he looked up again, a dry shadow of his grin was starting its crooked path. "So, I'll see you around, Professor." He nodded, a farewell and an acknowledgment of her anger, and headed down.

She waited for him to disappear so she could vent her fury. She longed to kick something—a wall if not C.J. Draper.

At the landing halfway down the flight of stairs, he stopped a moment, looking over the banister. He glanced back at her, then again at something beyond the banister, as if trying to weigh the possible impact they'd have on each other. He seemed almost bemused as he shook his head once, then turned and came back to where she still stood immobile. "C'mon, Professor, let's go out the other way."

The odd tightness was gone from his face and voice; the amusement that now tinted them infuriated her. She jerked her arm away. How could he laugh?

"I'm going this way. Good night, Mr. Draper."

"Aw, c'mon, Professor." He had a hold on her arm again, preventing her from taking the last step to the landing.

"What are you doing? Let go of me."

"Shhh. Not so loud."

"Why should I be quiet?"

He gave a deep sigh. "If you'd cooperate . . . but I guess you won't be satisfied . . ."

She couldn't shake his grasp on her arm, but he gave her enough slack to advance the last step to the landing. The idea of refusing to look over the railing just to thwart him tempted her momentarily. But such childish pleasure was beneath her, she sternly told herself. Better to go along for now so that he'd release her before the warmth of his hand penetrated right through her coat and blouse to skin that was already traitorously softening.

She peered down to the dark hallway below them and barely distinguished a couple entwined on a couch that served as a reception area for several tiny offices. Much too intent on each other to be distracted, they showed no sign of noticing Carolyn or C.J.

Instinctively she stepped back into the corner of the landing. Her first thought to not disturb the couple quickly gave way to the realization that seeing them disturbed her, reminding her of too many temptations.

"You should stop them," she whispered as C.J. followed her into the corner.

"Me? Why?" he whispered back. He was so close he didn't need to do more than whisper.

Why? Because a man held a woman just a stairway away. Kissed and touched. And C.J. Draper stood so close to her she could hear the rhythm of his breathing, could feel the brush of it on her face. He was so big that he cut off the rest of the world. Only this small corner, with the two of them, existed.

"They probably both have roommates and don't have anywhere else to go," he said.

"They shouldn't be doing that." *I shouldn't be thinking what it would be like to do that with you.*

"They're just doing a little necking." His broad shoulders deepened the shadows that seemed to swallow her.

"They shouldn't be doing that," she repeated haltingly. She tilted her head back to look up at him.

"Shouldn't be doing it here? Or not at all?" C.J. bent closer and looked into her eyes with an intensity that held her.

She wished he'd look away. Her throat went dry. Swallowing didn't help. "What do you mean?" Her question had a small crack in the middle.

"Don't you believe in necking, Professor?"

Now he was looking at her lips, and that was worse. She wanted to lick them. She couldn't, not with his eyes resting on them. Resisting the urge cost her breath, burning her lungs as if she'd been running.

"I do, Carolyn." His voice barely had sound. It was just a thought, a desire, hanging in the few molecules of air that separated their lips.

Carolyn remembered the feel of his lips from their kiss at Angelo's. The warmth and firmness of them against hers.

She wasn't aware she'd tipped her head back farther to receive his kiss until she felt its light touch. Then she wasn't aware of anything except the texture of his mouth moving on hers, the warmth of his hands and arms underneath her coat, wrapping around her, urging her body to curve into his.

So big, yet so gentle. He enveloped her, the strength of his arms cradling her firmly against him.

He held her tightly as his lips grazed her ear, then traveled down the side of her throat. She heard him breathe her name before his mouth came back to hers.

His tongue traced the outline of her lips, then slid along their seam, patiently requesting entrance. She parted her lips because that was what he wanted . . . no, because that was what she wanted.

Enticingly his tongue slid over the smooth, sharp line of her teeth. He explored the intimacy she allowed him with luxurious leisure. This could go on forever, he seemed to be telling her.

And as kiss followed kiss, she wanted it to. But she also wanted more. She needed more. She stretched up to wind her arms around his neck. Her body pressed against his so that she felt the power of his thighs against hers, the hardness of his chest against the swelling softness of her breasts.

The first hesitant touch of her tongue to his shocked her with waves of longing. There was no thought in this. Thought was for plodding along the earth. This took her up to the sky, circling around and around, higher and higher. She could only hang on.

Her fingers raked the hair at the back of his neck, urging him closer, closer. The warmth of his hand on the bare skin of her back fed her senses, but with no remembrance of his easing her blouse loose from her slacks to slip underneath it.

His tongue plunging deeper and deeper into her mouth drew a groan of mingled satisfaction and frustration that she didn't recognize as her own. The swift climb left her light-headed—and wanting still more.

He pulled back to frame her face with his long hands. She felt the slight roughness of calluses on the tender skin of her cheeks. He tilted her head back. She stared into the desire that he made no effort to hide and the question in his eyes that no amount of studying would give her an answer to. And she felt the beginnings of vertigo.

She glanced away and the dizziness rushed in.

"No." She couldn't get enough oxygen, not with the hardness of his body still pressing against her. "We shouldn't." She twisted away, leaning her right shoulder against the wall as she struggled to drag air into her lungs.

"What's the matter, Professor? Did your brain kick in?"

"Don't."

He hated the harshness in his own voice, hated it even more when he heard the confusion in hers. He knew what had happened as clearly as if she'd told him. He'd seen the fear in her eyes when she'd opened them and seen how far she could fall. He'd been up there with her, but that wasn't enough for her, so she'd brought them both tumbling down.

Anger sparked from the friction of coming so suddenly back to earth. Gently he straightened the collar of her green silk blouse that his urgent hands had disturbed. Then he stroked her hair away from her neck.

He knew he'd threatened the delicate balance between them when he'd asked what she was doing here. And he'd expected her to react that way to his telling her to stay away from the media. Hell, maybe that was why he'd done it. He'd been so damn pleased to see her, like a high school kid with a crush. And he'd felt like such a fool; just one reference to his being tuned in to her and she'd frozen. So he'd stepped on her toes good and hard with his size fourteens. Last time she'd run away; this time he'd given her a push.

Oh, the warning about reporters had needed saying. He couldn't risk her inadvertently hurting the guys just because hearing her laugh made his veins burn. But he could have done it another way, without kicking whatever remained of their truce to smithereens.

The players needed her; that was what he had to remember. He had to work with her for the good of the team; that was what was important. Then how come he felt like he'd just lost ten games single-handedly?

"No, maybe we shouldn't," he said softly as he drew away from her. "I'm sorry. I shouldn't have . . ."

Damn, he didn't want to say he was sorry. He didn't regret kissing her. God, he wanted to hold her, stroke her hair, tell her everything would be okay. But who was he to try to tempt her out from behind that marble mask? He hadn't come here for that. His top priority had to remain the opportunity he'd worked for all these years. He knew that.

She'd retreat behind the marble now. Just as well. Only it wouldn't stop this damn ache for her.

He knew that, too.

She thought it out that night, lying in bed and staring at the ceiling. The first step was to gather the facts.

Fact: when she closed her eyes, she could hear his voice, low and soft in her ear, and feel the stroke of his hand, tender and soothing on her hair.

Her lips tightened grimly.

Fact: what bothered her about the night they'd scouted the game wasn't so much falling asleep on his shoulder—that could happen to anyone lulled by the warmth and rhythm of a car—but that for a moment between waking and moving she'd known exactly where she was and what was happening, and she'd allowed it. More than that—reveled in it.

Fact: she'd made no move to stop him from kissing her outside Angelo's the other night.

Fact: she was more than a recipient of his kiss tonight; she was a participant. He'd apologized... *I shouldn't have.* But he'd done nothing alone. She'd welcomed the pressure of his lips on hers, the texture of his tongue, the heat of his body. She'd responded to it.

She felt a burning emptiness at the center of her, an emptiness she'd tried to ignore for weeks. Instead it had grown, spurred on by thoughts of C.J.

Enough facts. The obvious conclusion: she was attracted to C.J. Draper.

She was a grown woman. It was all very natural that she have sexual desires. That she should want a man's kisses, the solid warmth of his body, the shiver of his caresses, and all the things they promised.

Natural. All natural.

She twisted onto her side and stared unseeingly at the red glow of the digital clock.

Natural but not reasonable.

She and C.J. Draper had nothing in common. Two beings from different worlds with different interests. Their only mutual concern was the basketball team—and they battled over that. C.J. Draper wasn't the sort of man she could really talk to or hope to share a future with.

Not that she contemplated a future with him, of course. But she held a certain image of the type of man she should include in her life, an image C.J. Draper didn't fit. And she could well imagine that he generally dated a very different sort of woman. She rolled over, turning her back on an imaginary line of long-legged blondes.

He'd just hurried her along from one unsettling encounter to another, never giving her time to think things out. Like tonight, when her feelings about him had swung around like a compass gone mad. First friendly, then angry, then cool, then . . . hot.

But now that she'd thought things through, she realized she didn't run her life that way. She never had, and she didn't want to start. She always looked at the facts, came to a conclusion, then decided on a course of action.

The conclusion: C.J. Draper was basically overbearing. Sometimes masking it in charm, but always trying to hustle her into something.

Course of action: stay away from C.J. Draper.

"Brad, your French professor tells me your attendance has fallen off."

Carolyn contemplated the unconcerned face across the desk in her office. With Thanksgiving break past that didn't leave him much time to catch up before exams. To avoid a D he would need to improve his class participation and turn in a more than respectable final exam. He'd better develop some concern—and fast.

"They don't play much basketball in France," Brad responded when she demanded an explanation.

She wanted to throttle the attractive young man lolling in the chair on the other side of her desk. So much potential and not the slightest urge to use it.

If she could interest him in French... His lips twisted a little grimly. Unfortunately she didn't know of any attractive female French exchange students on campus. But there was one other way.

"If you don't improve your grade, there won't be *any* basketball played by Brad Spencer."

The lack of a threat in her voice seemed to make him sit up a little. She spoke with certainty, not bluster.

"You can't do that."

"If your grades don't meet Ashton's standards, I can and I will."

"Coach won't let you."

She battered down a surge of irritation before she could speak again. C.J. Draper had no say in anything she did. "It's not up to Mr. Draper. It's up to me. I'm the one who decides if you're academically eligible to play." She paused. "Or ineligible."

He stood up. "You'd do that to me?"

"No. You'd do that to yourself if you don't get your grades up. You've got ability. All you have to do is use it." She saw him waver and knew the precise moment he decided on bravado.

"I don't believe you. You can't do this," he said as he exited the room with a swagger.

On the way back from closing the door he'd left open, she glanced out the window. She saw him half jogging up the long slope, past the dormitory quads, heading toward the ridge where the gym sat. Going to appeal to C.J.

Let him say what he liked, she reminded herself. It didn't matter. She'd hammered this out with Stewart at the beginning—if a player's grades dropped below a certain level, he didn't play. They'd set broad outlines, but she decided the specifics.

Less than an hour later Brad Spencer, considerably chastened, knocked on her office door.

As they worked out a program to make up for wasted time, she wondered about his conversation with C.J. Resolutely she pushed aside a shard of resentment. So what if Brad had listened to C.J. and not her? The result mattered, that was all.

The reporter from the *Milwaukee Tribune* called on Tuesday, more than three weeks after her confrontation with C.J. in Ripon Hall. She agreed to an interview, not out of spite, although C.J.'s high-handedness *had* rankled a little. The point she really wanted to make was that the basketball coach didn't rule the academic adviser. She gave the reporter an appointment the same afternoon. She had the time.

The campus was nearly empty, although a weekend tournament would delay the players' Christmas break for seven more days. With the semester winding down toward the holidays, and the players' exams finished, she'd suspended daily study halls.

Overall their grades pleased her. Frank still lagged in English, but Brad Spencer had his C in French.

As Scott Gary introduced himself and described the story he planned for the *Tribune*, Carolyn studied him. The reporter didn't impress her. For one thing, he wore entirely too much polyester, except over a black-haired chest where his shirt seemed to lack buttons. For another, his smile was insincere and much too self-satisfied. But neither did he seem the type of ogre C.J. had drawn.

"I'm looking for background for a projected story after the first of the year about academic adviser programs," he said. "You're of special interest because the program's just getting started. And, of course, because of Ashton's strong academic background. Some of the programs seem to mostly just keep the players in the easiest classes so they'll stay eligible. I mean, lots of basket weaving, plus a string pulled here and there to get players in—and keep them in."

"That doesn't happen at Ashton," she said coldly.

"Oh, no—I mean, I wasn't saying that about Ashton. Hell, no. With Ashton's rep you're more likely to have nuclear scientists than pro basketball prospects, right? I mean, I just said that to show what a contrast Ashton was to some other schools. That's why you, I mean, your program and all, are so interesting."

He was backpedaling so fast that Carolyn thought he'd be out the door in another minute if she didn't step in. She told him how the program operated: the study halls, the liaison with professors, the individual sessions.

"So all the players are about the same level?" he asked.

"No, of course not. First, they range from freshmen to seniors. Plus, in any group of students some have backgrounds that just aren't as strong as the others."

"Some of Ashton's players have weak backgrounds," he paraphrased.

"That's not what I said, as I'm sure you'll discover when you replay that tape recorder you have under your notebook. I said that some have backgrounds not as strong as the others. Some need extra help, as is the case in any cross section of students. But all of Ashton's players are progressing well. No one is in jeopardy of academic ineligibility and no one is enrolled in basket weaving."

He pressed for names, and she firmly refused.

When Scott Gary left her office twenty minutes later, Carolyn fought down the urge to call C.J. Draper and ignobly flaunt an "I told you so." He was so sure she couldn't handle the media.

The interview had even ended cordially enough that he had promised to call before the article appeared and wished her happy holidays.

To Carolyn, the holidays really started the night of the faculty Christmas party held at the festively decorated Ashton Club. Around the huge ornamented tree and in front of a roaring fire in the big flagstone fireplace, everyone warmly exchanged season's greetings. These were the people she worked with; these were her friends; these were the people who had watched her grow up.

But her pleasure sustained a jolt when she turned around from receiving a cup of eggnog and saw C.J. across the room. Tall and elegant in a tweed suit, he was talking to the voluptuous new associate professor of economics. Although Dolph Reems always came, it hadn't occurred to her that C.J. would.

As always, attention centered on him. She tried to ignore him. But how could she miss knowing where he was and who he talked to with such a large group around him?

She wished happy holidays to Edgar and Dolph, Marsha Hortler and Mary Rollins from the registrar's office, and her other favorites. But the effort it took to ensure that her path and C.J.'s barely crossed drained some of her holiday spirit. She even imagined that he seemed always to be standing just a few feet away.

When Stewart caught her at the door just before her early departure and invited her for an informal dinner with the basketball team the next night at the president's house, she said no.

"They're the only students left on campus. I feel sorry for them," Stewart said. "They're going to come and help

Helene and me trim the tree. I'm sure they'd like to see you. You're a great favorite with them."

"Right now they'd probably like to lynch me after all the studying I made them do for exams," she countered with a small laugh. "Besides, I'm going shopping tomorrow. I'll probably stay there till the stores lock their doors."

But by 4:30 the next afternoon she'd had enough of shopping. She'd brought presents back from Europe, and she didn't have a very long list.

She'd spend Christmas on the farm with her grandparents, along with two aunts and an uncle and a few cousins she hardly knew. She'd return the day after to work on her essay for the seminar collection, spend New Year's with Stewart and Helene and relish the campus's quiet.

Driving the main campus road was a pleasure reserved for days like this. Usually packed with pedestrians and bicycles, it was something avoided when classes were in session. Now it formed a broad open boulevard through a winter world given a fresh coat of white by last night's snow.

She stopped the car to watch the last, thin lavender and rose rays of December's sunset on a tree-dappled hill. To her right the classroom buildings allowed glimpses of the Meadow and Lake Ashton. To her left the ground rose to the ridge that overlooked the lake and the lower campus.

The corner of her eye caught a movement that pulled her head around. A solitary figure, tall and lean, walked through the dusk, heading along the ridge path a hundred yards from the road it paralleled. It took Carolyn a moment to realize it was C.J.

Characteristically, he walked with his hands dug into his jeans pockets and the open flaps of his jacket puffed out in the wind. He limped.

Not heavily, but with a definite favoring of his left leg. He'd never limped before. Had he just hurt his leg? Her hand reached toward the ignition. She could drive up there in two minutes and give him a ride.

Could the limp indicate an older weakness he allowed to show only when he thought he was alone? Somehow she knew that was the right question.

Her hand dropped back to her lap. He wouldn't appreciate knowing that anyone had seen him limping. She watched his slow progress along the ridge, mildly surprised that the surge of concern she'd felt when she thought he'd just hurt himself grew stronger as he moved out of sight.

Ringing the doorbell of Stewart's house two hours later, she asked herself why she'd changed her mind. Then wished she hadn't asked the question. But before any troublemaking part of her could offer an answer she didn't want to hear, the door opened.

"Carolyn! I'm so glad you decided to come. Come in and let me take your coat."

Even before Stewart, smiling and repeating how glad they were she'd come, slid her coat off, her gaze collided with C.J.'s. She didn't even try to decide whose expression softened first, but silently they forged a tacit agreement to let the spirit of the holidays rule.

That one look at C.J. ruled out her first thought about his leg. He climbed up and down a footstool to hang ornaments on the tree with no sign at all of weakness or discomfort.

The sight of her in the doorway filled him with weakness and discomfort. Her eyes warmed and gentled as she smiled at the greetings of the players. Snowflakes glinted a final moment of miraculous existence in her hair. Her cheeks were chilled a perfect pink. Desire for her was instantaneous.

Later, escaping to the kitchen with the excuse of a second cup of postdinner coffee, he acknowledged that it was
also enduring. Lord, he wanted her. The sight of her, the
smell of her, the thought of her constantly reminded him of
just how much he wanted her. He tried everything he knew
to escape it. Long, exhausting workouts, cold showers, hot
showers, elaborate game situations to mentally coach
around. He'd even contacted a long-standing friend in Milwaukee who always welcomed him and never asked when
he'd come back. In the end he'd spent the evening talking of
basketball and academic advisers. He didn't think he'd be
going back.

Carolyn's laugh filtered through to the kitchen. Even the
sound of her.

A scrap of poetry taunted him:

There be none of Beauty's daughters
With a magic like thee;
And like music on the waters
Is thy sweet voice to me . . .

He closed his eyes and swore. Then a soft sound snapped
his eyes open and spun him around to face Helene's specu-
lative look.

"Everything okay, C.J.?"

"Sure, sure, everything's fine. Just got some hot coffee
on me, that's all."

Helene looked at the empty mug sitting on the clean
counter, then glanced back at the door she'd left open to the
sound of Carolyn and Stewart singing their rendition of the
Twelve Ashton Days of Christmas.

"That can hurt all right," she said, pouring coffee into his
mug. She looked directly into his eyes as she handed him the
mug. "Sometimes you just have to give it more time, to see

if it's going to heal or if it needs more attention." C.J. muttered something, but Helene waved it away.

He followed her back to the living room. She didn't miss much. He resolved not to give her anything else to wonder about.

When one of the upperclassmen suggested Carolyn come to Chicago for their three-day holiday tournament, C.J. congratulated himself that he responded with just the right lukewarm endorsement.

She'd turn them down. Carolyn at a basketball tournament? There was no way she'd say yes.

Then Ellis suggested she take them to a museum and make it an educational trip. Brad objected, but the rest of the team backed Ellis. And it was settled.

Conscious of Helene's watchful eyes, C.J. fought down the impulse to imitate Brad and groan aloud.

Carolyn recognized Rake Johnson immediately. He seemed to fill the hotel lobby. Everything about the man was big. His smile, his voice, his body, his following, his appeal. And his hug was huge; it had to be, because when he wrapped his arms around C.J. in greeting Friday morning, all six foot six seemed to disappear.

When C.J. introduced her, she discovered a gentle handshake and an intelligent, understanding manner.

"And this is Professor Trent," C.J. said, drawing her forward with a hand at her back that he quickly removed. "I hate to tell you, Rake, but this is one lady your fame and fortune will leave cold. You can trot out all your fancy stats, but they won't make a dent. The professor doesn't speak 'basketball.' Just English, as in literature."

"Please call me Carolyn," she said with as much dignity as she could muster. She felt dwarfed between the two towering men. "I'm pleased to meet you."

Rake looked down at her, then with raised eyebrows back to C.J., who grinned wickedly.

"Don't mind C.J.'s teasing, Professor," he instructed her kindly. He strung the letters of his friend's name together to sound like "Ceege." "He's just casting about, hoping to get a rise or two out of us. But we both know this good-for-nothing better than that, don't we?"

She intended to deny any particular knowledge of him at all, but could think of no tactful way to phrase it before C.J. responded.

"Hey, don't go talking me down in front of my players." He gestured to the ten young men hovering nearby, who looked torn between awe for the man they'd just met and fear at showing it.

"I'll make you a deal. I won't tell these fine young men the truth about their coach if you and the professor come eat with me before the game. You know it can be hard to find a good place to eat dinner at 4:30 in the afternoon, and I live a twenty-minute cab ride from the arena."

Carolyn tried to decline the invitation, but Rake wouldn't hear of it. C.J., she noted, said nothing one way or the other, but Rake insisted she come—and to "wear a striped shirt if you have one because we always end up needing a referee."

She didn't see C.J. again until she arrived at Rake's. He'd left with Rake while she and Dolph and the team spent the afternoon at the Museum of Science and Industry. The players had picked this destination. She preferred Sunday's planned visit to the Art Institute.

They whispered messages down the length of the acoustic hall, cheered chicks pecking their way out of shells in an incubator and stared in fascination at the working coal mine.

Frank and Ellis carefully read the label on each display and frequently consulted a guidebook. Thomas Abbott and some of the upperclassmen found an exhibit on electronics. Brad, she noted, wasn't with any of the others. She suspected he'd found either the cafeteria or a susceptible girl.

But she was proven wrong. With memories of a field trip from her junior high years, she found her way to the submarine display—and recognized Brad doubled over to enter the submarine's low opening. Quietly she backed away.

At the appointed meeting time, he sauntered up with a yawn. With a private smile, Carolyn noticed a book on submarines in his back pocket.

While Dolph and the players returned to the hotel for a rest and their pregame meal, she headed for Rake's penthouse apartment.

Nerves stung as she stepped into the elevator. What was she doing here? An outsider at a reunion between two old friends. On top of that she didn't know Rake Johnson at all, and she'd resolved to stay away from C.J.

But she'd agreed to come. She pressed the button for the twenty-second floor. As the numbers of the floors flicked past—two, five, seven, eight, eleven—she reached out toward the Stop button. She could go back down. Turn around, leave. She wanted to. She shouldn't. Not when she said she'd come.

Somewhere between the sixteenth and twenty-second floors she settled for promising herself she'd make some excuse and exit early. That gave her enough confidence at least to smile when Rake met her at the door and drew her into his apartment.

From that moment she didn't think about leaving until they headed to the game. She didn't even waste time wondering why she felt so at home. The food was too good, the company too easy, the view too spectacular, the conversation too interesting.

After they finished the chicken-and-rice casserole that Rake proudly told them he'd cooked himself, they took their coffee to the living room where two walls of windows presented a front-row seat for the setting sun's reflection on glacial Lake Michigan.

The table conversation had roamed across sports and movies, travels and friends, philosophy and politics. Now, from a story about a former teammate, Rake slipped into a new subject.

"You know, I thought I'd really enjoy just doing nothin' when I retired. All those years, all that work. At last I'd get a chance to relax."

Rake included her, but Carolyn knew the words and the laugh were mostly directed at C.J., who leaned against the corner pole where the windows met, staring idly out at the wind-whipped water. He'd eaten little dinner. She sensed a growing, coiling tension in him.

"I didn't even last the summer before I was dying for something to do," Rake said. He looked across at his friend and added with dignity, "I've found something."

He told them both of the drug rehabilitation program he helped establish. In addition to a link with the pro basketball league, it would help the poor in city neighborhoods. He talked about how frustrated he felt seeing kids give up their lives to drugs, how good any small victory felt. "I feel like I'm really accomplishing something."

"You've already accomplished something," C.J. said without turning from the window. "You're Rake Johnson. You're going to be remembered a long, long time in basketball."

His voice held no envy, but she couldn't help remembering what Stewart had told her about these two men. They'd started off together. Rake had gotten rich and famous, C.J. injured. It could have been the other way around. It could have been C.J. who possessed the penthouse and the fame. She looked at him, his long frame as comfortable in the white shirt and tan slacks he wore now as in his jeans or his tailored suits, and she wondered if he'd have been different if he'd had Rake's success.

Not so very different, she decided. C.J. Draper wouldn't let circumstances have the last word.

"I've been lucky," Rake said. "I've gotten a lot out of basketball, out of life. I want to give something back. Do some good in this world."

He hesitated a moment, then continued in a carefully light tone. "Let's just say I'm following your fine example, Coach Draper."

C.J. gave an inelegant snort of disbelief.

Rake turned to Carolyn sitting next to him on the couch. "You know, C.J.'s the one with experience getting folks off drugs."

Her eyes flashed to C.J., but he still looked out to where the sky and water swallowed the sun's last light.

"When he got his knee all busted up, Lord, they gave him pain pills every which way from Tuesday. He wouldn't take 'em. No pills, no way." Rake winked slowly at her and pitched his voice at C.J.'s back. "Why was that, C.J.?"

C.J. turned back to face the darkening room. The light behind him made only his silhouetted shrug visible. Illogically she was convinced that if she could see his eyes at that moment, she'd discover some key to the man. "Hell, I didn't know the damn things were covered by insurance. I thought I'd have to pay for them. If I'd known they were free, I'd have gobbled 'em like candy."

"No need to," Rake answered with his booming laugh, "with everybody eager to supply the 'star' everything he wanted, I was already doing enough of that for the both of us.'' The laugh eased away and left something warmer in his voice. ''I tried to stop, but I couldn't do it alone. He carried me through that off-season. Knee busted all to hell, but he carried me on his back.''

Rake seemed unembarrassed by the tears that glinted in his eyes and thickened the affection in his voice. C.J. turned to look back out the window.

''Why'd you do that, huh, C.J.? What excuse you got for doing that good thing, man?''

''Hell, I thought I'd get back on that damn team, and I didn't want a junkie for a teammate, much less my roommate. I didn't know they were going to cut me after all that, or I'd never have bothered.'' C.J. got the flippant words out, but his voice betrayed him.

Emotion tightened Carolyn's throat. If he hadn't stood across the room, if he'd been closer, she might have given in to the urge to soothe him with a touch.

Rake rose and went to stand next to C.J. ''I just want to do for somebody what you did for me, C.J.''

The bear hug between the two men brought a burning to her throat and eyes that in another second would have overflowed if C.J. hadn't pulled her from the couch.

''C'mon, you two sentimental crybabies. I've got a game to coach.''

Chapter Seven

Rake and Carolyn sat behind the Ashton team, three rows up in the gym for the holiday tournament. This wasn't Carolyn's customary spot. The angle made seeing the plays and patterns more difficult but made understanding the mistakes easier.

From across the court, C.J.'s face had always seemed calm, unaffected by the vagaries of the action on the court. Seeing him from the back as she did now, she realized how much he kept hidden. He leaned back in his chair, seemingly at ease. But he held his squared shoulders stiff, his back ramrod straight. He relaxed only when a time-out or a conference with a player coming off or going on the court gave him an excuse to move.

After a seesaw first half, the teams left the court with Ashton trailing by three points. Rake clucked his tongue and sighed. "Hardest thing in the world for that man to do is sit still and let someone else do the doing. But when he knows that's the best way, he'll do it. No matter what it takes out of him. I think it came from seeing his mom doing so much for him and Jan when they were young. He tried to take as much of that on as he could, but he was just a kid. He's still trying now."

"He seems to get along very well with his family," she offered leadingly.

"They're great folks, and they adore him. Jan had a tough time after her husband died, but she and the boy seem to have settled in fine near Mrs. D. down in Florida."

A question about C.J.'s father again stopped just short of her lips. If C.J. wanted her to know, he'd have told her himself. The thought left a tiny hollowness in its wake.

Rake laughed at his own amateur analysis. "Don't go telling C.J. I played psychologist on him. He'd split a gut laughing."

Carolyn smiled abstractedly. "But then why isn't he the kind of coach who runs all the plays from the bench?"

Rake shook his head. "Because he knows better. That may win games, but it doesn't teach much. And no matter what he says, he's coaching 'cause he wants to help those kids. Don't let C.J. fool you. He's sort of a con man in reverse. That man's got one blind spot—himself. He doesn't know how good he is, and he won't believe anybody else. He puts up a hell of a front with some people."

Like their first encounters, she thought. But also, on a deeper level, like this evening, when C.J. had turned aside Rake's attempt to express appreciation for his friendship and help. To the world, C.J. Draper appeared an open, easygoing sort. Inside there were rooms shut off—what had Rake just called them? Blind spots. Or tender spots. What could leave such emotional scars in someone so outwardly healthy?

"C.J. took some tough knocks as a kid," Rake said, unaware that his words fed Carolyn's wondering. "Sometimes I think he's still fighting that. It's what drives him, but he needs to steer it better. He'll drive himself too hard, too fast, unless he's got someone looking out for him."

Under Rake's direct look, Carolyn shifted uneasily on the hard bench. These backless seats really did get uncomfortable after a while.

The roar of the crowd welcoming the teams back for the second half drew a relieved sigh from Carolyn. Rake seemed wonderful, but he really shouldn't have told her all those things about C.J. She was curious, certainly, but nothing more.

She felt Rake's assessing look and was glad the second-half excitement prevented much more discussion. All the conversation focused on Ashton's last-second surprise victory and preparations for the next game at noon on Saturday.

The team played poorly Saturday afternoon, and Rake explained that after the excitement of the previous night's victory, a letdown would be predictable. That made it no less frustrating to sit in the stands and watch. And from the rigid line of C.J.'s shoulders and back, Carolyn judged that sitting on the bench and watching was worse. But Ashton won. Ragged play, blown shots and all, the Aces advanced to the tournament's championship game.

As soon as they showered and changed, the players, C.J. and Dolph joined Rake and Carolyn in the stands to watch the rest of the game that followed theirs. Ashton would play the winner Sunday night.

As they watched the number three ranked team in the country take apart a respectable opponent, Carolyn felt the Ashton players getting edgy. With twenty-eight hours until they took the court, they had plenty of time to worry how they'd fare against such an impressive team.

Their restlessness peaked during the team dinner at the hotel. Carolyn feared for the glassware and crockery with so much fidgeting going on.

"All right, guys, listen up," C.J. instructed at the end of the meal. "Ellis has something he wants to say."

Ellis withstood the gauntlet of raucous kidding with equanimity as he rose from his spot down the table. C.J. stepped behind Carolyn's chair, leaving Ellis his spot at the head of the table. The noise subsided.

"I'm not making any speech," he said with enough determination to make it apparent someone had wanted one. "It's just that the guys wanted me to say thank you for all your help this semester, Professor Trent. And merry Christmas."

Automatically Carolyn accepted the gaily wrapped red-and-green package. Surprise robbed her vocabulary of any but the clichés of "For me?" and "You shouldn't have." So she kept quiet.

Looking down the table at the double row of expectant faces, she started smiling. She didn't care what the package held. She treasured the gesture that it represented more than she would have thought possible.

"Go ahead. Open it," Brad urged.

Meticulously she began prying the tape off one corner.

"Aw, c'mon. Rip it," Brad pressed. But looking up, she saw the same sentiment on the other faces. She ripped it.

The froth of paper pulled away to reveal a framed eight-by-ten color photograph of the team in uniform, flanked by C.J. and Dolph in their Ashton blazers. An autograph went with each picture.

"We wanted you to remember us in case you decide not to stay on as adviser next semester," Ellis said.

Oh, it wasn't fair to capture her that way. But caught she was; she knew it. "It's a wonderful Christmas gift. Thank you all."

Under cover of the relieved babble that her thanks let loose, C.J. leaned over and rested his hands on the back of her chair. "How do you like the frame, Carolyn?"

She stroked a finger down the silken finish of the cherry wood frame. "It's lovely."

"I thought maybe I had it this time, but it's not quite right, either."

She tried to gather a frown as she turned to him. But she imagined it came out more quizzical than fierce. Their gift touched her, and she didn't quite know how to react.

"A little too dark."

Her mind comprehended the sense of his words, but the huskiness of his voice and the intensity of his eyes mesmerized her.

She stared at him. She felt his fingers, where they brushed her shoulder, tighten around the chair back. So tight. It must hurt, she thought a little fuzzily.

She sank into the blue of his eyes, diving deeper and deeper. Even when he broke the stare by dropping his eyes to her mouth, she couldn't escape. She didn't try.

"Just don't throw darts at it when you see our exam grades," Brad begged.

Blinking the room back into focus, Carolyn wrenched her eyes from C.J.'s and turned to the players.

"If she did that, there'd be a big hole where your head was from all the dart points," Jerry cracked. "Course you've got the biggest head, anyway, so it'd make a good target."

"That's enough," C.J. ordered.

She thought she caught a different note in his voice, but no one else seemed to notice. Except perhaps Rake, watching them from the other side of the table.

"Since you guys don't show any signs of settling down and getting a good night's sleep, which I can understand," C.J. went on. "And since you sure didn't burn off much energy on the court this afternoon—" the gibe drew sheepish groans "—I think the best thing is to devote tonight to wearing you guys out with some supervised exercise." This time the groans were heartfelt. "So we're going dancing."

When they arrived at the spot Rake had recommended, the crowded circular dance floor held people from their teens to their fifties, moving to the pulsing beat of a keyboard, two guitars and a drum. The Ashton players hung back by the entrance lit in purple and green neon and watched.

"C'mon," Brad urged his teammates. No one moved.

One song ended and another began, and still none of the players moved. Looking over her shoulder, she saw C.J. and Rake at the back, grinning broadly at the players' shyness.

She was as astonished as anyone when she heard her voice over the music, saying, "Okay, Brad, let's dance."

He needed no second invitation. Before she could reconsider she was on the dance floor trying to follow his energetic moves. *This is fun.* That was the only thought that formed as she listened to the music and tried to avoid collisions in the crowded space.

After two songs Thomas Abbott appeared at her side. "Hey, Spencer, my turn to dance with the professor."

"Thank you for the dance, Professor Trent," Brad said, and bowed from the waist as if they'd just completed a waltz at an inaugural ball. Then he winked and headed toward a group of young women off to one side.

She danced with each of the players. Frank tried to refuse, but she wouldn't let him. And she felt a vicarious pleasure when she saw him dancing later with a pretty brown-haired girl who smiled all the way up at him.

She moved to music that shifted from the Beatles and the Rolling Stones to more recent songs she vaguely recognized. She danced with Rake. She even danced with Dolph.

But not with C.J.

She noticed him talking to a woman in a sleek royal blue dress with no more front to it than her teal dress had a back, then spotted them once on the dance floor. She wouldn't admit to herself that she looked for him or that she wished she'd changed from the soft blue sweater and dark slacks that had seemed so practical for attending a basketball game. But she'd lost track of him until, as the band began the Beatles' ballad "And I Love Her," C.J.'s arm slid around her waist.

They danced without talking. Their movements meshed. Odd, she marveled dreamily. He was so tall that she'd have expected having their arms around each other could prove awkward. Although when they had danced at Homecoming and that night he'd held her in Ripon Hall...

Hurriedly she pushed aside the memory, only to have a question of how they might fit together in an even more intimate embrace come whispering into her mind, and be promptly shouted down.

The dance finally quieted the chatter of her thoughts until she felt only the music, movement and C.J. He circled her out of the middle of the floor through a maze of tables and chairs. As the first pulses of the next song's driving beat overtook the last fading notes, he led them in one last circle that carried them into an alcove not quite shut off from the room.

"Whew, I haven't been able to get anywhere near you tonight," he teased.

"Perhaps you were too preoccupied to give it much effort."

He quirked one eyebrow but gave no other indication of recognizing the trace of tartness. She gave a little sigh of relief to have it ignored.

In the shadows she couldn't be certain if she imagined the intensity in his eyes. He pushed a strand of hair behind her shoulder with a casual touch. Standing so close, she had to tip her head back to meet his eyes. He seemed to take up all the oxygen.

"For somebody who doesn't like to party, you're doing pretty well for yourself, Professor. Dancing with all the guys. The belle of the ball."

She leaned back against the arm still encircling her waist to laugh up into his face. "Perhaps I'm just finding out I do like to party. Perhaps I should thank you for showing me that," she tossed back.

"Maybe you should." He challenged her with a grin.

"I will!" She felt giddy with the thrill of the game, her body's movement to the beat of the music and, yes, the sensation of his arm around her. She stretched up to kiss one lean cheek. "So I thank you, Mr. Draper." She kissed his other cheek.

For a moment he remained perfectly still. Then he said, "And maybe I should tell you more things about yourself, if that's the reward I'm going to get."

"Oh, yeah? Like what?" she asked in challenge.

He slipped his free hand under her chin. "Like you're afraid if you're not serious all the time, then everyone'll find out you're just like everybody else—still wondering when you're going to grow up inside."

He'd changed the rules of the game. She tried to back away, but he held her firmly. "And if they do," he continued, "you're afraid nobody would ever treat you seriously again. Right, Professor?" His eyes narrowed and his fingers on her chin tightened. "And you're afraid that if they knew you felt like a woman sometimes, they wouldn't respect the professor anymore, so you hide the woman." She pulled her chin free, but his grip on her waist kept her wedged between his body and the wall. "And you want to know something else?"

She lifted her chin and arched one eyebrow at him. But the belated attempt at defiance was halfhearted. She didn't really want to fight him anymore.

Rake's deep voice suddenly boomed into the enclosed space. "Hey! What's this? C.J., what are you doin', man? You tell me I gotta keep everything like the Boy Scouts and then you go off in the corner with the professor? Nothin' doin', man. No way."

She welcomed the interruption, despite a stubborn inner voice that labeled it an intrusion.

"You want to know something else?" C.J. huskily repeated as Rake tugged them back into the swirl of dancers. C.J.'s arm tightened around her waist, pulling her up against him long enough for her body to respond to his hardness.

A rush of heat swept into her. She looked away. "No," she answered in a small voice.

In the moment before the movement of the dance pulled them apart, he spoke directly into her ear. "Okay, Carolyn. No more truths." His words sounded as intimate as a whisper amid the din of the music. "For now."

C.J. jogged across Michigan Avenue ahead of the early Sunday afternoon traffic, then realized Carolyn, Dolph and the players remained on the other side, waiting for the traffic light.

Glumly he stared at one of the lions guarding the Art Institute entrance while he waited, and reviewed the incremental crumbling of his resolutions to stay away from Carolyn.

He hadn't been able to stay away from her completely, so he'd vowed to limit their meetings. When he'd encouraged happenstances that brought them together, he'd promised himself he'd act distant. He might hold her in his arms, but he wouldn't sweep her off to a tower somewhere with a door that never let the world in.

He swore under his breath.

The big red bow around the lion's neck suited the season but not its solemn expression. Nor his own mood, C.J. thought. Everything he'd told her last night was true. But he'd been out of line. That peck on the cheek had pushed him too far—he wanted a hell of a lot more than that.

The light turned, and Carolyn and the others started across the wide avenue. Just watching her walk toward him... He couldn't take this much more. He could work his tail off, he could be patient as hell for something he had a chance for, but this... He'd better accept reality or he'd go nuts: whether or not fire existed behind that marble mask, she sure as hell didn't want him to play the part of Pygmalion bringing Galatea to life.

At least she seemed willing to have peace between them, maybe friendship. Take what you've got, Draper. Quit trying for too much.

Carolyn listened with surface attention to the guide tell the team of the Art Institute's recent expansion. She carefully kept her eyes straight ahead or to her left. C.J. stood to her right.

Trailing the guide, the group filed into a gallery filled with Rembrandts.

Of all the irritating stunts C.J. Draper had pulled, she decided that making outrageous statements, then pretending he'd said nothing out of the ordinary, topped the list. She wanted to tell him, with remote dignity and words she'd practiced long into the night, that he was entirely mistaken in his interpretation of her. But how could she when he acted casually polite this morning, as if nothing had happened?

Through connecting galleries they walked past portraits of eighteenth- and nineteenth-century English ladies and gentlemen.

She couldn't bring the subject up without making a big deal of it. He'd left her no choice. And she wanted to throttle him.

The idea of taking all six foot six of C.J. Draper and shaking him until that grin disappeared for good brought a glint to her eyes. The man had purposely plagued her since the first moment they'd met.

The guide brought them into the gallery that held *Sunday Afternoon on the Island of the Grande Jatte* by Seurat and immediately gathered the full attention of all but two of her audience.

All right, Carolyn acknowledged as the players first moved in close to scrutinize the tiny dots of paint, then backed up to see how they fitted together to form a whole, he could be charming. And he seemed a good friend to Stewart. He certainly cared about the players. Also, he'd helped when a friend most desperately needed help. Maybe all those things Rake had said about him were true.

After an introduction to the Art Institute's collection of Impressionists, the guide said they were welcome to look around on their own. She'd remain available for questions, she added with a smile at the attractive young men surrounding her. Carolyn drifted toward the Monets and Van Goghs, her thoughts still working. Whatever his good points, C.J. Draper was the most irritating individual she'd met in her twenty-eight years. She'd led an ordered, planned existence. Before she made changes she considered them carefully. Like Monet's studies in the altered light of different seasons, the changes were subtle, gradual. Not radical.

She'd known her goal and how she'd get there from the time she was a child. C.J. Draper wouldn't change that. Eventually he'd get the message that the outrageous things he said and did had no impact on her.

All right, they had some impact on her. But she wouldn't let them affect her. Not really.

Her gaze moved to a bright sea view by Monet—*Cliffwalk: Pourville, 1882.* Two women stood on the cliffs looking toward the sailboat-studded ocean and a fleet of white clouds. The blue of the sky tugged at Carolyn's attention. It was the blue she'd seen in a canvas sky over a field of bright tulips in Paris. Monet blue.

"That's nice," C.J. murmured from just behind her.

She turned to look into his equally blue eyes with a sense of inevitability.

No more truths, he'd said. Then why did he look at her that way? Why did she look back?

It didn't mean anything. It couldn't mean anything.

Beyond its own mechanical hum, the bus was quiet. Carolyn stared out the frost-patterned window at black night air so cold it seemed it would shatter. Inside it was warm. Everyone seemed to be asleep except her and the driver.

The team had filed on the bus after the game, subdued but not down. They'd lost. But they weren't beaten. They could hold their heads up, knowing they'd given the number three team in the country a close game. They'd contained the other team's star. He'd scored only fourteen points, and he was good. Perhaps the next Rake Johnson.

Earlier Rake had given her a kiss on the cheek and a big hug, which he'd used as a cover to whisper, "Take care of him."

Carolyn had pretended she hadn't heard. Taking care of C.J. Draper—if, in fact, he needed taking care of—formed no part in her plans for the future, immediate or otherwise.

As if her thoughts had stirred him awake, C.J. rose from a few seats in front of her. He seemed a little stiff. Slowly he walked down the narrow aisle quietly checking on everyone. Carolyn wondered if moving helped ease his knee.

He came back up the aisle and sank down next to her. "Couldn't sleep?" he asked softly.

"Didn't try."

"I tried, but I couldn't. Too much to think about."

Carolyn glanced up at him quickly. But before she could respond, he went on.

"This coaching is hell on the nervous system, you know. Don't sleep when we lose—too depressed. Don't sleep when we win—too excited."

"Same thing for eating?"

Surprised, he met her eyes. Caught by the light of a passing truck, they glowed—tiger's eyes softened by concern. The combination clutched at the ache he seemed to always carry for her.

Dangerous, Draper. Dangerous. You risk blindness, or worse, by looking directly into those eyes in the dark. He'd sat down, resolving to forge a real friendship with her, and already he was on shaky ground.

"You didn't do justice to Rake's chicken and rice, or the steak at the hotel last night," she explained. Did he think she was prying? Is that why he turned away so abruptly?

"I didn't want to tell you before," he answered with a lazy drawl that reassured her, "but I remember some brownies Rake used to bake back when he was living wild, and I wanted to see what that chicken and rice did to you before I dug in."

Carolyn smothered her laughter before it woke the others, but it left a comfortable afterglow in the silence. She was totally aware of where his shoulder and knee touched hers, and felt no need to change it. It felt good, solid and dependable, like his slow voice.

"When do you leave for your grandparents'?" he asked. "Indiana, isn't it?"

"Yes, Indiana. Tomorrow. How about you? What are you doing for the holidays?" It seemed intimate and cozy somehow, talking softly in the quiet bus.

"I'll go down to Florida in a couple of days." His mouth twisted into a wry smile. "An Indiana farm sounds a lot more like Christmas than a Florida rambler, but it's not Christmas without family, is it?" He paused, then added, "You'd like Mom, and she'd like you."

Such casual words. Polite, really, but they settled a warmth around her that was totally unexpected.

"I'll spend a few days with them, then tournaments start again on the twenty-seventh. There are a couple I want to hit. Do some scouting, make some connections..." His voice drifted off as his mind seemed to shift to another track. "Watching the guys play tonight, for the first time, I thought maybe this team could be something. Not just respectable, but a good basketball team."

Just above a whisper, his voice still vibrated with energy. "That loss did more for this team than any damn practice I ever held." He turned to her. "I saw a team tonight. Not just a group of individuals, but a team. They thought like a unit and played like a unit." He grinned in light mockery at himself. "I never thought I'd be so happy with a loss."

"'There are some defeats more triumphant than victories,'" she quoted softly. "A sixteenth-century French essayist named Michel de Montaigne said that."

His self-mockery deepened. "Yeah? Well, Michel must have known his basketball."

He shifted a little to straighten his left leg into the aisle, and his arm, hip and thigh came into firmer contact with her. Lost in languorous content, she didn't move away.

"When I first came to Ashton, I thought if I could just make the team respectable, I'd have really accomplished something. But now...well, there's something to be said for having players with brains. Those guys don't have a lot of talent, most of them, but they make the most of what they've got. They could be the base for some really good teams. Add a little more raw physical ability and Ashton could be one of the premier teams at a tournament like this one instead of the cannon fodder they thought we'd be."

"You like that, don't you? Surprising people."

"You bet. That's how you grab their attention enough to show what you can really do."

Had he tried that with her, surprising her to get her attention? She shook her head clear of the notion to focus on his words.

"If we make a splash this season, then back it up next season with a good record, I'd have a name. Then I could write my own ticket to whatever I wanted in basketball. Coaching big-time college or pros. Whatever I wanted."

She understood. He'd build his opportunity brick by brick. And when he finished, he'd follow it right out of Ashton University. Then Ashton could return to what it was before. And so could she. That was what she'd wanted. A happy ending for the school, for her, for him.

As C.J. spun his dreams, Carolyn shivered just once.

Chapter Eight

January brought snow, the new semester and changes. By the third Thursday in February the snow was replenished, the semester was old and the changes were routine.

She'd mailed her essay for the seminar's publication in England, and now she was teaching an advanced seminar as well as lecturing to other classes on her studies abroad. In addition, she was continuing as academic adviser to the team.

The upperclassmen no longer came to the basketball study hall, except Frank Gordon. He expressed no resentment at being the single exception to the all-freshman group of Thomas Abbott, Ellis Manfred and Brad Spencer.

Carolyn leaned against the frame of her office window, staring out at the campus wrapped in a mid-February layer of snow, and wondered if Frank would express resentment even if he did feel it.

He rarely said much to her. He'd give her that half-shy smile readily enough, but even when he asked questions, she had the impression they came almost against his will.

His work kept improving, and that was the main thing. Thomas and Ellis continued to do well; Carolyn had no concerns about how they'd do in subsequent years.

Brad Spencer, however, would have to be watched as long as he stayed at Ashton. When a topic sparked his curiosity, he went beyond assignments to learn about it. Otherwise, he required continual prodding. And if he thought she'd let up on him even when he finished playing basketball in his senior year, he had a surprise coming. She intended to see every one of these players graduate.

Carolyn blinked into the reflected dazzle as the snow caught the last afternoon sun. That sounded as if she intended to continue as academic adviser. She hadn't made a decision about that yet. At least she hadn't sat down and considered the facts, drawn a conclusion and decided on a course of action. How could she make a decision without even realizing it?

She'd told Stewart she would continue her duties through the season because of the difficulty of anyone trying to pick up in the middle and, yes, because she didn't want to relinquish her stake in the players quite yet. She hated to leave things unfinished.

But would it be finished until these freshmen graduated? By then, of course, new freshmen would have replaced them, and they'd need four more years of guidance. Would it ever be finished? Did she want it to be?

If she wanted to join the ranks of the academic elite, she needed to get back to teaching top-level classes, attending prestigious seminars, writing well-regarded articles. A year off might not hurt too much, but more than that?

Carolyn moved away from the Wisconsin cold seeping around the window's edges. She pushed the questions back. No need to work all that out now. She'd sit down and think it out after the season. For now, everything was going smoothly.

The players were doing well in class and steadily improving on the court. Since they'd upset the team ranked number eighteen in the country two weeks before, media attention had definitely increased. A lot of the questions went to C.J. He made a good story, and she appreciated how he acted as a buffer for the players, sparing them the roller-coaster emotions of media attention.

In fact, she felt quite charitable toward C.J. Draper these days. He'd even stopped his efforts to unsettle her...or had almost stopped. A tiny stuffed koala bear did appear one day on her desk, but that hardly counted. Though she'd waited for some comment from him on his color-matching effort, he'd said nothing.

So she couldn't really blame him when she'd found herself stroking the little fellow's soft fur against her cheek when she'd only meant to check the color against her hair. Too brown, she'd thought, and smiled a little self-consciously at herself in the mirror.

If the sight of the koala bear now residing with the teal-bowed teddy bear in her bottom desk drawer where she saw them every time she opened it, or a stray memory of strong arms and firm lips disturbed her peace now and then, she firmly reminded herself that these days she and C.J. talked to each other compatibly and companionably. That was all she wanted from their dealings.

The phone on her desk rang.

That might be C.J. now. She smiled. But the man's voice wasn't C.J.'s. She didn't recognize the name at first, either.

"Scott Gary. From the *Milwaukee Tribune*. We talked back in December about the team, Professor Trent."

She remembered. Polyester and too many buttons unbuttoned. "Oh, yes, Mr. Gary. What can I do for you?" She'd gotten enough of these calls to know the routine now. "I'm sure you know that all interview requests for the players are handled through the athletic department."

"I know."

She frowned at the phone. An undercurrent in his voice jangled at her nerves.

"Actually," he continued with confidence, "I called because there's something I can do for you. I mean, since you were so helpful last December, I thought I'd let you know we're running a story in the morning about the Ashton basketball team."

She waited, frozen in premonition.

"I mean, it's about Frank Gordon and how he got admitted despite Ashton's vaunted academic standards."

She knew what he was going to say. Her heart pounded angrily with the certainty. Her head throbbed with it. But she made him tell her. "I don't know what you're talking about."

She sat in the chair and listened to the voice telling her that neither Frank Gordon's grades nor his test scores met Ashton's stringent requirements for admission.

"I remember you telling me last December how things like that just aren't done at Ashton. I guess they are now—for basketball players. Or is it just a coincidence that the exception was made for a seven-foot center?"

Cold, hard reason told her he hadn't called just to lacerate her. There had to be a reason. *Think, Carolyn. Think.* Of course. He wanted a reaction from her—fury or denial, anything to spice up his story.

"Records like that are confidential. What are your sources for this alleged information?" Her voice tightened to keep the anger and pain out of it.

"The records are confidential, but there are ways of finding out. I mean, there are always sources. If you don't believe me, why don't you check yourself, Professor Trent? Or did you already know—"

She hung up, then shook her head to clear the thoughts that whirled in jagged fragments. With her hand still on the receiver, she sat as the winter sun retreated and lights popped on around campus. Nearly five-thirty. She just had time; Mary Rollins never left the registrar's office till six.

The smile she assumed to keep Mary from asking too many questions hurt. The muscles of her jaw ached from being held so tightly. Mary looked at her a little oddly, but made no objection to Carolyn's request for the academic records of one of the basketball players.

She opened the folder on Frank Gordon, which Mary had pulled from a drawer in the file room, and started reading reports of his progress at Ashton. She'd seen all this before, but if she was patient . . .

"I'll be in front if you need me, Carolyn."

"Fine. Thank you."

As soon as Mary disappeared down the hall, Carolyn went to the section marked Confidential. These were the personal files compiled before admission—transcripts from high school, reports from counselors, assessments from admissions experts—and any other sensitive material. Access was strictly limited, and the files were shredded with each graduating class.

She knew she should get Stewart's permission first, but she wanted to have the facts before she faced him with this terrible disappointment. Perhaps some part of her still hoped it wasn't true.

Frank's file was easy to find; it was the only one in the long drawer marked with a red tab. Here were the pieces she'd been missing.

The numbers and words on the form stabbed at her. Still, she recognized the careful and clever editing done on the information she'd received. Frank Gordon wasn't stupid—she knew that from firsthand experience—but his background left him far below Ashton's entrance requirements.

Carefully she returned the file, wondering who had added the red tab that marked Frank so clearly as a special case.

C.J. Draper had arranged to have him admitted to play basketball. It was as simple as that—with no thought to what it might do to Frank's confidence to constantly struggle against better prepared students; with no thought to what it meant to Ashton's long-standing and carefully guarded reputation.

Her voice barely shook when she called the athletic department, but the young secretary seemed to sense the urgency behind it. "Coach Draper's at practice right now, Professor Trent. But I can send him a message when they're done at 6:30—"

"Send him a message now. Tell him I want to see him at President Barron's office. Right now."

"But they're in practice—"

"Then interrupt practice."

Mary Rollins stared at her as she slammed down the phone.

"Thank you, Mary. Sorry to keep you so late." Her voice steadied, but she knew she couldn't manage a smile.

"No problem. But, Carolyn, you can't take that."

She looked down at the academic file she still held crushed against her coat. "No. Of course not." She didn't need it. Each item in that file—and the confidential one—was imprinted on her memory. The facts repeated in her mind in the few minutes it took to cross to Stewart's office.

C.J. had gotten Frank into Ashton despite the rules. C.J. had lied to her. C.J. was doing just what she'd feared.

Her first suspicions about the basketball program were finally confirmed. She should feel vindicated, but she didn't. She felt angry. Oh, yes, anger strong enough to pump any bitter disappointment out of her system for good.

Marsha Hortler, occupied on the telephone, nodded for her to go into Stewart's office. The smile that Stewart had begun to form when he glanced up from his desk withered when he saw Carolyn's expression.

"I've sent for C.J. Draper, Stewart. I'm sorry to break in on you like this and seem so high-handed, but there's a serious problem that needs to be addressed immediately."

"Carolyn—"

"You're damn right there's a problem." C.J.'s angry voice pulled their attention toward him as he strode in. He was only wearing a lightweight jacket open over his sweatpants and sweatshirt, but a temperature barely into double digits apparently hadn't cooled his anger. The door slammed behind him, but he didn't pause until he faced Carolyn in front of Stewart's desk. "What the hell do you think you're doing, Professor Trent?"

The snarl was like a physical blow, but she refused to recoil. "I'm fighting to protect Ashton and its reputation."

"Is this how you do it?" He held up a tightly wadded sheet of newsprint. The grooves bracketing his mouth were white with rage. His eyes narrowed in disdain. "A printer at the *Tribune* brought me this." He threw the sheet down on Stewart's desk. "So that's how Carolyn Trent fights for Ashton—by smearing a kid in the press."

The words *Ashton*, *Gordon* and *Admission Irregularities* showed in headline type. A flash of pain struck her for

Frank. He, too, was a victim in this. She'd find a way to help him, but first she had to protect Ashton.

"If Frank is hurt," she said, "it's by the people who cheated to get him admitted to this school. It's by you, not me. And I won't allow it." She faced C.J. squarely, tilting her chin up to trade glare for glare. "You're so intent on feeding your own ambitions, you're making Ashton into the kind of school where athletics come before academics, and I won't sit back and watch it.

"Frank Gordon shouldn't have been admitted to Ashton," she continued, "and he most certainly should *not* be playing basketball. He should be getting extra help to make up for that background you so carefully omitted from the file you gave me. Frank has ability—real ability, the kind of ability Ashton is supposed to develop. That's the kind of place Ashton always was until you—"

He took a step toward her. Reflexively she stepped back, then stopped immediately. "If your beloved Ashton's the kind of place where women like you use boys like Frank Gordon to get what you want—or to get rid of what you don't want—I don't give a damn for the place, or you."

The door he slammed on his way out reverberated into silence before Carolyn turned to Stewart. He sat as he had when she'd entered, seemingly frozen by C.J.'s eruption into his office.

She drew a deep breath. This hurt Stewart, too. He cared as much about Ashton as she did. He also liked and admired C.J. Draper.

"Stewart, I'm sorry you heard it this way, but you must have gathered Frank Gordon shouldn't have been admitted—"

"Sit down, Carolyn."

"C.J. must have pulled some strings in admissions. We have to check that so that it doesn't happen again, but the first thing is what to do—"

"I said sit down, Carolyn."

He'd never used that tone to her. Not in all the years growing up in his house. Not in all the years studying and teaching at his school.

He took his glasses off and rubbed the bridge of his nose with a weary sigh. Then he looked directly at her. "I was the one who oversaw Frank Gordon's admission."

The decision to sit or stand was beyond her control. Her knees made the decision for her: sit or fall down.

"I was involved almost from the beginning. C.J. told me about the boy and I looked into Frank's background carefully. I decided he suffered from poor test-taking skills and a very poor school system. He didn't lack for intelligence, but he did lack the usual Ashton background. That's part of what intrigued me so much."

Even through her astonishment she sensed his excitement. "This school has made great strides, but we're becoming rigid. If we don't keep growing, trying new challenges, then we'll start teaching by rote. And that's not teaching at all."

He stood up to come around the desk and sit in front of her. "There are fifteen others, Carolyn. Fifteen other students whose grades and scores didn't meet Ashton's standards in some area. But they had something else. There are some gifted musicians, a very promising artist, a brilliant math student, two wonderful writers. And others. We're tracking these sixteen very carefully, hoping their success will help us launch a permanent program."

The red tag, she thought. Now she understood the red tag on Frank's file.

Stewart leaned forward to meet her eyes. "I didn't do this lightly. I talked to administrators at other schools. And I consulted with some of our top people in admissions."

She hated the pain welling up in her, but she couldn't stop it. "But not with me."

"No." He sat back. Then, seeming to come to some decision, he leaned forward again and took her unresisting hands in his. "I knew your feelings about athletics, and Ashton's academic standing. I feared you'd be too—"

"Rigid?"

He met her angry look steadily. "If you like. I was going to say adamant. But that was only with the abstract idea. I knew that when you dealt with Frank—or anyone—as an individual that you'd do your best for them. I hoped it would open you to some new ideas, ideas you haven't had much chance to examine because you've moved so quickly up the academic ladder. That's one of the reasons I wanted you to work with the team. The other reason is that you're a damn fine teacher, and you're the best one to help the boy realize his potential. And it's working."

His look challenged her to deny it. "Did you listen to what you said to C.J., Carolyn? First, you said Frank shouldn't have been admitted, but then you said he should be getting extra help to develop his potential—the kind of potential Ashton should develop."

She remembered saying the words, and being too furious to consider what she was saying. Or to be bothered that she'd contradicted herself. She'd believed in Ashton's standards, and Frank didn't meet those standards. But he *did* have potential. And she'd fight anybody who tried to prevent her from helping him.

"What you just said about Frank's potential tells me that you want to keep the boy in school. And from what I've seen of his grades he's making remarkable progress under your guidance. Wouldn't you say his progress is good?''

"Yes."

"Is he in danger in any of his classes?"

"No," she admitted. "But he could do better. He's operating under a tremendous handicap. It's as if he started a race a mile behind everyone else."

"I know that. So does C.J." He stilled her impatient reaction to his defense of C.J. with a raised palm. "And, most importantly, so does Frank. But he made the decision to try to catch up. He's quite a kid. In all of this his welfare is what should come first."

Stewart stood up and placed an affectionate hand briefly on her shoulder. "Now that this is out in the open I think you and C.J. should discuss how to handle it from here. Whatever else there is between the two of you—" with his back to her as he returned to his chair, she couldn't tell if he'd added special meaning to those words "—you both owe it to Frank and the rest of the players to get along. I think you should go talk to C.J."

Oh, yes, she would talk to C.J. Draper. That she was sure of. He would know just how she felt about his lying to her, keeping her in the dark, accusing her of being underhanded when he'd manipulated her all along.

And she knew where to find him. A gym rat. Shooting hoops.

Both sets of double doors from the foyer to the gym were threaded with steel chain and padlocked for the night. Still, she could hear the distinct bounce of a ball against a hardwood floor. He was in there. She fought down an urge to futilely rattle the doors for admittance. She wouldn't give him the pleasure. She backed up two steps, staring at the unhelpful doors. He was inside, so there had to be another way. Of course . . . through Dolph Reems's office.

C.J.'s office was open and empty. Shrugging off her coat and tossing it aside as she passed through Dolph's office, she headed for the gym door, held open by a rubber wedge. She kicked it away as she crossed the threshold and heard the faint click of the automatic lock behind her.

The bleachers were pushed back against the walls, all except one partially opened section, the closest to where she stood. C.J.'s discarded sweatpants and a key ring were thrown across the bottom step. The gym was empty, except for C.J. in shorts and sweatshirt, playing one on none.

He dribbled the length of the court toward her, feinting away from imaginary opponents, driving through an imaginary defense. She knew he was aware of her, but he never faltered as he leaped and released the ball on a delicate, arcing path to the basket. The net made a swishing noise as she said, "I want to talk to you, C.J. Draper."

The ball bounced once, barely reaching knee level before he scooped it up and headed toward the opposite end of the court. Again the ball arced neatly into the basket. Again he scooped it up and headed back. But this time he found Carolyn squarely in his path.

"I want to talk to you!"

He pulled up in front of her, close enough for her to see the sweat glistening on his bare arms and neck. "Get off my court with those shoes."

"C.J.—"

"Get those shoes off if you're going to stay here." He bounced the ball just inches from the toes of her pumps, then drove around her for another basket.

He wouldn't get rid of her that easily. She stood on one foot to remove a black pump, and threw it with the force of anger. The other quickly followed. The twin thuds pulled C.J.'s head around, first to the shoes lying in the corner formed by the partially opened bleachers, then to Carolyn's defiant stance in the middle of the court.

One corner of his mouth twitched. He dribbled toward her, slower and slower as he got closer. Then, just as she dived for the ball so enticingly near, he bounced it past her with a quick flick of his wrist, sidestepped her and continued dribbling toward the basket without missing a beat. Her slick nylons on the smooth floor slid her off balance, and she barely prevented herself from falling.

"Better take the hose off, too . . . if you're going to stay."

She glared at his back as he lazily approached the basket. She pulled off her panty hose with no regard for their delicacy, jammed them into the pocket of her suit jacket and, with quick, long strides, got close enough to send the flamered jacket in the same general direction as her shoes.

"You know, you seem angry, Professor." The lazy drawl of their first encounters was back. "When I get angry, very angry at someone very aggravating—" he shot her a laser look from his blue eyes as they faced each other at midcourt "—I come out here and shoot hoops. Sorry, that's *baskets* to you, Professor. Usually I don't care much for company when I shoot hoops. In fact, I went to some pains to make sure I wasn't interrupted. But I guess you didn't get the hint."

She grabbed for the ball, but he was too quick for her. "Maybe that's what you need. To shoot some baskets." He moved to the basket, soaring toward it to lay the shot in. Then he recovered the ball and returned to midcourt.

"I know what I'm angry about, Professor. I'm angry that someone I asked not to do something—"

"Demanded!" she amended as she lunged for the ball.

"Went ahead and did it with no regard for who it might hurt."

She started a move toward his right hand, and he dribbled behind his back to switch to his left. Too late, he saw it was a fake. She grabbed the ball before he could secure it, then stepped back with her prize. "Now, Mr. Draper!" she said, gloating with victory.

"Now, Professor Trent," he said, acknowledging her upper hand mildly.

"I wasn't given the information about Frank Gordon that I needed to do my job."

Her pride wouldn't let her point out that she also hadn't had the information to betray Frank as he'd so unjustly accused her of doing. How could she tell the reporter anything about Frank's background when she seemed to be one of the few who didn't know?

"Maybe not. Why don't you go ahead and shoot the ball? You're not bad for someone who doesn't like basketball."

Absently she dribbled the ball with the long-forgotten movement of high school physical education classes. "The information I needed—"

"Of course, I was forgetting you were a swimmer, weren't you? Once an athlete always an athlete. Go ahead, shoot."

"You didn't trust me. You lied to me." She pushed the ball toward the basket with all the force behind those words. It came up short, hitting hard against the front rim and ricocheting back to midcourt.

C.J. easily pulled it in and headed for the basket. "Maybe not, but you didn't trust me, either. You were so sure you knew more about everything than I did that you couldn't believe I would know why a reporter might want to talk to you."

"You could have told me!"

"I did tell you."

"Not about reporters! About Frank!"

"Yeah, and you could have raised a stink about it. Look what you did today."

He put the ball up, but it caught the right rim and squirted away. C.J. grabbed for it, but this time Carolyn was there. She wrapped her arms around the orange leather sphere and twisted away with flying elbows. "That's because you lied about it."

"Shoot it, Carolyn. Don't just stand there."

Stung, she dribbled from the sideline around to the free throw line and let go with a shot. To her deep amazement—and gratification—it swished through the net without touching the rim at all.

"Not bad, Professor." C.J.'s voice held genuine praise.

He dribbled out to her at the free throw line. They faced each other and started a fast-footed drill of feint-and-follow.

"That's how you reacted now," he said between moves, "after knowing Gordo for four months. What would you have done back in October?" His movements were dizzyingly fast, but she followed every one. "I didn't know—" his words came out in pants, but the movement never stopped "—if I could ... risk it. Gordo's just ... getting his feet ... now."

Her breath came hard, her heart raced, but she wouldn't give in. "I...wouldn't...hurt him." Lunging, she knocked the ball away. She was a step quicker because he had to pivot on his weak left leg. She got the ball and held it with one hand against her side.

"Not even to get rid of basketball at Ashton—to get rid of me?" he asked.

He thought she'd do that? He thought that of her? "No, not even for that," she snapped.

She stood with her hands on her hips, the ball tucked casually under one arm. Her breathing lifted her breasts high under the demure white blouse.

He stopped just inches from her and stared down. He'd never seen her like this before, and he was willing to bet she'd never looked like this before. She'd never looked more beautiful. Sweat ran from her temple down to the side of her cheek and neck, then disappeared under the collarless neck of her blouse. Her hair was mussed and wild. Tendrils clung to the dampness around her face.

He'd stayed away from her for months, playing at being only colleagues. He'd welcomed her presence at the games and pretended it didn't drive him nearly mad. But never did the ache go away.

Then some fan had marched in with a clutch of newsprint in his hand, saying he worked at the *Tribune* and had seen the proofs of this story. Accusations in oblique headline style. Coyly worded questions. Facts and figures that didn't add up. And her name coming out at him as if it were in boldface. He hadn't even seen what the article said about her—just her name.

He'd seen Frank's hunted look, and something had exploded in him. Was it four months of evasions and secrets? Or four months of frustrated longing?

Vaguely he was aware of her looking up at him now, her eyes opening wider, their color turning to an amber glow. Impulsively he reached his fingers to twist a curl at her temple.

Some stronger instinct pushed his mouth to follow. Exploring, learning, his tongue reached out to touch the dampness of the skin beside her eye. With a groan deep in his throat, he tasted the saltiness, and something more, a tart sweetness that was hers, that came from inside her. His tongue followed the dampness, replacing it with its own mark, tracing it in her hair, along her temple, over her cheek.

Just below the point of her jaw, he found the hammering of her pulse. He could hear her breath, sharp and shallow. His lips closed on her skin, tasting, teasing. The heated air around them seared each breath, but no matter how he burned, he needed more and more breaths to fill his lungs.

He fired kisses along her jaw, her chin, her cheek, her forehead, tormenting himself with the nearness of her mouth. Then he pulled back just enough to see her eyes again. The amber fire in their depths gave one answer. He needed another.

Urgently he pulled her hands off her hips. The ball's hollow bounces echoed away from them in the silent gym. He slid his hands up the soft material of her blouse, gripping her arms to raise them to his shoulders. She hardly seemed aware when her arms continued the motion, winding around his neck, drawing them closer.

But it wasn't close enough to satisfy him. One hand on her back, one on the curve of her hip, brought them together along the lengths of their bodies. He saw the realization of his desire blaze into her eyes.

He watched her struggle with emotions she couldn't master. He waited—dreaded—the moment when the mask would slide into place over the vulnerability. But it didn't.

She made no attempt to deny her answering heat. He saw it there in her eyes, felt it in the slight tremor of her body. Now he allowed himself to bend over her to cover her mouth with his, swallowing her gasp into his own. Her lips parted under his, their tongues meeting tip to tip, sliding together, then parting to explore farther.

They were moving, turning around and around in a slow waltz of desire. His fingers wound in her hair, gently tipping her head back into his wide palm to leave his mouth open passage to her throat. His lips and tongue caressed it, tasting, nipping. His mouth dipped lower, seeking below the neckline of her blouse. His fingers met hers, fumbling to open buttons, push aside silken straps and clear his way.

Slowly, slowly, they were moving toward the cool, smooth hardness of the floor. He knelt over her, looking at her hair, a darker fan on the warm brown of the wood that cradled it. He dragged his sweatshirt over his head, feeling jolts of desire as her fingers trailed up his chest in its wake.

He slid one knee between her legs, then bent to her bare breast, encircling the taut nipple with his mouth's gentle heat. He could feel the smoothness of her palms as they skimmed over the ripples of his shoulders and spine, pressing him closer and closer to her.

His hand found the hem of her skirt, reaching under the silk of her slip to caress the silk of her thigh. He moved up to brush his bare chest against the aroused peaks of her breasts, then claimed her mouth once more. His hand circled higher and higher, edging the skirt up.

A metallic clank reverberated across their heated bodies—an icy shock of realization.

Some instinct for self-preservation—or sheer blind luck—had led them to the corner by Dolph's office, near her shoes and jacket. The bank of bleachers nearly sheltered them from view.

The rattle of the padlocked chain on one of the foyer doors was unmistakable. C.J. urged Carolyn closer to the protection of the bleachers and curled his body above her. All the doors were firmly locked. Nobody could get in, but the move to shield her was an instinct too strong to ignore.

Good God, he'd have made love to her right here on the gym floor, and she would have let him. What had he been thinking? He wasn't thinking—that was clear.

Desire hummed through him. He'd wanted her—wanted her that very moment—with a desperation he'd never experienced. But, damn, what had he been doing? How could he do that to her?

A disgruntled voice seeped through the wooden doors. "I tol'ja there weren't nobody in the gym." A murmur responded, then the first voice offered, "Well, if you're so certain, open 'er up, then." Another rattle, less enthusiastic this time, came to them before the bare whisper of a sound drew the final rejoinder from the same voice. "Well, I tol'ja there weren't!"

The sounds faded into silence that grew wider and wider until it seemed to encompass the entire world. It held him and Carolyn as captives, chained to immobility by the quiet. Something had to break it. Sound. Movement. Something.

"Carolyn." The syllables forced past his frozen lips galvanized their universe.

She sat up abruptly, pushing aside his protective arm, gathering her clothes to her with trembling fingers.

"Carolyn, I—"

"If you say—"

Her voice shook badly. He held out a hand to her, but she slapped it away, hard. And he saw with astonishment that it was rage that shook her.

"If you say y-you're s-sorry," she stuttered as she struggled to her feet, "as if it was all your doing, and I had nothing to do with it, I'll kill you."

He cursed himself silently. He'd taken her mask away all right. He'd made it impossible for her to pretend her emotions didn't exist, but she didn't believe she could deal with these emotions.

If he could talk to her, soothe the panic in her...

On one knee he tried to hold on to her arm, to stop her from walking away with her blouse only half buttoned and her skirt still awry. She backed away from his reach, snatching his keys from the bench.

"I'll buy rat poison, I'll put the entire bottle in your Gatorade and I'll watch you die a terrible death! With pleasure."

Numbly he watched her fumble a moment before fitting the key into Dolph's door. She firmly rammed the wedge home to prop open the door, but he saw her hands tremble as she pulled on her coat.

The slam of his office door behind her pushed the full realization of what had happened—and what had very nearly happened—into his brain. He rocked back on his heels and muttered an oath.

Chapter Nine

Anger, carefully tended, kept other emotions at bay for hours. But in the time after midnight, enfolded by her terry-cloth robe, curled into a corner of the couch, Carolyn's mind took a look at her heart.

Like a boxer regaining consciousness back in the dressing room, she relived each individual blow that had combined to knock her out.

It had started with the phone call. Even before Scott Gary had told her about the newspaper story. It had started with her disappointment that it wasn't C.J. She'd wanted it to be C.J. She'd grown accustomed to hearing his drawl; she liked the sound of it.

That was what made the pain of Scott Gary's news, confirmed by the files in the admissions office, all the harder to absorb. Then had come the scene in Stewart's office. C.J.'s rage. Stewart's revelation.

She drew her knees up on the couch and hugged the blue pillow tightly to her as some sort of armor against the hurt. But the hurt came from inside. The hurt came from knowing that people you liked and cared for didn't trust you.

She'd been conspired against. She stared unseeingly at the bookcase with the silver-framed portrait of her parents and the child Carolyn. No, she'd been excluded.

Stewart, C.J. and Frank had decided she wasn't understanding enough, not open enough. Go ahead and say it— not loving enough to see the value of a person beyond his academic credentials.

Perhaps they were right. Perhaps she'd grown rigid about how she thought things should be. At Ashton, in her life. About what she wanted—thought she wanted. Oh, God, she didn't know what she wanted anymore.

Yes, you do, whispered something at the edge of her consciousness. C.J. *You want C.J.*

She wanted the feel of his hands skimming her skin. She wanted the power of his mouth claiming hers. She wanted the weight of his body pressing into her softness. She was done with denying the longing. Not even anger could defend against wanting him.

And no amount of reasoning could change that.

She'd thought she had very good reasons to deny the fierce tug of desire. But the past few months had proved that the differences in their interests, their worlds, their backgrounds didn't prevent their working well together. They respected each other's individual abilities. With all the obstacles, they'd become friends.

When all the reasons blew away, what she really had was fear. But fear of what?

C.J.? He wanted her. She hadn't encountered this type of man before, but she wasn't naive. She knew his desire for her was real. And knowing it fed a warmth deep inside her.

There had been a desperation to his kisses, to his touch, that had shocked and thrilled her at the same time—he was desperate for her. Her light touch had set his hard muscles jumping, the feel of her lips on his brow had closed his eyes in pleasure, the movement of her body under his had sent his pulse hammering.

Was it his reaction that had frightened her? Remembering his instinctive move to protect her body with his own, she shook her head. No. She trusted C.J.

It was herself she didn't trust. This went beyond the physical pleasures she'd known before. She was just as desperate for C.J. as he was for her.

Fright and exhilaration rushed over her at the same time, just as when she'd taken a long-ago roller coaster ride as a child with her grandparents at the state fair. What terrified her was that taking this ride required letting go. No holding on to reason. No clutching a safety bar of analysis.

She'd concentrated so long on honing her brain to reach her goal—a professor at Ashton University—that she'd had no training for roller coasters. In her code professors didn't ride roller coasters. But Stewart had called that code rigid. And that code had stopped Frank and C.J. from confiding in her. And had caused C.J. to apologize—apologize!—for their passion.

Could she let go of the rigid code?

She wanted to let go. Good Lord, how she wanted to. But what if it cost her all the respect and reputation she'd worked so hard to gain? Worse, what if, at the moment of letting go, her hands refused to open?

The sun rose on Friday with no answers.

Heavy-eyed, Carolyn called the athletic department secretary to say that she would miss the daily meetings with the players and the group study hall that afternoon. She would also miss accompanying the team when it left that night for road trip games on Saturday and Monday.

Then she switched on her answering machine and shut out the world. A shower refreshed her but brought her no closer to sleep. The doorbell rang just before noon. It rang twice before she moved from the couch. When she opened the door, a packet addressed to her fell in, and she saw a messenger bicycling down the drive.

Opening the packet, she pulled out Frank Gordon's complete academic records. No message, no explanation, but she recognized C.J.'s writing on the envelope.

She spent more than an hour studying them, checking back from one sheet to another. Stewart was probably right about Frank, she thought as she stood up and tried to stretch the kinks out of her neck and shoulders before going to change into jeans and a sweater. Right about his background masking his potential, and right about what Ashton could do for him. But wrong not to tell her.

With all the information that now covered the couch and coffee table, she could have helped Frank more. He could have come even farther in the past four months if she'd had it from the start. Even now she'd change his program. He excelled in mathematics and science, but his verbal skills lagged behind. He needed basic intensive work there. She grabbed a pen and legal pad and started making notes.

When the doorbell rang in midafternoon, she answered it automatically. Frank Gordon stood there. "Professor Trent, may I talk to you?"

"Of course, Frank. Come in."

His obvious discomfort deepened to something bordering on panic when he saw his records spread out. "Maybe I shouldn't have come. It looks like you're busy," he said miserably.

"No, it's all right, Frank. I think we need to talk."

She gestured for him to take a seat at the dining table. In the kitchen she poured soft drinks into ice-filled glasses and fixed a plate of cheese and crackers. She suddenly felt ravenous, and the players were always hungry. As she brought them in, she caught a glimpse of the clock. "Shouldn't you be at practice?"

"It's all right. I talked to Coach. He said what you said— that we should talk. Coach said it was more important right now that you and I get things straight than a couple of hours of practice."

Frank swallowed. It was the longest speech she'd ever heard from him. Obviously he would have preferred untold hours of practice to making it.

"You must have had a difficult time today with that article in the *Tribune*," she probed gently.

"It's not so bad. Most people here have been real nice. Students and professors saying hello like they always do. It's those reporters... But Coach is taking most of the heat. I wish..." But his wish was caught in a renewal of shyness.

"Why don't you just tell me about coming to Ashton, Frank. It's a long way from where you grew up. In Pennsylvania, right?"

He nodded. Slowly at first, then with gathering confidence, he told her about his parents, younger brother and two younger sisters. His family lived on a small farm in rural Pennsylvania that had been in the family for generations. It hadn't been self-supporting for twenty years or more. His father had gone to work in the Pittsburgh steel mills. He hadn't minded the hard work or the hour-and-a-half commute because it had kept the farm going.

"The steel mill closed right before my senior year in high school." Frank turned the glass around and around in his right hand. "We didn't go hungry. We grew food on the farm and we'd hunt. Mom always has been good at making do, and nobody complained."

He glanced at her quickly, then back down at the glass in his big hand. "There were some tough times. Especially hard for my pap. It's hard on a man not having steady work and seeing his family doing without. I wanted to try to get some sort of job, but pap insisted I stay in school and play ball."

"Perhaps he hoped you'd get a scholarship."

Frank nodded. "There were a couple of schools talking about giving me a scholarship to play basketball, but it wouldn't have done any good. Even with them giving tuition, room and board there wasn't any money for all the other costs of going to school.

"When pap said he was selling the farm, I knew it was to get money for me. I told him I didn't want to go to school. I had it all planned. I'd join the army, then I could send money home. That's the only time my pap's ever raised his voice at me." The glass in Frank's hand made figure eights on the table mat.

"Mom kept telling me how she and pap had discussed this, and they'd decided sending me to school was an investment in the future for the whole family. But how could I let them risk the farm that way? That's our past. All of us."

Carolyn heard how the standoff had continued to strain the family until C.J. Draper had arrived at the tiny rural high school just before the end of the season. Frank's high school coach had contacted everyone he could think of, trying to get aid for the best player he'd ever had. A friend of a friend had told C.J. about the situation, and he had stopped to see Frank play.

Frank looked straight at her and spoke earnestly. "Coach had just come back from playing in that Italian league to take a job as assistant coach with the pros. It wasn't like he was one of those college coaches trying to recruit me. He didn't have anything to gain by helping me. He just did it. He set it up so I could go to Transon Junior College near home on a scholarship and he got me a secondhand car from somebody and a construction job during summers so I'd have enough money for school.

"I worked hard at Transon, Professor Trent, trying to catch up. I owed that to my mom and pap. I want to play pro ball. But if something goes wrong—like the steel mills closing for my pap—I want to have something else I can do so I can take care of my family. I thought, maybe I could build things, be an engineer...."

His fingers tightened around the glass. "I know I don't belong here. But when Coach said maybe there was a way, well, I wanted to come here so bad. I asked Coach not to tell anybody about me, about how I don't have the grades or the scores like the other students. He said he had to tell Mr. Barron. But he promised he wouldn't tell anybody else."

Both hands encircled the glass, and he stared into the dark liquid with the concentration of a crystal ball reader. "I think some of the guys think I'm slow. Brad and Ellis are always helping me. But they never say anything. I've been trying so hard, Professor Trent. I didn't want to let anybody down. I didn't want to make you unhappy or hurt Ashton."

"Oh, Frank, I know." She fought tears as her hand touched his. "You haven't let anybody down. Your parents should be very proud of you. I know how hard you're working."

"I'll try even harder, Professor Trent, if you'll just let me stay at Ashton."

The meaning of his words hit her with unexpected force. "Is that what Coach Draper said, that you might have to leave Ashton?" Did C.J. really think she would sacrifice this boy to weaken basketball at Ashton—to hurt C.J. Draper? An emotion she could only describe as fear gripped her throat.

Apparently puzzled by her intensity, Frank stared back at her. "No. He just said I should talk to you. I thought . . ."

"Nobody's going to force you out of Ashton," she vowed. "We're just going to try to make it easier for you to do better. You have a great deal of intelligence, Frank. We just need to tap it. If I had known about your background, you could've had more help, and the right kind of help. We can make some changes in your schedule and get you more intensive tutoring to fill in the gaps from your earlier education."

"But how about basketball?"

She knew she must tread carefully here. "We can try to schedule around the basketball, but some things might conflict. Then you'll have to make a decision."

She looked into his troubled eyes before she took another tentative step. "I know you feel a great deal of loyalty and gratitude to Coach Draper."

"He did a lot for me." He wasn't defensive; he was just reminding her.

"Yes. And, as you pointed out, he did it when the only thing he could have expected out of it was that you'd have the opportunity to do what's best for you. That's still the one thing you owe him."

She saw his uncertainty and drove home the point. "And that's the one thing you owe your mother and your father." That took hold; she could sense it. But she wouldn't press it now. "Anyhow, that's something you'll have to think about, Frank. In the meantime, when you come back from this road trip, I'll have some ideas on how we can fill in those gaps."

Frank shot up from his chair with a hastily stifled curse. "The road trip! The bus leaves in twenty minutes, and I haven't packed. Coach'll skin me."

He reached the door before he turned back to her with a smile of relief at shedding the burden of weighty secrets. "Thanks, Professor."

"You're welcome, Frank. But don't be too thankful until you see what I have in store for you come Tuesday."

Working on a program for Frank gave her a purpose. Poring over his records, calling his professors for consultations, mapping out a strategy—all that gave her an excuse to block out other thoughts.

On Saturday night she listened for the late news and heard that Ashton had won its game. The sportscaster mentioned questions about Frank Gordon's admission to Ashton, but not until after pointing out the fact that he had scored twenty-one points. She hoped that was a sign the episode would be short-lived.

It was past midnight when the phone rang. The machine answered. After the beep there was a pause. "Carolyn. It's C.J." Nothing else. It was as if he knew she was listening, and he was willing her to pick up the phone. Her hand reached out, then stopped.

The machine cut off.

By Tuesday morning when the team returned to study hall, much of the furor over Frank Gordon had blown over. Stewart had calmly cited statistics to the media on the special exemption admissions that Ashton had allowed. Frank Gordon was one of sixteen admitted that school year under a special program established and administered by the president's office. The sixteen students were faring very well, Stewart had explained, and the program to broaden

Ashton's horizons and outlook would continue. And expand.

While Carolyn had admired his handling of the situation, she couldn't help but wonder if the speeches weren't at least partially directed at her.

The players, pleased over winning both games on the road trip, seemed untroubled by the storm that circled around Frank. They certainly treated him no differently. And Frank himself seemed more at ease with his teammates and with her.

Ellis adroitly stifled Thomas Abbott's passing reference to Coach acting weird all weekend, and Carolyn heard no more about C.J. Nor did she see him.

Indulging in a long, scented bath on Wednesday night, she came to the conclusion that he was avoiding her. Patting herself dry, she met her eyes in the mirror. To be honest, they were avoiding each other. It was no accident that she'd been using the campus paths only when he was most likely to be in practice. She wrapped the worn, soft terry of the robe around her comfortingly.

The doorbell rang. She knew it would be C.J. even before she opened the door. Still, the sight of him, his broad shoulders filling the frame of the storm door he'd already opened, caught her heart in midbeat.

"May I come in, Carolyn?"

She was immobile.

"You'll freeze standing there like that." His gloved hand reached out to her arm, but stopped short. "You're shivering."

She stepped back then, opening the way for him to enter. She watched as he took off his gloves, then his jacket. He moved slowly, as if not entirely sure of his muscles' responses to his commands. Then he pulled a small, flat package from the pocket of his faded, snug-fitting jeans.

"I'm still trying, Carolyn." His mouth showed no sign of his usual grin, though his voice was light. "I found this in a little shop at the hotel."

She stared at the package in his hands as if it were a hypnotist's charm. He held it out to her, but she made no move to take it. So he slowly unwrapped the tissue paper to show a small, polished tortoiseshell comb. Her eyes followed the movement of his hands toward her hair until she caught sight of his face. Without the grin he looked vulnerable, even a little frightened. Around his eyes faint lines of concentration, or perhaps strain, showed.

She felt his fingers tremble slightly as they pushed the comb into the hair beyond her temple. His voice sounded uneven as he considered his effort. "No, not quite right this time, either. It's too dark."

He'd seen the comb in the hotel shop the afternoon before the game and had thought immediately of Carolyn. Angrily he'd tried to thrust aside the instantaneous longing.

That night, when a blonde, showcasing long legs in a short skirt, had started flirting with him in the hotel bar after the game, he'd told his emotions to listen to reason. Here was a chance to forget Carolyn Trent—if only he could stop remembering her.

The blonde must have thought he was nuts when he'd abruptly excused himself. The night clerk had definitely doubted his sanity when C.J. had threatened bodily harm if he didn't open the shop for the purchase of one small tortoiseshell comb.

Why wouldn't he meet her eyes? Carolyn wondered with an edge of panic. He just kept staring at the comb. Her words came out in a rush. "I didn't tell the reporter those things about Frank, C.J."

"I know."

"You talked to him?"

"No. I know you. When I—" his lips pulled into the smallest of grins "—uh, cooled down the other day, I realized you'd never do that to Frank. It's not your way."

The lightening of the burden she hadn't realized she carried made her light-headed in its suddenness. His gaze moved to her eyes. She couldn't mistake the longing. It was desire. But more. It was want and need, and still more. "I know you think I hate basketball, but I don't—"

His finger lightly touched her lips to quiet her. "This is about more than basketball." She could feel the warmth of his body. "You know that, Carolyn. It's about time we were honest about it—both of us."

Her habitual half step back brought her against the overstuffed chair. "I . . ." She cleared her husky voice to try again. "I don't think I'm ready for you, C.J."

He stepped closer but didn't touch her, holding her instead with his eyes and voice. "I want to make love with you, Carolyn. Do you understand? Not make love *to* you, not sleep together, not have sex with you, not go to bed together." His voice dropped to a low, strong murmur. "Make love with you. I think we're ready, both of us." The crooked grin appeared, then slipped away. "Maybe we've been fighting the readiness even more than each other. But I won't hurry you."

Slow and deliberate, his kiss was as good as his word. His lips touched hers, feather light. Then again. One corner of her mouth. The other. The center. Her lips parted and the angle of his kiss changed, intensified without deepening.

He was heat and light, exploding behind her eyes, shimmering through her veins. With only their lips touching, the swell of sensations sweeping over her body swamped her thoughts. But they also overwhelmed her defenses against the fear. She pulled away from his kiss and leaned her forehead against his chest.

The cold from outdoors still collected in a thin layer over the heat of his body; she felt them both, mixed with the cottony smell of his shirt and the clean scent of his soap. His hands stroked her back, across her shoulders and along her upper arms. He kissed the hair caught in the tortoiseshell comb.

If she could just let the feelings take her... She didn't know if she could. She didn't know if she should. She tried to tell him, but he only felt the new tension in her body.

C.J. muttered a curse. Trying to see her face, he held her away from him. His voice was calm, but his fingers bit into her shoulders. "Is it because I'm a jock? I don't meet your standards? Is that—"

"No!" She tilted back her head so he could see in her eyes that it wasn't him, but her. She'd lived her life by her mind, carefully thought out steps, rational decisions. But this, with him, wasn't rational, had nothing to do with intellect. Her body, her heart, her soul pulled her to him.

"Oh, God, Carolyn, don't cry. I never wanted you to cry." Rocking her in his arms, his voice rasped. "Just tell me what you want. You want me to leave? You want me to keep a respectful distance? I'll try if that's what you want. By God, I'll try. But I don't know if I can do it."

His gentle touch and the rough, raw emotion of his voice short-circuited some barrier in her. She couldn't get words out. But her heart found another way. She shook her head, stopping only to reach up to press her lips against the skin at the base of his throat.

Electricity jolted through C.J. Reflexively he tightened his hold on her, and the feel of her warm, soft curves against his hardened body sent another surge through him. "Tell me what you want, Carolyn."

"I want you."

He'd longed for those words, dreamt of them—to his chagrin and discomfort. But now the words echoed with so much confusion. Gently he pushed the hair back from her temple and feathered his lips across the smooth skin. "But you don't want to."

It wasn't a question, but she tried to give an answer. "I'm frightened, C.J.," she whispered. "I don't know if I can just *feel*."

Oh, God, where had all her words gone? She had to make him see. She had to try. Looking up at those blue, blue eyes, she linked her arms around his neck.

She leaned against him as she stretched up to capture his lips. The feel of her body along his, the press of her breasts against his chest, the touch of her thighs against his, pounded desire through his veins.

His hand caressed the curve of her buttocks, then brought her tightly against his lower body. He strained toward her through the worn denim. He wanted her to feel his arousal, to know that she did this to him; to know that if she meant to back away, it had to be now.

The wordless murmur that escaped her lips before he captured them told him that there would be no backing away.

She tugged at his shirt, trying to push it out of the way and run her palms over the hard planes of his abdomen and chest at the same time. He pulled the shirt over his head and dropped it behind him.

Almost shyly she took his hand and led him to her bedroom. Just short of the bed, where the light from the hall splashed through the center of the room and whitened a corner of the bedspread, he pulled her possessively into his arms.

She wanted to feel. Tonight, at least tonight, they'd feel.

His kiss crushed her lips, and she welcomed the pressure. She tilted her head back farther and farther to take the feel of his mouth, a caress dense with emotions she had no thoughts to analyze.

When its heaviness was too much, she arched her neck and let her jaw and throat revel in the texture of his lips and tongue. "C.J." Her voice needed to whisper his name the way her fingers needed to tangle in the shining thickness of his hair.

The tie of her robe slipped loose under his hasty fingers. His hands moved to her shoulders, greedy to touch her but afraid, so afraid she would still turn away from him.

His hesitation brought tears to her throat. C.J.—so sure, so strong, so certain—needed her reassurance.

She shrugged the robe from her shoulders and stretched up for his lips once more. The friction of his body against hers stoked the heat deep inside and sent a stream of fire through her.

If his arms hadn't held her, she couldn't have remained standing. His lips crashed down on hers, then found the hollow at the base of her throat as he scooped her into his arms and placed her on the bed.

He knew she was frightened. Shattering a marble mask took a lot of courage, a lot of strength. But the need in her— the need in him—was too great not to be answered.

He stripped off the rest of his clothes and lay beside her quickly; he'd give her no time to cool. He skimmed his hands over the warm silk of her skin, just grazing the swell of her breast as he traced her side, then down the concave line of her waist to the curve of her hip and below to the smoothness of her thigh.

He'd craved the heat of her body, the heat of her desire. He needed it. The light touch of her fingers on his shoulders was hesitant, shy. She'd said she was scared. So was he.

He moved up to meet her eyes, to let her see his weakness and let her draw strength from it.

He saw the uncertainty seep from her eyes, replaced by passion. No longer shy, her hands pressed his head down to her, where she met his mouth with lips already parted. Her tongue tantalized his, dueling and feinting before dipping deeply in a kiss that left them both breathless.

Bending over her, he trailed kisses down her throat and pressed his mouth to the trembling pulse at its base, then journeyed on. Slowly, tenderly, his lips circled the softness of her full breast. When, at last, the deliciously torturous progress was over and his lips grazed the hard, tender button, she arched under him. Closer. She had to get closer. He drew her nipple deep into his mouth as she pressed against him.

Almost languidly he paid the same loving attention to her other breast, circling her higher and higher. But this time there would be no vertigo, no fear of heights, not as long as she held on to him.

His long body settled between her thighs with a sigh drawn from both of them. When his gentle hand found her moist and heated for him, her hips surged in a response that nearly pushed him over the edge.

"I...I want to go slow for you, Carolyn."

His breath, ragged and shallow, stroked her breast with his words. She could feel him throbbing against her thigh. She twisted her hips to bring him closer to her and heard him groan.

"I don't know if I can wait," he gasped.

"Don't wait." Her fingers found the base of his spine and urged him toward her while her hips invited. "Now, C.J."

"Carolyn...Lord—" Abruptly he moved away from her. For an instant she felt only disorientation and loss. Then small sounds came together in explanation of his movement. Protection—something she'd nearly forgotten. The gesture drove home to her how much he cared.

When he came back to her welcoming arms, he held just enough control to enter her slowly, to watch the widening of her eyes as the length of him filled her. She gave a small cry when he pulled back, and tried to hold him inside her. But he had only withdrawn to stroke into her again, deeper. Again and again. Slowly at first.

"C.J." She wanted to tell him so many things, but she could only whisper. She wanted to tell him how his taste, his smell, his feel, his look filled her dreams. Those were the things she wanted to revel in, to relish when they made love—oh, yes, in her dreams she had always wanted to make love with him.

But he took all her senses reaching out to capture him and turned them inside her. So everything she was and could be was focused on the sensations he was creating in her.

Tension coiled tighter and tighter in her with each quickening thrust of his body. She strained to reach some goal she was certain was unattainable, but still his sweat-filmed body—and her own—drove her toward it.

And then they were there. Together. Spinning through waves of pleasure. From far away, but very near, she heard him call her name. And she answered.

"C.J.!"

It was astonishment, wonder, ecstasy and even a little fear. It was pure feeling.

Slowly she glided toward earth through this foreign atmosphere where nothing as coherent as thought existed. She didn't want to move—ever. How could she move when she wasn't sure where her flesh ended and his began, and felt no reason to find out? She had no sensation of his body on top of hers, but only of the two of them joined.

She felt the pulse of his heartbeat gradually regulate. She wasn't sure hers ever would.

Sometime she would have to think about what had happened, how it had changed her. For certainly she was changed. But for now she drifted in happiness.

When he could move, he eased most of his weight off her, but couldn't bear to leave the comfort of her body. He kept one leg across hers and claimed her rib cage with one long arm. His head found the curve between her neck and shoulder so his lips could always take the taste of her skin.

Nestling closer, she remembered her idle thought about how she might fit with someone so tall, and smiled to herself. They fit perfectly. She shifted a little to feel more of the delicious friction of his skin, still warm and slightly damp, against hers.

"Don't do that." The low growl into her shoulder was barely intelligible.

A stiletto stab of fear pierced her contentment. Did he regret it? "Why not?"

He lifted his head to look into her eyes, with their amber darkened to a passion-filled glow. "You'll make me want you again."

"Is that bad?"

Propping himself on one elbow he studied her. There was no coyness in her. She really wanted to know. So did he. He stroked the damp hair back from her temple. "It's not if you don't think so."

She lifted her head to quickly kiss the nearest part of him, which happened to be his chin. His grin flashed into existence, then faded to seriousness.

"You know this doesn't solve everything, Carolyn." Again he stroked the hair at her temple. Slipping deeper into her hair, his fingers found the comb caught in thick, twisted strands. Disentangling it would require concentration

"There are still things we need to straighten out between us." His fingers gently tugged at a stubborn lock of hair. "About Ashton. About Frank and the team." He looked down into her gaze that hadn't left his face, and his voice dropped to a husky note. "About you and me."

"I know."

He saw the single crease in her brow and felt a clutch in his gut. He couldn't let her slip away from him now. He wouldn't. For four long months he'd wanted her. Now he knew he'd continue to want her. The ache for her wasn't sated. Would it ever be?

"We're going to work those things out. All of them." The comb came free of the last silky knot, and he tossed it aside. "Do you understand, Carolyn?"

His kiss prevented any answer. It was an openmouthed demand that she answered readily with no consultation with reason.

As long as he didn't regret this, she understood only that they would work out anything. She told him so with the means of communication he left her. Her lips softened under his. Her tongue made bold forays to discover the sensitive caverns of his mouth. Her hands stroked and clasped. Her body writhed and tempted.

"Oh, God, Carolyn." He pulled back while his lungs made valiant attempts to pull in air. "You feel so damn good. You make me...you make me forget everything." He grinned in mild self-mockery. "All the lectures I've given the guys on their responsibilities and I nearly didn't—"

She shushed him with her fingers on his lips. "But you did."

The self-mockery remained, but it didn't totally hide from either of them the huskiness in his voice. "Sometimes I'm not exactly levelheaded around you, you know."

"Then I'll be the levelheaded one," she said with careful lightness.

"I'm not sure I'd like that, either."

Some instinct told her this emotion was something new to C.J., too, and he wasn't quite sure what to do with the volatile commodity. "There's just no pleasing some people," she murmured as her fingers trailed down his rib cage to his lean hip and onto his thigh.

"Oh, yes, there is. At least this person." He covered her body with his and showed her just how much she did please him.

Chapter Ten

Carolyn woke with C.J.'s chest as her pillow, C.J.'s body as her blanket.

To get enough room for his long body, he'd stretched nearly diagonally on the bed. She curled against one side. It was the most wonderful sleeping position she'd ever found.

She smiled and shifted slowly so that she wouldn't wake him. She wanted to watch him sleep. A stubble of light whiskers showed in the diluted sunlight of the February morning. The grooves his grin carved were just faint echoes of white in his cheeks. His strong mouth showed a sensitivity she'd never seen before. His mop of multishaded hair was tousled like a little boy's.

But the body exposed by the covers drawn down nearly to his waist looked nothing like a boy's. She remembered his broad shoulders deepening the shadows in the stairwell of Ripon Hall before he'd kissed her. And the way they'd looked in that sleeveless sweatshirt the day she'd interrupted practice. And the way they'd felt in the gym on Thursday and again last night.

Softly she feathered her fingers across the collarbone that stood out in high relief under his taut skin. Boldly she touched her lips to the webbing of muscle that connected his shoulder and arm. Her tongue made dizzying patterns on his skin.

C.J. woke with an unexpected heat emanating from his shoulder and pulsing through him. Only one person, one dream, had caused that sensation. He groaned out her name before he was totally conscious.

"I'm sorry I woke you."

She was real. And she looked adorably guilty, even as her hand trailed down his chest to taunt his male nipple into reaction.

"You can wake me this way anytime you want." His breath was harsh, irregular, but he wasn't beyond thought. Not quite. Not yet.

"Can I?"

To his ears, she sounded distracted, maybe preoccupied by the way the interconnecting muscles over his ribs contracted at her lightest touch. Still, a persistent mist of anxious thought tugged at him. It felt so damn good, but did she want to do this? Did she really want to touch him with so much tenderness? It didn't seem possible.

"Carolyn?"

"Hmm?" She'd just discovered how easily she could push the covers aside to explore the lean hips and long legs so artfully displayed by those indecent gym shorts she'd seen him wear.

"Carolyn!"

The haze of passionate absorption in the intricacies of his body was too thick to allow for anything more than another murmur.

Sitting up quickly, he grasped both of her wandering hands in one of his and used the other to take hold of her chin to look into her eyes. The amber glow was there, glazed with the heat of desire and a wondering kind of triumph.

She smiled at him, then leaned against him to flick her tongue enticingly across his lips as she freed her hands from his unresisting grip. Stroking down his chest, she followed the light covering of hair that narrowed to a line at his navel before flaring out.

He dropped back against the pillow, letting the agonizing tenderness of her touch wash over him. Last night she had opened herself to him, given herself to him. Now she took. She staked her claim to his body. Maybe she already had his soul.

A shudder racked C.J. as her exploration with fingers, mouth and tongue continued down the elongated muscles of his thighs. When she got to his knee, she stopped to examine the lines of scars.

"Oh! I should have thought. Does it hurt when you...I mean last night...?"

The nerves around the scars were dead. He knew they were, but they sent off crazy flashes of sensation under her touch that made it very difficult to focus on her words. "No. It didn't hurt." His half laugh, half moan was at his own expense. "It hurts a great deal more when I don't."

Satisfied, she rubbed her mouth across his knee as if to heal past hurts, then traveled on. He was so tight, every muscle clenched, every sinew tense.

She remembered what Rake had said about how hard it was for C.J. just to sit back and let someone else do the doing. But he was letting her do the loving now. Perhaps he just needed the reassurance that someone else would do the doing, the loving, if he didn't.

Her tongue circled his ankle bone, and C.J.'s body contorted in an effort not to explode.

"Carolyn! For God's sake."

She answered his plea by moving up his body with a string of hot, moist kisses. His urgent hands tugged at her shoulders, and he started to roll her onto her back, but she resisted, and he understood. She rose above him, and he gripped her hips with a gravelly groan. This time she was the one who took him inside her.

"Carolyn. I have wanted you forever."

He was sheathed in her, pulsing with the warmth of her surrounding him.

"Forever," she repeated with a moan.

As the crazy, tightening ascent built, he held on to her for dear life unaware of her fingers digging just as tightly into him.

Picking her way along a slush-filled path, Carolyn listened to Helene grousing about Marches that came in like lambs.

"It thaws just enough to cover the entire landscape in slush and mud, and then—just when you get a whiff of spring—wham, we're back to blizzards. I'm going to retire to Bermuda."

They'd left an alumni tea at Stewart's office and were headed across campus in the damp chill of dusk to Carolyn's car so that she could drive Helene home.

"You've said that every March for three years that I know of, Helene," Carolyn said with a laugh. "I don't think you've ever even *visited* Bermuda. And what would Stewart do without you?"

Carolyn looked up in time to see an astonished pleasure cross the older woman's face. Was what she thought of Helene and Stewart's relationship so important to the older woman? Had she—and possibly Stewart, too—read into

Carolyn's words and actions a disapproval she'd never meant to show?

Never meant to show. But did she disapprove? She remembered the dinner at Angelo's and C.J.'s suggesting that when Stewart was ready he'd have someone to love him. Then, she'd thought how inappropriate Helene seemed for a university president. Now, she could only see how well the woman suited Stewart.

"He needs you," Carolyn said deliberately. "You're good for him."

A film of tears appeared in Helene's eyes, and she seemed robbed of her usual chatter.

Taking Helene's arm to guide her over a particularly large patch of half-melted ice, Carolyn added more lightly, "Besides, what would you do with all your wonderful wool clothes?"

Helene patted Carolyn's gloved hand on her arm in thanks. "You wait and see, Carolyn Trent. I'll disappear to Bermuda one winter just like the robins. Not all of us have something tall and charming to ward off the chill of these Wisconsin winters."

She hardly heard Helene's discussion of C.J.'s visit with Stewart to view some old campus movies. Color—unrelated to the raw air—flooded her cheeks. In the past three weeks Carolyn had heard several vague comments about her relationship with C.J. She and C.J. had agreed to be discreet. But more and more she wondered if it was a matter of public knowledge that he spent more nights at her place than his.

"You know I can't get cable at my place like you do here," he'd said offhandedly one night while flipping from basketball game to basketball game. "You get a lot more games. I wish I could tape some of these."

"You could set your VCR up here."

The offer had been carefully casual. She'd adamantly shut off any efforts of her mind to analyze or label her feelings for C.J. Draper. But when his blue eyes had turned toward her, she'd felt her heart hammering. What was she getting herself into? Did he read this as a preliminary step to giving permanency to their relationship? Did she?

Either he didn't see her trepidation or he ignored it, because he simply said thanks.

The next day he brought the machine over.

It was just a VCR and some videotapes, she'd told herself. A simple practicality so that he could tape more games. But when she curled up in his arms to read while he watched the tapes, practicality seemed a very distant concept. And it was even harder to remember that other people observed her and C.J. and did their own analyzing and labeling.

"That doesn't change anything," she said, more in answer to her own thoughts than to Helene.

"Of course not." Helene's look of surprise took on a shade of appraisal. "There's no reason for it to change anything you don't want changed. What are you worried about it changing?"

What was she worried about? That other people knew she was involved with C.J.? She'd never particularly cared for her private life being known, but surely that was one aspect of campus life she'd long accepted.

"I'm not worried about anything," she assured Helene. And only a tiny voice whispered cautiously to her: except perhaps tempting the fates by feeling so happy.

"Helene! Carolyn! Hold up there." Dolph Reems came chugging up to them, already pulling open his satchel-like case. "Boy, am I glad I saw you, Carolyn. I've got to get over to my daughter's for my grandson's first birthday, or my life won't be worth living. I'm already ten minutes late, and if I swing by your place, too, it'd take another fifteen.

But I promised C.J. I'd get him these tapes from last season's conference tournament today. He wanted to watch them before tomorrow's practice." He pulled out four videotapes and tumbled them into her unresisting hands.

"You know, I really think we have a shot at winning that tournament." He continued on his way, still talking to them over his shoulder. "I really appreciate it, Carolyn. Tell C.J. I'm sorry 'bout not getting them to him earlier. I had to pick up the cake. Bye. Bye, Helene." He climbed into his car, backed up and waved goodbye to them.

"My God, if Dolph Reems knows, *everybody* knows," Carolyn sputtered at last.

"The secret is definitely out," Helene said with barely controlled laughter. "Do you mind so terribly?"

Carolyn looked down at the tapes in her hands and said with a trace of wonder. "No." She was just surprised. "It's just Dolph...I mean, I've known him since I was a little girl, and he's always seemed so straitlaced, but he..." She searched for a phrase to explain Dolph's attitude and fell back on understatement. "He didn't seem to mind."

"Mind? He positively beamed. The man looked like Christmas and the Fourth of July had arrived together! You'd think he expected a commission as matchmaker!" And now the laughter did overtake her. "When everybody knows Stewart and I are splitting it down the middle!"

C.J. noticed the tapes on the table, but not right away. First, when he deposited the cartons of Chinese food he'd brought for dinner, he wrapped his arms around Carolyn from behind and kissed her neck. With the lettuce she was washing for a salad dripping in her hands, she could do no more than lean back against him and sigh.

That was enough.

He spread the fingers of one hand and let them graze the bottom curve of her breast. "Mmm. Salad'll be good."

"There's not going to be any if you keep doing that."

He loved the way her cool voice grew husky under his touch. His hand covered her breast, sensing it tighten through the slippery silk.

"If that's the choice, I'll take this," he murmured against her neck. "I like this blouse." His fingers began adeptly unbuttoning the white mother-of-pearl buttons down the front of the peach silk.

"Then why are you taking it off?"

"I like what's underneath better." His fingertips slipped inside the opened blouse and delved under the lacy edge of slip and bra to the ivory-smooth skin. One touch brought the rosy tip to tight attention.

"Oh, C.J." She dropped the lettuce into the sink and twisted in his arms to face him, trying, still, to keep her wet hands away from him.

He bent to trail his lips along her jaw, then down her throat and lower. Slipping the straps from her shoulder helped him clear the way for his mouth to follow where his fingers had prepared. Wet hands were forgotten in the need to hold his head closer.

The phone jolted her back to the present. The sound of water running and the smell of Chinese food slipped back into her consciousness.

"Let it ring," C.J. growled.

"We did that last night, remember? And never got any dinner. Tonight we eat, first," she said as he helped her restore her clothing. Then she picked up the phone. "Hello? Oh, hello, Stewart." She listened just a moment, then handed the phone to C.J. without looking at him. "It's for you. Stewart."

Even as he talked to Stewart about arrangements for the team's tournament trip, he watched her. Searching, she knew, for some reaction to Stewart's easy assumption that C.J. could be reached at her apartment. She wasn't sure herself if her lack of reaction resulted from the numbness of shock or disinterest in something basically trivial.

Quickly she finished the salad and set the table. By the time she'd brought the food, C.J. was hanging up. He sat down with his usual easy motion, but she sensed an added tension in him. Perhaps Stewart's assumption bothered him. He wasn't a man accustomed to being considered part of a twosome.

"What are these?" He patted the stack of videotapes as she served the salads.

"Dolph gave them to me." Her casualness was impressive. "I ran into him this afternoon and he asked me to bring them ... here to you." She'd almost said "Home to you," but had faltered at the last second.

He tightened momentarily. More a stillness of his face than an obvious tension in his muscles. Then he relaxed.

Carolyn felt her breath come again as they dug into the cartons of Chinese food. Some milestone had been passed. She didn't have to identify it to be glad it was behind them.

"Must be the tapes of last year's conference tournament. I wanted to look at them again. With only a week left we've got a lot of practicing to do."

He talked on about basketball while they ate chicken cashew and shrimp and vegetables, but all the while one level of his mind tried to weigh her reaction. For his part he didn't give a damn who knew. She was the one who wanted discretion. He'd shout it from the chapel's bell tower if they'd let him. But she didn't want it that way.

Her marble mask had been held in place by a lot of ideas of what a proper professor should and should not do. He'd wondered—and tried hard not to—how she'd feel when the pairing of Professor Trent of the English Department and Coach Draper of the basketball team became public knowledge. He hadn't acknowledged the possibility that she'd recoil, but it had been there.

Having the tacit declaration of that public knowledge delivered virtually back to back by the two men who were the closest things to father figures in her life should have really thrown her for a loop. But she'd hardly batted an eye.

It didn't reassure him. C.J. didn't consider himself an insecure man. This was something different.

He told her the team had a real shot at some upsets in the conference tournament, maybe even winning the title and the automatic berth to the national tournament that went with it. Even without the title the team could get invited to the national tournament as a wild card.

And he thought about how much he wanted her. All the time. Any time. Never had a woman excited him so easily, so unwittingly. Watching her in the kitchen, finding excuses to brush against her as they cleaned the dishes. Hearing her voice. Just knowing she was in the living room reading.

He'd lie in her bed holding her, stroking her soft hair. Totally satisfied, yet never having enough of her. His desire for her was a constant pool of gasoline that needed only the tiniest flick of flame from her for a conflagration.

"Okay, we've eaten first," he declared, grasping her hand and tugging her toward the bedroom. "Now it's time for seconds."

She wasn't a jealous woman, but she could be jealous of basketball. A game for heaven's sake. A boy's game played by overgrown boys in shorts, squabbling and fighting over a silly orange ball. Good Lord, she even sounded like a jealous woman spitting venom at a rival.

In the afterglow of their lovemaking, lying naked with C.J.'s warm chest against her back and his arm thrown across her, how could she doubt his feeling for her? She didn't. But when he talked about the conference tournament and what the team could do, she remembered his ambitions. Ambitions that all led away from Ashton and her.

What would happen after this season he was making such a success of? Would other schools want him sooner than even his dreams had foretold?

"Frank got a B plus on that history paper," she told him, only partially aware of the impulse to remind him that his accomplishments with the team went beyond the court. "I don't know why the old skinflint couldn't have given him the A," she grumbled. Where he nuzzled the back of her neck, she felt C.J.'s mouth lifting up into his uneven grin.

"Why do I feel like Ward Cleaver learning the Beave just got a good grade? Think I should take him out for an ice-cream sundae?"

Carolyn reached back to slap at his fanny, but found instead the hard muscle of his upper thigh. "Seriously, you should be proud of these guys. They're really working hard—in the classroom, too, I mean."

How could he be serious about anything but the feel of her fingers lightly trailing up and down the back of his thigh? "Uh-huh," he mumbled, feasting more deeply on the taste of the skin at her shoulder. "That's the guys—Classroom All-Americas."

"Well, there is an academic All-America team," she objected. The unevenness of her voice betrayed the effect of the charges set off in her body by the feel of his muscles and the sensation of his mouth and tongue branding the back of her shoulder.

"Uh-huh." The words were automatic. His mouth crested the ridge of her shoulder to the front, starting a slow, sensual descent toward another peak, already rose-tipped and pebbled. "But no coach. Doesn't help the coach any to have academic All-Americas."

"Some coaches have clauses in their contracts for bonuses based on graduation rates. More and more schools are doing that, so the coaches who keep their players in school are rewarded." She sensed his heightened interest in her words and felt unaccountably shy.

"How do you know about that?"

"Oh, I read it somewhere." She pressed the flat of her palm against his buttock to draw him closer. His body hardened in delighted response. But the attempt at evasion and diversion seemed to intrigue him more.

He leaned over her to see her face. "Where'd you read it?"

"Some magazine," she muttered.

He used the simple expedient of pressing her shoulder down into the mattress so that she lay on her back. That way, with his body half over hers, he could see into her eyes. "What magazine?" His grin popped in and out like sunshine behind fitful clouds.

There was no reason for embarrassment. Still, she felt a little silly. But he wouldn't let it go. She knew him too well. "*Sports Illustrated.*"

He looked into her mildly defiant face and laughed. Amusement, and something deeper, swelled his heart. He dropped back but pulled her with him so that they lay facing each other, side by side. "Professor Trent buying *SI* in a plain brown wrapper. I can see it now," he teased, but without malice.

"I thought I should know more about the players' interests," she said defensively. "Their world." *And yours.*

He saw the unspoken words in her eyes and experienced a glow, swift and warm, of a deeper emotion calling for a name he wasn't quite ready to use. He trailed his hand lightly down to her breast, circling the nipple with infinite care. Then he slid one knee between hers and pulled her top leg up across him until it hooked over his narrow hip.

When his hips moved and she felt the smooth, hard heat of him touch her, her system went haywire. She gasped and arched toward him, instinctively seeking deeper contact. She had just enough rationality left to know he was equally affected. She hardly recognized his voice—only the emotion—when he spoke.

"You're quite a woman, Professor Trent."

He slid inside her.

Chapter Eleven

C.J.'s predictions about the conference tournament nearly came true. The team won its first game easily, pulled an upset in the semifinals and just missed another one against the favorite in the championship game.

From the first game on Friday until after the championship game on Sunday night when Ashton received an atlarge bid to the national tournament, Carolyn was convinced her blood pressure never dropped below a hundred and fifty. She was fascinated, and awed, by the excitement, noise and passion of the conference tournament.

"I still have the marks on my palms where my nails dug in from clenching my hands," she told Stewart the next Thursday afternoon in his office.

Marsha Hortler had called saying Stewart would like to see her, but so far they'd only talked about basketball. C.J. and the team were already at the tournament site just outside Chicago preparing for their first-round game Friday afternoon. She planned to drive down with Stewart and Helene in the morning.

"Wait until you see the national tournament," Stewart advised. "The conference is just a warm-up for the nationals."

She groaned. "I'm not sure I can take that."

"Hope your nerves are steady now because I have some more news for you. Exciting news, I think."

Carolyn straightened in the chair. His words said one thing, but his voice said he wasn't entirely happy with the news, whatever it was.

"I received a call from England this morning. This year's seminar organizer contacted me as a professional courtesy to ask permission to approach you about returning there to teach. Permanently."

Astonished pride surged through her. They wanted her. One of the most prestigious gatherings of literature professors in the world wanted her.

Permanently. The word swept in another set of emotions. Live in England. Leave Wisconsin. Leave Ashton. Leave her friends . . . Leave C.J.

"I could play the heavy if you want." Stewart offered. "I could tell them no, that you're contractually bound to Ashton."

"Am I?"

Some of the hopefulness went out of his voice. "Not in any way that would prevent your going."

She had a choice to make. She'd make it. She couldn't decide this by default. "No, Stewart. Thank you, but no. I have to make the decision."

"I'm very proud of you, Carolyn. But I would hate to see you leave." He sighed heavily. "I guess it's good practice for me. I expect other schools—bigger schools with bigger programs and better jobs—to start calling about C.J. any time now.''

The reminder that C.J. might not be at Ashton left a jagged pain. ''Stewart, please don't say anything about the offer from the seminar to anyone.'' He peered over the top of his glasses at her, and she looked away. ''Nothing may come of it, and I'd prefer we kept it between us for now. Just us.''

''All right, Carolyn, if that's the way you want it.''

''Yes. That's the way I want it.''

''Can you believe this, Carolyn?'' Helene shouted over the noise.

Sitting right next to her, Carolyn barely deciphered the words. She knew Stewart, on the other side of Helene, was speaking because she saw his lips move. But the flood of sound swallowed the words.

The arena was under siege from noise. Every decibel in the world was here, caught in the shouts and roars and whistles and claps. It was enough to tear the world apart on this Sunday afternoon in March: Ashton University was on the verge of the biggest upset of the season.

After reaching the conference tournament final the week before, then winning the first-round game in the national tournament Friday, the Ashton Aces possessed a wide following as a sentimental favorite.

But this, this was totally unexpected. Leading Bracken State, the number two team in the country, by three points with nineteen seconds left in the game.

The Bracken State coach called his final time-out as soon as his team gained control of the ball. His players gathered around him while he rapidly diagrammed plays designed to prevent the loss.

Anxiety sent Carolyn's heart thudding against her ribs. Nineteen seconds. There were so many ways a win could disappear in nineteen seconds.

A three-point shot would tie the score and send it into overtime. Did Ashton have the endurance for that? A foul at the wrong moment could give Bracken a chance at tying. Or winning. If Bracken got one basket, then stole the ball back for another try...

Her stomach churned with the possibilities as she watched C.J. crouch down, with the Ashton players encircling him.

Frank, Ellis and Jerry had played every minute of the game so far. All three bent at the waist, resting their hands on their knees and sucking in air as they listened to C.J. Despite the frown of concentration between Brad's eyes, his mouth couldn't suppress a wide grin. Holding still was impossible for the rest of the team as jolt after jolt of adrenaline pumped through their systems.

She saw C.J. look from face to face as he tried to prepare them for the crucible of the next nineteen seconds. She could practically hear the slow drawl that could calm even at a shout.

Helene's words came through erratically, like a poor long-distance connection, one faint, one clear, one unintelligible. "They win this and they go to the regional semifinals! Then just two more victories, and it's the Final Four! I've always wanted to go to the national tournament."

Want. The word buzzed around Carolyn's head. Wants conflicted and canceled out. She couldn't wish for Ashton to lose, but wanting them to win amounted to wanting C.J. to leave. How could she not want him to get his opportunity, to move on to his dream of the big time?

She, too, had a chance at a dream. Prestige, honor, recognition in her profession. Hadn't that always been her dream?

At that moment she knew only two things that she wanted unequivocally. She wanted the Ashton players—her players—to do themselves proud. And she wanted to put her arms around the tall, lean figure in the red Ashton blazer sending his players back to the court.

She loved him.

She held her breath, waiting for a reaction, but there was none. No surprise; it would have been like being surprised that her lungs functioned. No astonishment; it would have been like being astonished that her heart pumped.

She loved him. And she knew he felt an agony more intense at that moment than his knee had ever caused him. He could do nothing but wait and watch. And let someone else do the doing.

The Bracken State coach got to his feet and hollered instructions as his team brought the ball in. Despite Ellis's arms-spread efforts to distract the passer, the ball found its mark. The Bracken player eluded Brad and dribbled across midcourt.

Bracken State snapped out two more passes, so quickly that the Ashton players had to scramble to catch up. The third exchange went to Bracken's tallest player, in position just to the side of the net. He pulled in the pass, soared over Frank and slammed the ball home.

Noise became a physical pressure on Carolyn's chest, pushing out her breath. There wasn't time to worry about breathing.

One point. Twelve seconds on the clock.

Ellis passed the ball to Brad, who immediately sent it back to Ellis. He was the one Ashton wanted to handle the ball. He was hard to steal from; and if Bracken State fouled him, he was steady at the free throw line.

Ellis brought the ball up the court with precise care. With a one-point lead the clock was his friend—as long as he held on to the ball.

Nine seconds. Bracken State tried to hem Ellis in so he'd have to pass the ball or risk a foul for holding it too long. He slipped away just in time.

Seven seconds. The Bracken State coach stood and screamed at his players to foul. The player closest to Ellis lunged at him, hacking him across the forearm.

A foul was called, and soon Ellis stood at the free throw line, measuring the familiar distance with his eye. The noise in the arena took on a different quality, undiminished but breathless.

The ball left Ellis's hands in a perfect arc. As it curved through the air, time slowed. Carolyn saw Ellis turn an anguished face to C.J. on the bench, saw C.J. rise from the bench and holler something. He clapped his hands twice, then motioned for Ellis to get back on defense.

The ball touched the outside of the rim and time returned to its usual excruciating pace. The ball squirted to the right, directly into the hands of a Bracken State player.

"Oh, Ellis," Carolyn gasped. How long would he punish himself for that miss? But for now he couldn't allow himself the luxury of blame.

Six seconds. Bracken State brought the ball up the court as quickly as they could. These players were experienced and confident. They expected to win. All they had to do now was get the ball to the basket.

Five seconds. The Ashton players spread under the basket, arms wide, trying to form an impenetrable barrier. From up above Carolyn saw the open Bracken player a split second before his teammate passed the ball to him in the left corner.

She tried to shout a warning, but the wall of sound swallowed her words like a single drop in a downpour.

The Bracken State player gathered himself for the shot. He released the ball from his fingertips. Brad hurtled toward him with arms extended and his body nearly parallel to the ground.

The ball slammed against Brad's hands and rebounded to the shooter. But the opening was gone. His balance already regained, Brad closed in to corner him. The shooter passed the ball back to a teammate.

Three seconds. Ellis shouted something, pointing for Frank to change positions. Carolyn saw C.J., still standing on the sidelines, half reach toward the players as if to move Frank back. His arms dropped abruptly to his side. She saw in every line of his body what control it took to stop the gesture, to hold himself off the court—to let his players play.

Two seconds. Bracken State made one last pass away from the basket, then sent the ball toward the big player, once more positioned beside the basket. He would need only to reach up for the ball and continue his trip to the net for the winning points.

One second.

Frank rose from the players around him like a puff of smoke. It wasn't a leap; it was levitation. It was a liquid movement that pulled the ball into his chest and guarded it with extended elbows as he floated back to the court.

It was victory.

The final buzzer sounded, and Frank flung the ball above his head. The Ashton players, racing from the bench and the corners of the court, piled onto him, pyramiding in ecstasy.

C.J. moved more slowly to where Ellis stood alone near center court, head thrown back, arms extended in exultation. He reached out a hand to his player, then pulled him into a hug.

Carolyn knew she was crying, but couldn't feel the tears. She could hardly feel the tug on her arm as Stewart tried to keep her and Helene ahead of the wave of humanity surging onto the court.

Dolph Reems's bear hug caught her as she came off the last step of the bleachers. He was shouting, but she couldn't separate the words.

Out in the middle of the court the players milled around and pounded one another on the back, shouting their joy. Brad draped his arm around Jerry. An upperclassman who rarely played pumped Ellis's hand unceasingly. Thomas Abbott erupted into periodic whoops of triumph. Frank withstood his teammates' congratulatory pummeling on his shoulders with a face-splitting grin and a glistening in his eyes.

From the edge of the melee Carolyn saw Rake enfold C.J. in a hug. When he looked up and saw her, warmth lit C.J.'s face.

He loved her. He might not even know it, but it was there, in the blue eyes and crooked smile. The wonder of it made her heart want to float up among the rafters and her knees want to buckle.

Two long strides brought him within range to wrap his arms around her. Her body fitted against his, and he felt complete satisfaction.

"Coach Draper! Coach Draper! How are you feeling after that tremendous upset? What do you have to say?" The television interviewer's microphone nearly tangled with Carolyn's hair as he tried to get it up to C.J.'s mouth.

"I feel terrific. But all I have to say is you should talk to the players. You can talk to me after we lose. When we win, go talk to the guys. They're the ones who did it."

He gave a last smile, then pivoted away from the camera, still with a secure hold on Carolyn. He'd no more let her go now than he'd give back that one-point victory. He pushed the hair back from her cheek as she looked up and smiled at him.

"I don't think I have the nerves for this." Her voice shook a little.

"I didn't hear you calling any refs jerks this time."

She laughed, and his grip on her tightened. "You couldn't possibly have heard me even if I had."

"I'd hear you."

She found herself believing his certainty. She loved him, and almost told him then. But that was for a private moment, which this most certainly was not. "I'm so proud of you, C.J. Draper."

Warmth leaped up to a blue flame in his eyes, but he kept the words casual. "Hey, I wasn't the one out there making the plays. The guys won the game."

"You taught them how to win. And then you let them do it."

He saw the understanding in her eyes, and he knew she appreciated the extent of his accomplishment. Who needed awards or trophies when someone looked at you that way? "Hardest thing I've ever done," he murmured.

"I know." She put both arms around his waist and hugged him hard.

"All right, all right, you two," Rake boomed over her head. "I'm always having to break you two up."

She released one arm's hold on C.J., just enough to clasp hands with Rake and accept his hearty kiss on the cheek.

"Hell of an accomplishment, C.J. I'm braggin' all over how I know C.J. Draper."

"Still a couple to go before we wrap up the big one." C.J. sounded like a boy afraid that hoping too hard might jinx his wish. But to Carolyn the words seemed faintly ominous.

Two more games to reach the Final Four. The last weekend of the basketball season, when, of the nearly three hundred teams that had started off the season, only four remained with a chance at the national title. The semifinals on Saturday, then the final game on Monday night were watched by millions on national television. Getting to the Final Four meant exposure for the players, added revenue for their schools and the sort of attention that could put a young coach on the fast track to glory. A track that led straight away from Ashton.

But not as far away as England, a nagging voice reminded her.

"In my book the biggest win of all is the one you've got wrapped up in your arm right this second," Rake said. "Don't let go of that one, C.J."

She felt his arm tighten around her, and her heart made a silent plea. *Don't let me go, C.J. Don't ever let me go.*

"Can I open my eyes yet?" Carolyn squirmed impatiently against the backrest of pillows on her bed.

"Not yet. This is a surprise. Don't you know the rules about surprises?"

She made a face at C.J.'s chiding tone, but didn't know if he'd seen it since her eyes were obediently closed. "I know what you're doing, you know," she said with a trace of smugness.

"Oh, you do, do you?"

"I can hear the VCR." If he hadn't sounded so abstracted, she wouldn't have tried to rub it in. "It's a special tape, isn't it? Is it last night's game, C.J.?" One eye popped open rebelliously, but she saw only C.J.'s broad back blocking the TV screen. She closed her eye again.

"You think I'd do that to you? Make you watch another basketball game?" He'd teased her about that ever since he'd caught her watching one of his scouting tapes a couple of weeks ago. "And the name's Christian Jeremiah."

She knew immediately what he'd given her. His name. *Christian Jeremiah.* She mouthed the syllables. How like him to slip in the giving of a gift so quietly. She hadn't forgotten what he'd said that November night at Angelo's: he trusted his name only to the people he trusted with his life. "Christian Jeremiah? That's what C.J. stands for? I think it's a wonderful name."

"Give the lady a prize—she didn't even give the hint of a giggle. Now keep still and keep those eyes closed." She wanted to hug him, to touch him, to kiss him, but she held perfectly still.

She sat up a little straighter in triumph. "It's last night's game, isn't it?" She could hear him coming closer and joining her on the bed.

"Nope."

Being wrong wasn't so bad, she thought mistily, not when his voice was a breath in her ear, not when his arm was circling her shoulders.

"Okay," he whispered, taking time to trace the delicate patterns of her ear with his tongue. "You can open your eyes now."

She opened her eyes as she opened her arms to his embrace. For twenty-eight years she'd lived without him; now, after just a few weeks, the solid warmth of his body was a familiar comfort that she clung to.

Reluctantly he drew away enough so they both faced the television. He seemed nervous. "Here." He handed her the remote control. "Turn it on."

She looked up at him, puzzled by the faint anxiety filtering into his voice and eyes. "Not basketball?"

He just gestured for her to turn the power on. Her thumb pressed the button, and the machine hummed to life.

The screen glowed for an instant, then the slightly grainy background of old home movies resolved into the figures of a young man and woman. The woman had the crisp bone structure that would tempt an artist, and the man's hair held a shine that promised gold even in the black-and-white film. They smiled into the camera for a moment, then turned to each other and, clearly, immediately forgot the camera.

Carolyn's heart constricted, pushing out the words and the tears together, "My parents."

"Oh, God, Carolyn, I'm sorry. I thought you'd want—if I'd known—"

He reached for the remote control, but she jerked it away from him. "I want to see."

"Carolyn, honey—"

"I want to see."

The tears didn't stop, but they didn't prevent her from seeing the eighteen minutes of film. A graduation showed her parents looking very dignified in their professorial gowns—until her mother mugged at the camera. At a faculty picnic, her parents and younger versions of Stewart, Elizabeth and Dolph Reems participated in a spirited softball game; and a child, she realized must be herself, toddled along the sidelines. Then came a sequence of first her father and then her mother pushing her in a swing while they took turns filming. They must have found a cooperative stranger to run the camera, because the film faded out with the three of them laughing as the swing went higher and higher with two pairs of hands pushing.

It wasn't until the screen went blank that she became aware of C.J.'s hand stroking her hair.

"I'm sorry, honey. I should never have sprung it on you that way. If I'd thought—"

She pulled in a deep breath and wiped at the tears with her fingertips. "It's all right, C.J. I'm okay now. It was just the shock...."

The shock of seeing her parents as living, breathing, laughing, running people. She'd thought of them the way they were caught in the still photographs she knew. Serious-faced for the faculty section of an Ashton yearbook, or smiling warmly as they did in the photo with her in her living room, but always two-dimensional figures. Her professor parents.

"How did you find these...?"

"Stewart had them. We were talking about your parents one day, and he said he'd taken some movies. I wanted to see them. I wanted to know what they were like...."

Her heart turned with an odd kind of joy that only made the tears come faster. He'd wanted to know what her parents were like. He cared so much about her that he wanted to know them, too.

"There are three. This is the first. I thought it would be nice to have them on tape so you could watch them whenever you wanted..." He trailed off into the miserable knowledge that he'd made her unhappy. He'd brought those tears and that paleness in her face.

She turned in his arms and entwined her own around his neck, speaking between light kisses along his jaw. "Oh, C.J., I love you. Thank you."

Bewildered by the change in her, he heard the last words first. A weight eased off his heart. Then the other words took hold.

He cradled her face between his big hands to force her eyes up to his, to try to read those words, those dizzying, dazzling words there, too.

She knew she wasn't ready for that examination. She hadn't meant to say the words so soon. She wasn't sure if he'd be testing her, or she'd be testing him. But she couldn't bear the idea that either of them might fail, so like a coward she avoided it by pressing her lips to his. That took no courage at all.

Her tongue slipped between his parted lips, the tip branding-iron hot on the sensitive caverns of his mouth. She dipped deeper, enticing, driving the breath out of his body in short, shallow gasps.

She felt bold and shaken, all at the same time. Brazen with desire, she gently drew his tongue back into her mouth. He took the invitation with a rhythm her whole body took up. Their rhythm. The beat of their love.

Clothes formed no barrier; they flung them away without finesse. Nothing was a barrier. They joined, moving together toward the goal she knew only they could reach. Only together. They were there. Together.

Together. The word still echoed softly with the passion that continued to throb through her. She wouldn't wonder how long together. She couldn't. She rested her cheek on his chest and heard the strong, solid pulse of her love beating in his heart.

C.J. held her tightly but consciously kept his touch light as he stroked her back. Every time between them was fantastic. This time was different. Deeper. Richer. There was an added resonance.

He didn't use the word love, even to himself, but the sound of it vibrated between them. He knew it.

Love was a miracle—that was what people said. But miracles could disappear if you didn't believe. God, he wished he'd spent time in his life practicing believing in more than his ability to make a basketball do tricks.

He shifted a little to pull the covers over them, and she raised her head. "When will the other tapes be ready?"

"A couple of weeks."

"I want to watch it again, okay? I promise, no tears this time."

"That's a deal."

He held her against him as she watched the tape in silence twice more. As she rewound it after the second time, she sighed deeply.

She caught him studying her face, anxiety drawing his brows down in a frown. Dear C.J., how he hated her tears. She smiled reassurance at him and the crooked response pulled at her heart.

"You know," he said thoughtfully as she clicked the tape back onto her parents' smiling faces. "I think they would have liked you."

Unexpected and swift, tears pricked her eyes. "Nobody's ever said that before," she said with a tremor in her voice. "They all say—"

"How proud they'd be of you," he finished for her.

She looked up in surprise at the disapproval in his tone. "They've probably been saying it since you were old enough to understand. And all those well-intentioned 'compliments' had you trying harder and harder to make your parents proud."

The words clicked in Carolyn's head like tumblers in a lock. Of course. That was just how it had been her whole life. She'd never seen it until he'd said the words. But she'd felt the frustration of searching for something unattainable. Oh, yes, she'd felt it.

"I knew I wasn't like my grandparents. By the time I was seven years old I knew I was different." The words came haltingly. "I never knew what kind of person I should try to be. Then, when Stewart and Elizabeth brought me here, it felt familiar, comfortable."

She looked at him to see if she was making sense. Even if she wasn't, he understood. It showed in the blue depths of his eyes. She felt a grateful swell of love for him.

"I was intelligent. That was one kind of person to be. One kind of person I *knew* my parents must approve of because they were intelligent. I decided to become a professor."

Then everything had seemed so clear. If she followed the rules, if she did all the things a professor should do, and if she did them perfectly, surely her parents would have loved her.

As if in answer to her thoughts, he said, "There's no magic formula for pleasing somebody. And there shouldn't be. Even if your parents are around to tell you what they want from you, it doesn't mean you'll make them happy. You've got to make those decisions yourself."

She read a sadness in his eyes and knew he was talking about himself. The old unspoken question opened her lips, but she hesitated.

"Go ahead, ask," he urged softly. He wanted her to ask, to have enough curiosity, if nothing else. *No, be honest,* a voice inside him challenged. *You want her to care enough to want to know. You want to tell her.*

Carolyn swallowed. "What happened with your father, C.J.?"

He let out a long breath and stared at the lifeless screen for a moment before drawing in more air. "He left when I was nine. Just walked out on my mom and Jan and me."

She settled the palm of her right hand over his heart, but didn't say anything.

"I thought he was God when I was a kid. Later on I saw what a jerk he really was. I remember him talking about all the great things he could do if he didn't have us hanging around his neck. What a big man he was, and what a sap

Mom was for always helping other people. So he took off, and he left Mom to try to make it alone with two kids.''

"Have you seen him?''

"No.'' He pulled the covers more tightly around them, taking the time to tuck the corner around her shoulders. "When I first made it to the pros, I kept expecting him to show up, asking for money. But in my second year I found out he'd died four years before, about ten years after he left. He died broke.'' He seemed to try to shake off the memory with a move of his shoulders. "But I wasn't ever worried about getting his approval. More like worried how to get away from him.''

His derision was supposed to show how little it bothered him, Carolyn knew. She knew, too, how he still ached with a boy's loss.

"But the rest of the family's great,'' he told her. "You'll like them.''

"I'd like to meet them,'' she said, the wish a little tentative.

"You will,'' he answered with a firmness that wiped away her momentary uncertainty. "If we make it to the Final Four, I'll have them all come to the semifinals.''

She kissed him softly and let him lead them both to a place where love wrapped around them. No scar, no matter how old or how deep, could hurt either of them there.

The first ring of the telephone pulled Carolyn just far enough out of sleep to hope the sound was a dream. The second ring was undeniably real.

The cocoon of warmth created by the covers and C.J.'s body was disrupted when he reached across her for the receiver, and ruptured completely when he sat up abruptly. He asked two terse questions: "How bad?'' and "Where?''

Then he got to his feet, jerking his clothes on even before he'd hung up.

"C.J., what is it?"

"Rake. He's hurt. He was in an accident last night in Chicago."

"Oh, God." Big, gentle Rake. "Is it bad?"

"Yes."

She swung her legs out of the bed. "I'll go with you."

He snapped his jeans shut and looked at her for the first time. She was softened and rumpled from sleep. "No."

She ignored him. "What happened?" she asked as she started getting dressed.

Sitting on the edge of the bed, pulling on his socks, he started swearing. Low and vehement. "Some jackass he was trying to help in that damn fool program of his was going ninety-five miles an hour on Lake Shore Drive when they crashed into the guardrail and flipped over onto the rocks. Why the hell did he try to help?"

He tied his shoes and stood up.

She had a blue shirt on and socks, holding her dark slacks ready to step into them. She looked delicate and young and exhausted. Smudges under her eyes were a reminder of the tears of the night before.

"You're not going, Carolyn." His voice was harsh with anger at a world that would let people like Rake and her be hurt.

The tone, more than the words, stopped her.

"I don't know when I'll get back. The guys need one of us around with all this tournament buildup. They need you."

He kissed her fiercely at the door. She watched him clatter down the stairs in the near dark of the winter dawn and wondered, How about you? Don't you need me?

Chapter Twelve

When he called that evening to say Rake was holding his own, she felt as if he'd been gone for weeks and was a thousand miles away. He sounded so tired. And so unreachable.

The next twelve hours were critical. He'd call if there was any change. He'd be back as soon as he felt he could leave.

She heard his car at about 6:30 Wednesday evening. She had the door open long before he came up the stairs. Tight grooves cut into his cheeks and hard lines around his eyes chilled the blue. But the lines were from exhaustion, not grief—there was that to be grateful for.

Rake would make it. He faced months of rehabilitation, and maybe more surgery on broken and crushed bones, but he'd weathered the initial trauma that threatened his life. The driver escaped with bumps and bruises.

"Too damn high to get hurt," C.J. said as he paced in her small kitchen.

She reached out a hand to him, but he might not have seen it as he passed her. He hadn't touched her since he'd come in.

"C'mon, let's go out," he said abruptly. "Let's go have rigatoni at Angelo's, and you can tell me about the guys."

At Angelo's he downed barely enough rigatoni to keep the chef from being insulted and listened avidly to her small pieces of news.

It had been a remarkably quiet two days for a team about to play in a regional semifinal. There were only sixteen teams left in the country, but fifteen of them were given better odds than Ashton of getting any farther.

"Carolyn. C.J." A thread of cigarette smoke preceded Edgar Humbert's economical greeting. "What have we here? An anticipatory celebration dinner? Awfully confident, aren't you, C.J.?"

C.J. smiled dutifully at the well-intentioned kidding.

Edgar tried unsuccessfully to snap his fingers around the inevitable cigarette. "Oh, no, of course not. How stupid of me. You must be celebrating Carolyn's coup. What an offer, my dear!"

Carolyn saw C.J. tighten, and she tried to stem Edgar's flow. *Not now,* she silently pleaded to the fates. This wasn't the time. Perhaps after the season, after she'd thought it out by herself. Perhaps then would be the right time to tell C.J. about it.

"Edgar, how did—"

"How did I know? Through my network, of course. I know it's not official, but that's just a technicality. My sources tell me they're practically drooling in their eagerness to get you to teach there. I always said you'd be a department head by thirty, but this—this is way beyond my meager predictions. We'll miss you, my dear, but now I can always brag I knew you when."

He took a breezy farewell, unaware of the tense silence he left behind.

She followed the track of wax dripping down the rounded side of the bottle holding the candle. Why couldn't she find something easy and clever to say? Why didn't he?

"What offer?"

He sounded as distant as he had on the telephone. His eyes were blank.

How could this happen? How could they have gotten so far apart since just Monday night? She loved him, but she didn't have any idea what was in his mind at the moment. She couldn't read his face, couldn't decipher the meaning behind his stark words.

Could that have been relief in his voice? Was he glad she had the offer? Did the expectation that she'd be leaving take a burden away from him? She'd said she loved him, but he'd said nothing back. Wouldn't he have said it if he'd felt anything? Was she wrong about his feelings? Or was he unable to admit them? Did the scar from his father's desertion go that deep?

Clearing her throat didn't diminish the lump of panic blocking it. "From the seminar I attended last summer. They want me to come and teach. They contacted Stewart, and he told me."

"When?"

"Last week."

"Congratulations." He looked right at her, and yet she hadn't a clue to his reaction. It was as if his eyes had become a steel-blue vault door. "It's a hell of an opportunity."

"Yes."

"Hard to pass up that sort of opportunity."

She swallowed hard. God, he was practically pushing her away. He hadn't wanted her with him when he'd gone to

Rake; he hadn't needed her, the way she'd thought he would if . . . if he really loved her.

Her chin came up. She'd hold back the tears. "Yes," she repeated. "A hard opportunity to pass up."

They came together with desperation that night. Needs crying out were answered physically, but left a deeper void. Carolyn whispered his name once, but he didn't answer. She curled up on the side of the bed with her back to him.

Long after her breathing steadied into sleep, he stared up at the ceiling. Closing his eyes just brought pictures of Rake, the strength broken and battered, tubes from IVs and monitors snaking around him.

But when Rake had come to, and the doctors had let C.J. talk to him, Rake had just said, "They say I'm gonna need some rehabilitation. I told these doctors my friend C.J. is one helluva expert in rehabilitation."

He had seemed to slip into sleep again, and C.J. had let loose a low stream of curses at the driver who'd put Rake there. Then Rake's eyes had opened again, and he'd softly scolded, "It wasn't his fault, C.J. Don't blame him."

Don't blame him? Then who the hell was he supposed to blame? C.J. demanded now of the ceiling.

All that nonsense Rake had talked back in December about trying to do good; this was what came of trying to do good. People hurt you.

He knew that. You couldn't grow up in the kind of neighborhood he did and not know that. What you had to do was try to make something of yourself, of your life. And get away. Take the steps that led to the big time. That was what he'd wanted from Ashton. Just to get his chance.

Maybe Rake had forgotten that. Maybe after being a big star the way he'd been he'd lost that drive. But Carolyn hadn't lost her drive. After tonight C.J. knew that.

She had her chance, her offer.

God, how he'd hated asking her about it. But she'd just sat there in silence after Humbert had let it out and, God help him, he'd had to know.

When he'd asked how long she'd known, he hadn't realized he'd been praying she'd say, "Today" or "Yesterday," until the prayer had died with her answer. Last week. She'd known for a week, yet she hadn't told him. Not sure how to break it to him. Not sure how to tell him she was leaving.

At least he knew now. At least he could get used to the pain. And he would.

In the morning C.J. sounded almost casual when he told her not to bother to come to the tournament. Together they'd planned that she'd leave the next day. Now he said she shouldn't bother making that long trip to Kansas City.

"It's a hell of a long trip, and you can see the game better on TV." Light words that tore at her.

"But I have the reservations—"

"Cancel them." He seemed to hear the harshness in his own voice, then tried to soften it. "They'll let you cancel. It's just not worth the trip. It gets pretty intense, and there wouldn't be any time for us to spend together." He looked at a point just over her shoulder.

He was telling her she'd be in the way, she thought. She'd be in his way. Just at the tournament, or beyond?

"I've got— The guys and I have got our opportunity, and we have to make the most of it now. With no distractions."

After a tepid goodbye kiss, he left her standing at the front door of her apartment. He hesitated at the top step, seeming to consider the orderly pattern of Ashton laid out below.

Raw and dank, the March wind matched the chill of loneliness inside her.

Abruptly he turned. Two strides brought him back across her small porch. He jerked her into his arms roughly and kissed her with a fierce need edging toward violence.

Stunned, she couldn't react for a heartbeat. Then, as she raised her arms to him, he just as suddenly released her and was gone.

Carolyn's weekend passed in a fog of misery. It only lifted long enough for a few sharp moments to penetrate.

The campus thrummed with excitement. Every snatch of overheard conversation considered the team's chances. On Thursday night a car caravan set off for the overnight trip to Kansas City. All day Friday every greeting among those left behind included the question, "Where are you gonna watch the game tonight?"

Carolyn had hoped for solitude in her apartment, but that was impossible. C.J. existed in every corner. She stroked a notebook that he had left on the coffee table. A lingering hint of his smell was on the pillowcase when she made the bed. A shiny strand of light brown curved across the bathroom mirror.

By the time Helene discovered Carolyn hadn't gone to Kansas City after all and insisted she join their game-watching group that night, she was willing to do anything rather than be alone with her six-foot-six ghost. And that was what he looked like as the TV cameras zoomed in on him during the regional semifinal.

Ellis handled the players with aplomb, and Brad swished his long-distance shots in with authority, leaving Frank to stake out territory under the basket. The Aces operated as a unit, a team. Each seemed to know where the others would be even before they moved.

As Ashton methodically took control of the game, the camera focused on the coach more and more. The announcers gabbled about up-and-comer C.J. Draper and how well he handled all the hoopla.

Carolyn wanted to shut off the glib voices. Were they blind? Couldn't they see how tense and drawn he was?

The final seconds to victory were counted down with adolescent relish by the adults in Stewart's den, and a cheer went up along with the whoosh of televised sound. Stewart gave a modified little jig of celebration.

"One more game and we go to the Final Four!" Edgar Humbert whooped.

She forced a bright smile while the pressure of tears pounded behind her eyes. She saw Helene's frowning gaze resting on her. But when she slipped away from the celebration early, Helene made no move to stop her.

Saturday's mail brought the official offer from the seminar organizers. Sitting on her couch, she stared at the formal phrases.

Was this what she wanted? She looked at the paper without seeing it. She'd wanted it once, she knew. For such a long time she'd wanted just what this piece of paper provided—prestige, respect, position, honor.

She turned the thin overseas envelope over in her hands, staring at the address as if it might have been delivered to the wrong person.

Surely this would have pleased her parents. *No!* What would please *her*? What did she want of herself?

She thought she'd known. All those years she thought she'd been working toward it, carefully accumulating the right credentials. And reaping an odd feeling of restlessness.

What did she want? What did she *really* want?

That was the problem, she thought with a twist of her lips. She lacked much experience at deciding that.

Ashton lost on Sunday in the regional final. The team that stopped the Aces was bigger, stronger, more experienced. There would be no trip to the NCAA Final Four for Ashton, but the outmanned players did reap plenty of praise. The announcers gushed over their spirit and the strategy of their young coach.

The postgame interviews were a blur to Carolyn, punctuated only by the recognition of how worn C.J. looked and his answer to a question about his ambitions: "Sure, I've got ambitions."

The interviewers asked the players about the experience of playing for someone who'd made such an instantaneous impact on the basketball scene. To her ears, they made it sound as if C.J. had left already.

The players looked to Ellis, who said how grateful they all were to Coach Draper for what he'd taught them over the season. The interview ended with Brad's defiant rider: "And we'll be even more grateful after next season when we've learned more and win the national championship!"

The team bus returned on Monday night to cheers and congratulations. Surprised smiles lit up the players' faces as they came off one by one into an impromptu celebration. C.J. came last. Carolyn watched from a distance as he scanned the crowd. It cost her to resist an urgent hunger to put her arms around him and feel his long arms encircle her. But he didn't need the discomfort of an unwanted declaration. If he wanted to see her, he'd come to the apartment that night.

He didn't. But Frank did.

Frank accepted her offer of a soft drink gratefully and sat down at the dining room table with an assurance very different from a month before. He responded to questions about the tournament enthusiastically. But she knew he couldn't give her the answers about C.J. she wanted, so she didn't ask the questions. Besides, he obviously had something else on his mind.

He drained the last of the cola and looked at her with a shy smile. "I've told Coach I'm not going to play in the summer league." He swallowed a little at the enormity of his decision. "Or even in the fall semester. I want to get my grades in shape. I thought by then, with some help—" he shot her a hopeful look "—I'd be caught up, and then I could play in the second semester."

A real smile lightened her face for the first time in a week. "I think that's wonderful, Frank. I know you'll catch up by then. You've come so far already...."

One level of her mind began plotting study programs. If he worked like mad all summer, there really wasn't any reason he wouldn't catch up by the start of the fall semester and then he could play—but would he be playing for C.J.?

Whether she stayed or not, C.J. could give the players so much...if he stayed.

"What did...Coach Draper say?"

Frank made a figure-eight pattern on the cloth place mat with the bottom edge of the empty glass. "I don't think it matters much to Coach, because it doesn't look like he'll be around much longer."

When she opened the apartment door to C.J. on Wednesday night, she remembered Frank's assessment. No, it didn't look as if he'd be around much longer, she thought as she watched him restlessly pace her living room. He was like a caged panther.

"I've missed you, C.J."

"I had some things to think about."

"I know." She also knew he'd been to Chicago to see Rake. She wasn't sure how she knew, but she did.

He didn't seem to want feelings from her now. But she had too many feelings, and they were too strong to be quieted. "Oh, C.J., I'm so sorry."

He shook off her sympathy. "There'll be other games."

"I meant about Rake being hurt," she said softly.

The pacing stopped. Without the steady pulse of his stride, Carolyn heard her own heartbeat as a solo drum. He met her eyes for the first time. Across his face flashed a momentary revelation of tremendous pain. And fear. What was he afraid of?

He started to turn away from her. Moved by a need to make some contact, she caught his hand. For an instant she thought he meant to jerk away from the touch. Instead, he sank down on the couch next to her, with his face turned away.

A curse came out. "He was just trying to do good. He was just trying to help somebody." His voice hesitated, then strengthened to bitterness. "That's what comes of trying to help."

The bitterness came from anger; Carolyn knew that. And she knew anger at the injustices of the world could become corrosive. But he hurt so badly.

Her arms slipped around him the way they'd longed to, and she rested her cheek against his taut shoulder. Through the layers of clothing she felt the tension of his back. Her hands stroked his chest. He caught one in both of his and held it a moment, as if deciding what to do with the captive.

Then he clasped her hand tightly to his side and a breath, long-held, escaped him slowly. For a long moment Carolyn felt his ribs shudder. Her own eyes stung with the tears he refused to let fall.

Then, although he didn't stir, she sensed his withdrawal. It was like a cut of cold air. "C.J.?"

"I'm leaving tomorrow for the Final Four." His words pushed her away. She released him. "The top coaches, top athletic directors from around the country, will be there. Some great programs are looking for coaches. They'll be there...."

"I see." She sat up straight. She wouldn't let the hurt seep into her voice. "You've made your opportunity and now you're going to take it."

"That's right."

"What about me?"

He twisted around to look at her. A fire burned through the fog in his eyes, and for a moment he was her C.J. again.

"Come with me," he said.

It was as close as he'd come. But it wasn't close enough. And the fire in his eyes disappeared with her next gentle words. "No. I'm not going with you."

"So the opportunity's just too good to pass up, huh?"

It took her a moment to sort through the cynicism to realize he meant the position in England. She shook her head. "It has nothing to do with that."

"Doesn't it?" He looked beyond her. "Doesn't it have to do with Carolyn Trent, the perfect professor? Isn't that what it's been since the moment you were told you'd be stepping down from your academic pedestal to deal with the basketball team?" His eyes focused on her again. "And the basketball coach."

She wanted to tell him that he was wrong, that he'd always been wrong. His eyes wouldn't let her tell anything but the truth. "It was in the beginning. But it hasn't been that way for a long time—"

He stood up abruptly, his movements jerky. "Yeah, it's just a coincidence you've got this fancy offer."

"The seminar doesn't have anything to do with why I won't go with you, C.J. *You're* the reason. This isn't right for you. This isn't the right time for you to leave. These aren't the right reasons."

If she could just make him see... He'd taught her not to restrict herself to one dimension, but now he was prepared to judge himself on wins and losses.

"If you stay here...you said Ashton could really be great. You said what an opportunity this is. All it needs is some time."

He wouldn't look at her. "Yeah, time I can't afford to waste."

The harsh words squeezed at her heart as she watched him prowl in the small open area beyond the coffee table. He stopped and faced the window.

"C.J., what happened to Rake doesn't mean..." Doesn't mean what? What could she tell him? That he wasn't mortal? That he had all the time in the world? But he already knew, all too well, that the world could topple years' worth of work and dreams in an instant.

"What happened to Rake just woke me up out of the little dream world I've been in. Sitting up here at Ashton like I'm living in some damn *Leave It to Beaver* episode. If I let this chance go by, there might not be another one. I'm not going to stay here forever. Because, by God, before I'm done, I'm going to be somebody!"

Carolyn looked up at the strong bones of his face, unsoftened by any trace of the crooked grin or the usual laughter in his eyes. Restlessly he moved away from the window.

This man, she realized with something close to shock, was as bound up by his own self-imposed rules as she had been.

And his expectations of himself were just as unreasonable. Why hadn't she seen that before?

Frantically her mind tried to absorb this new understanding. Was the side of him that tried to weigh issues by wins and losses one of those unreasonable expectations? Was he trying to "be somebody" because that was what he thought he had to be?

Carolyn stood up slowly. She spoke deliberately. "This isn't about Rake, C.J. It's not even about Ashton or me. It's about your father."

Fury burned his eyes blue-hot as they faced each other across the space of the coffee table.

"You're still the boy trying to be somebody so your father will approve and come back," she said.

"Who the hell are you to talk?"

Color drained from her face. She saw her own pain reflected in his eyes. She knew with every fiber of her heart that it hurt him to hurt her, but he didn't relent. Her easygoing C.J., she thought with a new twist of pain. So easygoing on the outside, so driven on the inside.

"At least I know my parents are dead, C.J.," she said very softly. "I never tried to win their approval so they'd come back. And now, with your help..." *And your love, C.J. Dear heaven, I need your love.* She caught her bottom lip between her teeth to control the tremor in it. "I'm learning to be the person I want to be and not guess what they might have wanted."

He was silent and still. She had to say this now, to try to make him see. There might not be another chance. "You're talking about being caught just like your father did. You're talking about getting away so that you can 'be somebody' just like he did."

How could she make him see? Rake had said C.J.'s one blind spot was himself. How could he be so smart about everything else and so blind about himself?

"You are somebody, C.J. You're the coach. You're the friend to all those guys on the team. This whole university admires you and likes you and respects you. They love you." Her voice dropped. "You're important to Ashton. You're important to me, C.J." She put out a hand to touch him on the arm, but he stood just out of reach. "Don't you understand that?" Her fingertips, just inches short of him, fell to her side. He stood motionless, expressionless.

"I'm going to that tournament," he said flatly. "I'm going to find myself the best and biggest job there. I'm going to be on the cover of all the magazines. You may not see them over in England, but I'll be there. I'm going to have a team that's number one in the country. I'm going to win the national championship. I'm going to *be somebody*. Do you understand that?"

He flung the last words at her and spun away. Then he grabbed his coat off the back of the chair, not bothering to put it on before slamming out the door and rattling down the stairway.

Carolyn folded onto the couch. Her legs would no longer hold her. Her heart could hardly hold the pain. C.J. Draper was somebody; he was the man she loved.

And he had just walked out of her life.

Chapter Thirteen

Carolyn had no chance to decide if her misery wanted company. Edgar Humbert called the next morning and asked her to take two of his classes because he didn't feel well. That night Mary Rollins insisted she needed Carolyn to read over a fifty-page grant proposal she'd written. Helene recruited her for an alumni tea Friday afternoon. Stewart wanted her for a Friday evening panel discussion. And every one of the ten basketball players discovered a need for individual consultation.

When Frank, Ellis, Brad and Thomas arrived at her doorstep on Saturday with bags of chips and cans of soft drinks just before the start of the national tournament's first semifinal game, she didn't know whether to laugh at their heavy-handed tactics or cry over the cause of their ministrations.

Missing C.J. was a void that didn't go away for all her busyness. Her heart pulsed pain with each beat. How would this hurt ever heal?

"You were the only person we knew with a VCR," Brad lied. "This way we can tape the game."

"I could tape it for you and give it to you later," she countered with some halfhearted notion of ending the charade.

"Yeah, but this way we can rewind and watch the best plays during commercials," he improvised.

She was no match for them. Especially not when they were trying to be on their best behavior.

When she came in with a tray of ice-filled glasses, she found the four players carefully arranged around the television in her bedroom, sitting decorously on straight-backed chairs they'd brought in from the dining room. They reminded her of little boys who'd had their cowlicks plastered down for a church service.

How C.J. would have enjoyed this performance! The grin would have fought to come out, his eyes would have gleamed with humor and his drawl would have slowed in an effort to control the chuckle in it.

Carolyn blinked her eyes hard to push back that saltwater thought. There was no use thinking about that. Being weepy didn't change a thing.

Instead, she set her mind to making her guests relax. First, she slipped her shoes off and settled on the bed cross-legged. Halfway through the first half, the straight-backed chairs were pushed to the edge of the room and long bodies sprawled on the floor, the bed and the easy chair—when they weren't jumping up to exclaim over a play or rewinding the tape for a quick review.

The cowlicks were back standing on end the way they were meant to, she thought with an inward smile. Between games

they ordered pizzas, and Brad and Thomas made a run for
more soft drinks.

At halftime of the second game, the camera found C.J.
in the stands. Into the intense quiet of the room, the chat-
tering voice of the announcer reported that the talented
young coach who'd had such success with little Ashton
University was the hottest commodity at the Final Four.
Several programs seemed interested in the dynamic new
force in college basketball, but the rumor was that he'd be
taking the head coaching position at a major university in
the Southwest. Not at liberty to say exactly where or for how
much, the announcer could assure his listeners it was a big-
money, big-program, big-conference job that would give
C.J. Draper a real showcase for his talents.

Strangely the words hardly touched Carolyn's pain at all.
The job itself seemed so immaterial compared to the reasons behind it. But it had to be different for the players, she
thought as she looked at the faces of these manly boys.

The players had become very dear to her, and the knowledge that the affection was reciprocated warmed her. But
players such as Brad, Ellis and Frank hadn't come to Ashton to study under her; they'd come because of C.J. What
did his departure mean to them? A hurt? A disappointment? A betrayal?

Brad muttered a long, low curse under his breath and the
room came to life once more.

"Boy, that's the big time, isn't it?" Thomas Abbott said
in the tone of someone who understood giving way to such
a temptation.

Frank's defense was immediate, "He's gotta do what's
best for him."

"He's made his opportunity and now he's got to take it."
Brad's voice was so low that Carolyn wondered if he even
knew he'd spoken aloud.

"There's no denying that's a better deal than he's got here," Thomas pointed out. "He'll probably have five assistants, his own secretary and a whole suite of offices. Teams like that probably fly around in chartered jets, not old buses like us."

No private talks in a sleeping bus, no taping scouting games off the cable channel, no need for someone to spot numbers when he scouted a game. Carolyn found small solace in knowing that at least he wouldn't be doing those things with anyone else.

Ellis's quiet voice slipped into the contemplation of unknown luxuries. "We haven't done so badly for ourselves here. I know some guys from home who went to schools like that. It's as if playing balls' their job, and the school's their boss. Even if they want to study, they hardly have time. The coach sure doesn't make the time for studying. And when they get out, what do they have? Sure, a few go on to the pros, but what about the rest of them—most of them. No degree. No job. Nothing. Coach did all right by us bringing us here."

If the others disagreed, if anyone wanted to rail that C.J. could have, should have, given them more by sticking around, no one said it. Not one word of blame or disappointment.

She wished she could be so philosophical.

"C.J. stopped by the office before he left for the Final Four, Carolyn."

She looked up at Stewart from the coffee cup she held with both hands. The cold air that came in when she'd opened the door for him seemed to have settled around her despite the bulk of her heavy sweater and jeans.

At first she thought he was part of the keep-Carolyn-busy campaign. But she saw in his face that he'd come for something more.

"He offered me his resignation. He said he wanted to be free and clear when he talked to other schools about coaching jobs." He reached across the table and gripped one of her cold hands in his warm one. "I thought you should know."

"Thank you, Stewart. He told me, in his way, before he left." Her words had come out steadily.

She'd spent a whole sleepless night thinking things through, and she'd come to some conclusions. They didn't stop the pain, but at least they gave it some meaning. And for the first time in her life she felt as if her mind and her feelings formed part of a whole, not conflicting halves.

Stewart's voice held genuine regret. "I thought you two really had something."

"We did."

"I'm so sorry, Carolyn. I know how much it hurts to lose someone you love...." She turned her hand over and gripped his. "I wouldn't blame you if you held a grudge because I made you be academic adviser."

Admiration, respect, gratitude, affection—she'd always felt those things for the president of Ashton University. Now she felt a flow of love for the man who'd loved her and accepted her for seventeen years. He shared her pain. She'd never really seen that before.

"Oh, Stewart. No. I don't hold a grudge." She reached across the wedge of table separating them to hug him. "I'm glad you did it. It's opened my eyes—to a lot of things."

As she pulled back, she saw in his eyes a warm pleasure at her gesture, tinged with a little uncertainty. He needed some exuberant loving; the kind Helene could provide,

Carolyn decided. Just as she'd needed the kind of love C.J. gave.

"I don't regret anything about it. I learned so much more than I taught. From the guys. And from C.J."

Hours into the night, as she watched the tapes of her parents, she'd examined the person she'd been and the person she was now. She welcomed the fun-loving, colorful and sensual sides so long shunted aside by Professor Trent.

She would never shut them away again.

And, perhaps to the amazement of Professor Trent, Carolyn was no less respected, no less accepted, no less taken seriously.

You're afraid if you're not serious all the time, then everyone'll find out you're just like everybody else—still wondering when you're going to grow up inside.

She'd built walls around herself made up of all the things a professor should be so that she'd be loved and accepted— but the love and acceptance had been there all the time.

It had taken a basketball team to knock enough holes in the walls to let some air in. And it had taken one special basketball coach to knock the walls down.

"I just wish . . . I just wish . . ." If only she'd been able to help C.J. find the same freedom. Through a sheen of tears she looked up at Stewart. "I love him, Stewart."

He encircled her with a father's arms, and Wisconsin dusk turned to frigid dark as he listened to her.

When he got up to leave, she realized she needed to tell Stewart one more thing. "I'm not going to England. I've written to the seminar, declining their very flattering offer," she said with a small laugh at her self-quotation. "It would look great on a résumé, but I'll be happier staying at Ashton for now."

Her eyes welled with tears again, both at the pleasure in Stewart's face and the thought of how much happier she'd be if C.J., too, were at Ashton. She shook herself free of the thought. "Besides, I have some things I need to finish up—I've promised Frank Gordon the toughest summer of his life."

"You're quite a woman, Carolyn," Stewart said. "Your parents would be proud of you."

"I hope they'd also like me."

"I know they would," he said with conviction. He turned to leave, but her voice stopped him. "Stewart. I think they'd like Helene, too."

He looked at her, puzzled for a moment, then smiled with a trace of self-consciousness.

"She's very special," Carolyn added. "I like her a lot."

His smile lost some of its self-consciousness and deepened. "Me, too."

"You know our program, C.J. Our facilities are among the finest in the country." The athletic director didn't have to brag; he just told the truth.

"We're confident that with our facilities and your talent we could have the finest basketball program in the country, too. You'd have your choice of assistants, of course. And office support staff. We can arrange special financing if you're interested in buying a house. And we provide a new car every other year. You'll want your lawyer to look this over, but with performance bonuses, you'd be looking at something around..."

C.J. listened to his dream being detailed, luxury by luxury, bonus by bonus. A sparkling new field house instead of Ashton's anachronism. A flotilla of assistants instead of Dolph Reems and a team manager. An office staff instead of a shared receptionist and battered filing cabinets. A house, a car, a bonus. Everything he wanted. Everything it took to be somebody.

Then why did he find it so damn hard to concentrate on what the man sitting across the table in this posh hotel suite was saying? C.J. blinked away the image of a laughing face framed by glowing golden brown hair.

Have his lawyer look at it, wasn't that what the man had said? With Stewart it had all been done on a handshake. Submitting a resignation hadn't even been necessary. He'd just wanted to make it seem more real to himself. He was free—with no obligations, no commitments.

Sure, they'd had a good thing going, but things like that ended. Brown eyes, low-lidded with passion, invited him to come nearer.

She walks in beauty, like the night
Of cloudless climes and starry skies;
And all that's best of dark and bright
Meet in her aspect and her eyes...

C.J. shifted his long legs in the easy chair, completely unaware that the movement caused the man across from him to raise the bonus for winning a conference tournament by several thousand dollars.

Ashton. He was thinking of Ashton. And the basketball team.

It had been a hell of a season. C.J.'s cheek creased into the beginning of a grin. The weeks of studying tapes, the months of searching for players, the days of practices, the hours of straining on the sidelines all seemed rather fun from this short distance. That one-point victory in the second round of the tournament over Bracken State had made it all worthwhile.

He needed no tape to again see those final seconds. To see Brad move in to knock back Bracken State's open shot from the corner; Ellis adjust the defense; Frank rise to stop the pass; the players hug one another in the middle of the court with the exuberance of victory.

Their faces flashed in front of him, a season compressed into a moment. He saw the upperclassmen, who could so easily have resented a new coach and a new program, accepting lesser roles and contributing to the best of their abilities. He saw Brad learning to tone down his razzle-dazzle to a constant glow. He saw Ellis gaining the confidence to wield the leadership he was born for. He saw Frank grow until he was willing to expose his weaknesses in order to improve his strengths.

The time-lapse clicked off and he saw himself.

The one-point victory wasn't what had made all the months that had gone before worthwhile; it was all those individual moments of effort, triumph and failure that gave meaning to the victory.

The athletic director sitting across from him was still talking about his offer. But the remembered thunder of Rake's voice dimmed the athletic director's words. *In my book the biggest win of all is the one you've got wrapped up in your arm right this second. Don't let go of that one, C.J.*

Carolyn.

He nearly said the name aloud.

You are somebody.... You're important to Ashton. You're important to me, C.J.

Carolyn... Carolyn laughing. Looking down her nose at him. Fiercely fighting any interference with the players' studies. Carolyn at the basketball games. Reaching out to touch him in comfort. Dancing so close that their bodies moved together. Storming at him across a basketball court. Releasing her passion. Carolyn in his arms, kissing him awake in the morning, leaning back against him in the kitchen. Loving him. *I love you, C.J.*

Then how the hell can you leave me?

The question was a bayonet in his chest. A real, physical injury he could deal with. He could meet it straight on and defeat it. He could do the exercises, grit his teeth through the therapies, withstand the physical pain. But this was a wound to the heart.

How do you cope with that, Coach Draper?

Sometimes you just have to give it time, to see if it's going to heal or if it needs more attention.

Helene hadn't been talking about burns from any imaginary spilled coffee, and they both had known it. She'd been telling him he might need patience with Carolyn. Maybe a lot of patience. He'd thought the waiting was all over when she'd opened her heart to him. But it wasn't. And it wouldn't be until he had her head, too.

Right now her head told her to take that job. But that wasn't really Carolyn. That was just a leftover reaction from the marble mask she'd sculpted because she thought it would please the world. If he gave her time, she'd realize what was best for her. . . .

Who the hell are you kidding? his honesty demanded. Sure, she'd be happier at Ashton, but it's yourself you're worried about. You've grown to need her. You love her . . .

I love her.

His heart spoke with authority: then why the hell did you give up?

The athletic director's voice was insistent enough to break through his thoughts. From the edge to his words, he'd clearly said them at least once already.

"So what's it going to be, C.J.?"

Carolyn pulled into her driveway and brought the car to a stop in the dimness of the early spring twilight. The weather softened with another tantalizing whisper of spring, but the early sunset reminded her that winter hadn't let go entirely. She'd have to hurry to get changed before going to Stewart's for dinner. She'd watch the championship game on TV tonight with him and Helene.

She let out a sigh as she shut the car door. She'd promised herself to hold on to the good things about her time with C.J. and not let the pain obscure them. But she wasn't sure she'd be able to do that if the TV kept flashing pictures of his face to torment her battered heart.

With two steps left to reach the stairway, a form stepped out of the growing shadows, startling Carolyn. "Wanna shoot some hoops, Professor?"

C.J.

For its battered condition, her heart performed some amazing stunts. It somersaulted at the sight of him in his worn jeans, bombardier jacket open to an Ashton University sweatshirt and a basketball tucked under his arm.

Then it twisted with dread. Oh, God, he's leaving already. He's come to say goodbye for good. She'd thought she was ready. She'd thought she was reconciled to it. She wasn't.

"C.J., what are you doing here?" It was hard to find the breath for words. "The tournament's not over."

What a stupid thing to say. He knew that.

"I got done early." The fading light outlined the shrug of his shoulders but shadowed his face.

"So you found the job you wanted?" She forced the question out.

"Yup."

"Oh." She thought she was braced for it, but the pain brought a gasp only smothered by biting her lip. She would remember what he'd already given her; she wouldn't dwell on what else they might have given each other. That was what she had to do to survive. But, oh, God, how it hurt.

"That big university in the Southwest?"

"Nope."

"Oh? Didn't they offer it to you? The people on TV said—"

"Don't be insulting, Professor. They offered it."

She frowned, trying to see his face in the dusk. No bitterness lingered in his voice. Yet he sounded different from the C.J. of old. More grounded, somehow, if that made sense. If they offered it, but he wasn't going there...

"You turned it down?" Her voice was husky with a hope she couldn't deny.

"Yup. Told them I already had the job I wanted. Told them it was going to take a little longer to rebuild this program and to reform staid Professor Carolyn Trent."

"You did, C.J.?"

"I did, Carolyn." His voice softened and deepened.

There hadn't been much time to practice what he'd wanted to tell her. There had been a job to turn down, then an early-morning flight to Chicago to spend a couple of hours with Rake, followed by the drive back to Ashton and a brief meeting with Stewart to retrieve one letter of resignation.

But he didn't need practice to tell her what he needed. This move he'd make on instinct alone.

"You were right," he told her. "I should have known that. I guess I'm just not one of your quick studies. It took me a while to mull it over on my own to realize you were right, to realize I was still carrying some things my father had said around in my head. I didn't really believe them, but I let them get to me."

With practiced ease he used his elbow to swing the ball around in front of him. He held it there with his long fingers spread out on the familiar surface. "Then I realized that it's *my* standards that count, not his. And by my standards, I *am* somebody; I must be to have somebody like you care about me.''

A cymbal's crash of hope shook Carolyn. Surely he'd have to shout to overcome its din. But the low drawl came through just fine.

''So I'm going to stick around. I've got to satisfy myself that the job is done right.'' He took a step toward her, into the light that showed the yearning and the determination in his face. ''Stay with me, Carolyn.''

Joy wasn't a tender emotion. Not quiet and peaceful. It rocketed through her veins, hammered at her heart, burnt in her lungs. And made it very difficult to say the words that needed to be said. What she wanted to do was shout out loud—or say nothing at all, but to let her lips converse another language with his.

''I'm not going to teach at the seminar, C.J.''

For a moment he thought someone had tackled him from behind his weak left knee. Then he realized the weakness in his knees was accompanied by a soaring in his heart. His grin pleated his cheek, but he feigned condolences when he said, ''Didn't get the offer, huh?''

''Don't be insulting,'' she said, echoing what he'd said earlier. ''I just mailed the letter thanking them for their kind offer. But I still had some work to do here—a lot of work, taming Coach C.J. Draper.''

He dropped the ball and closed the distance between them, wrapping his arms around her. Her body fitted to his unhesitatingly. She slipped her arms under the jacket to enjoy the solid feel of him while his large hands spread across her back to bring her closer. The immediate heat between them burned away the chill of the past two weeks.

He found her mouth with his and claimed it. It was a kiss that remembered the differences and disagreements, and knew there would be more. But it was a caress that promised solutions and commitments.

The tip of her tongue, arcing along the roof of his mouth, was the head of a match igniting a fire. Before the flame flashing through him became something he couldn't control, he ended the kiss.

He had to, he thought with a wry inward grimace, or there would have been a major scandal when the basketball coach made love to the professor of English literature in the sodden remnants of last summer's flower garden.

He touched the crown of her head with his lips, then rested his cheek against the softness. "I love you, Carolyn."

She pulled in her breath with the pure, shuddering joy of it. "I love you, C.J."

They held each other there, letting the fragile, molten words harden into a vow strong enough to last a lifetime. He stirred first. "You know, someday one of us will want to take that other job."

"I know. We'll work it out. Perhaps you could become a specialist in coaching basketball at strong academic institutions."

He kissed the top of her head. "Yeah, and maybe you can become an expert at teaching literature to jocks."

"What are you going to do now?" she asked.

C.J. knew she was asking about his job at Ashton, but he chose to take it another way. "What I'd like to do is maybe have something to eat, then watch the game in bed with you—and I really don't care how much of the game I see."

"The game! I forgot. I'm supposed to be at Stewart's by now." She headed up the stairs, but she kept a secure hold on C.J.'s hand until he laughingly reminded her he had to retrieve a piece of Ashton athletic department property he'd let roll under the evergreens.

She was on the phone when he came into the kitchen with the basketball in one hand and a small paper bag in the other.

"Stewart, this is Carolyn. I'm not going to be able to come over tonight."

"I thought maybe you wouldn't."

"C.J.'s back, Stewart."

"I know. He came by my office first. Ostensibly to get his letter of resignation back, but actually to find out how you felt."

"He did?" Carolyn looked over her shoulder at the tall form closing in on her. She had so much more to learn about him, this confident, sure man with the streaks of deep vulnerability.

He wrapped an arm around her waist from behind and used the other hand to sweep back her hair to clear a path for his kisses along her neck. She found it difficult to concentrate on Stewart's voice.

"He said I should go ahead and tell the team that he's coming back, but I thought maybe you and C.J. would want to come over—"

"No," C.J. whispered into her ear before gently nipping the lobe. "Tell him maybe next week. Or next month."

Voices in the background told Carolyn that someone on the other end had claimed Stewart's attention but certainly not as seductively as C.J. had claimed hers. Stewart came back on with a laugh. "Helene says if I dare to suggest you should come over, I'll be drawn and quartered. With that in mind, I think I'll just say good night. We'll tell the team, and you'll probably hear the cheering over there. God bless you both, Carolyn."

"Thank you, Stewart."

She hung up the phone with a hand only slightly unsteady from the attentions being paid to the tender skin below her ear. When those attentions continued down her neck and into the V of her blouse, the unsteadiness extended to her knees.

Hunger was a live current in their lovemaking. Hunger for each other, hunger for touches that confirmed the spoken assurances, hunger to start fulfilling the promises of forever.

Clothes were pulled off with mutters of satisfaction. Hooks, buttons, zippers were met with frantic fingers and half-laughing mumbles of impatience. Finally, flesh to flesh, Carolyn sank to the bed, pulling him down with her.

When C.J.'s thrust joined them, they stilled, letting the miracle of being one carry them. Then another, more immediate hunger, nudged them into slow, rhythmic motions, and they continued their journey to pleasure.

Such pleasure, Carolyn thought, a long while later when her mind could find any thought beyond his name. Such dazzling, delightful pleasure.

He started to roll away to relieve the crush of his weight on her, but she held him tightly in place. She needed the reality of his body. She needed to hold on to the security of his long legs still tangled with hers.

She looked around at the darkened room to remind herself that this *was* reality. C.J. loving her was the most real, the most secure thing in her life. Feelings were as real as the curtains on the window, the bedspread half tumbled to the floor, the numerals of the alarm clock adding a faint red glow to the night table.

"Oh, it's almost time for the game to come on." She felt ready to play herself—and she knew she'd win. She was tall, powerful and invincible; she was loved. "Why don't you set up the VCR, and I'll get something for us to eat?"

He grumbled something into the soft skin of her shoulder.

"What'd you say?" she asked.

"I said—" he lifted his head to pronounce the words clearly "—that I think I've created a basketball monster. There'll be another one of these games next year. Let's just stay here."

She laughed. The look that sprang into his blue eyes drew her back into his arms for another long kiss. But at last she broke away and went to the closet for her robe.

"What about Frank, C.J.? He told you about not playing this summer or the fall semester?"

"Uh-huh."

"He said you didn't mind."

"Yeah, but that was before I came to my senses and decided to stick around. We're going to have to figure something out about that. You know," he said slyly, "if Frank doesn't play next fall, I'm going to have to spend a lot more time this spring recruiting, trying to fill his spot. Lot of time away from home. Nights. Lots of nights."

Perfectly straight-faced, she adjusted her robe and said, "I think with a special tutor he could make up the work in the summer—with the right tutor." At the door she turned back to add, "I thought I might do some tutoring this summer."

He grinned and called after her. "I knew that brain of yours would come up with something."

When she returned with sandwiches, chips, fruit and drinks, he was propped against the pillows with the remote control in hand.

"It's all set, you basketball junkie." He grinned a little smugly. "But I put it on automatic, just in case we find something better to do." He took the tray from her and looked at the drink suspiciously. "What's this? It's not Gatorade, is it? I've lost my taste for that stuff lately."

"Just keep that in mind if you're ever tempted to stray," she warned darkly. Then she laughed. How she loved him, that semidrawl, that crooked grin, those blue eyes. She wanted to be back in his arms.

"Ow! What's this? I stepped on it." From the heap of their clothing discarded on the floor, she found a small paper bag that contained the hard object her bare foot had encountered.

"Oh, that. It's for you." He leaned back for a better view of her face.

She glanced up curiously, but he just nodded at her to open the bag. Inside was a small square jeweler's box covered in soft velvet of an unusual warm golden brown. She looked at C.J. again, but his blue eyes were fixed on the box in her hand. Carefully she flipped open the lid.

It held a single sheet of paper. In C.J.'s handwriting were the words: "Redeemable for one diamond ring of your choice and one set of wedding bands of a mutually agreeable design."

She swallowed tears of joy and looked into his bright blue eyes.

He smiled back. And a final tiny, unspoken fear slid away from his heart. "I hear Tuesday's a good day to shop for diamonds."

She slipped an arm behind his waist and wrapped the other around his flat abdomen, cuddling closer until her hands clasped to complete her circle around him. "A perfect day."

She rubbed her cheek against his chest as he encircled her with one arm. With his other hand, he picked up the jeweler's box she'd dropped amid the covers.

"Now *this*," he said, tapping the box, "is the color of your hair. By God, I finally matched it!"

* * * * *

Silhouette Special Edition

COMING NEXT MONTH

#589 INTIMATE CIRCLE—Curtiss Ann Matlock
Their passion was forbidden, suspect . . . silenced by the specter of his late brother—her husband. Could Rachel and Dallas reweave the angry, fragmented Cordell and Tyson clans into a warming circle of love?

#590 CLOSE RANGE—Elizabeth Bevarly
Tough, disillusioned P.I. Mick Dante had long admired ethereal neighbor Emily Thorne from afar. But when she approached him to track her missing brother, temptation—and trouble!—zoomed into *very* close range.

#591 PLACES IN THE HEART—Andrea Edwards
When Matt finally came home, he discovered he'd relinquished far more than he'd imagined. . . . But would Tessa make room in her heart for her late husband, her sons, *and* the lover who'd once left her behind?

#592 FOREVER YOUNG—Elaine Lakso
Levelheaded Tess DeSain ran the family bakery—and her life—quietly, sensibly . . . until flamboyant Ben Young barged into both, brazenly enticing her to have her cake and eat it, too!

#593 KINDRED SPIRITS—Sarah Temple
Running from Ian Craddock's dangerously attractive intensity, Tara Alladyce sought emotional sanctuary . . . in a phantom fling. But Ian wasn't giving up easily—he'd brave man, beast *or* spirit to win her back!

#594 SUDDENLY, PARADISE—Jennifer West
Nomadic Annie Adderly kept her tragic past a secret . . . and kept running. Then incisive, sensual detective Chris Farrentino began penetrating her cover, pressing for clues, probing altogether too deeply. . . .

AVAILABLE THIS MONTH:

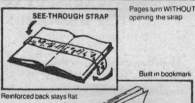